Warrior Fae Princess

Also by K.F. Breene

DDVN WORLD:

FIRE AND ICE TRILOGY
Born in Fire
Raised in Fire
Fused in Fire

MAGICAL MAYHEM SERIES
Natural Witch
Natural Mage
Natural Dual-Mage

WARRIOR FAE SERIES
Warrior Fae Trapped
Warrior Fae Princess

FINDING PARADISE SERIES
Fate of Perfection
Fate of Devotion

DARKNESS SERIES
Into the Darkness, Novella 1
Braving the Elements, Novella 2
On a Razor's Edge, Novella 3
Demons, Novella 4
The Council, Novella 5
Shadow Watcher, Novella 6
Jonas, Novella 7
Charles, Novella 8
Jameson, Novella 9
Darkness Series Boxed Set, Books 1-4

WARRIOR CHRONICLES
Chosen, Book 1
Hunted, Book 2
Shadow Lands, Book 3
Invasion, Book 4
Siege, Book 5
Overtaken, Book 6

WARRIOR FAE PRINCESS

BY K.F. BREENE

Copyright © 2019 by K.F. Breene

All rights reserved. The people, places, situations and craziness contained in this book are figments of the author's imagination and in no way reflect real or true events.

Contact info:
www.kfbreene.com
books@kfbreene.com

CHAPTER 1

STEVE HUMMED A little tune as he waited on the Brink side of the portal in the South Side of Chicago. He would get the rare opportunity of shepherding in the new guys Roger had sent to join Devon's pack. Rough and fierce, these three shifters were called in when things got hairy. Given Charity was getting strong magical surges and needed to be rushed through the dangerous wilds to the Flush, a place in the Realm where a subset of fae lived, so she could get aid from what was hopefully her people, Devon was going to need experience in his numbers.

Speaking of Devon—Steve checked his watch—he and his pack were supposed to be there ten minutes ago. Their flight from Santa Cruz must've been delayed.

It wasn't like Roger to trust Steve with authoritative duties. Hell, it wasn't like Roger to trust Steve with anything besides fighting. The alpha liked to keep Steve on a tight leash where he could. Then again, maybe Roger thought Emery would keep things in line. The Rogue Natural would be leading them through the wilds, trying to sneak around the elves who were patrolling in large numbers. It would be a longer and slower route than most other ways, but that was why there wouldn't be elves standing in the way. He knew the wilds of the Realm as well as anyone could. His knowledge made him indispensable. But his choice of company made Roger a little nervous.

Emery ran with a couple of magical chicks that could bring a grown man to tears. One of those chicks, a fire-starter with a joy of killing things, was shacking up with an elder vampire. Vlad's buddy, to be precise. If they didn't need his expertise so badly, no way would Roger use him.

Roger apparently didn't realize that Emery wasn't one to follow orders any better than Steve. He was supposed to be here too, but the mage had decided to wait in Seattle until the last minute, where he'd then use a couple of magical fast tracks, somehow skirting past loitering elves to do so, and rendezvous with Devon's pack at the agreed-upon time and place. It was dicey, Emery's plan, especially since he'd expressly forbidden those types of patrolled magical roads when Charity was in tow, but it wasn't Steve's place to say boo. Given that Emery wasn't pack, Roger couldn't do dick about his decision, which was how Steve had gotten the solo role of fucking with the new guys.

Roger should've known better.

Steve looked around the deserted warehouse parking lot. This place was a real dump. Trash littered the streets, show windows were boarded up or broken, and a couple of used condoms were draped over a cracked parking bump five feet away. A fixer-upper, but the people here sure knew how to party.

He hoped someone tried to mug him.

The portal shimmered white before a booted foot stepped through the jagged slice in the sky. Although Steve didn't know these shifters personally, he'd seen all three of them in passing and heard plenty of stories. Steve combined with these three would equal ten decent shifters on the battlefield—they were *that* good.

The first to step through was Dale, complete with a stupid-looking mustache and a bump in the side of his lower lip from his chewing tobacco. He trained his small black eyes on Steve before letting them drift away, sussing out the area.

"This place is a shithole," Dale said, taking a wide stance with his hands on his hips. "This where that chick's father lives?"

"The broken-down warehouse, yes." Steve pointed at the condoms. "This is her boudoir where she entertains menfolk. She wasn't here, though, so they just got after it themselves. Too bad you missed the action."

Dale shook his head, his gaze barely flicking toward the mess. "Do you got duct tape for that mouth?"

"My, my. Kinky. Sorry, Chuck, I don't swing that way."

Dale's eyebrows pinched together. "My name is Dale, and I wanted that tape to shut you up, dipshit."

Steve grinned. Nothing irritated self-important

pricks more than when you got their names wrong.

They were here to do what Alder, the beta of the North American pack, hadn't been able to do those few months ago—talk to Charity's father and try to get some proof of Charity's ancestry. They wanted to make sure she was actually *custodes*—a guardian—a subset of fae known to their people as protectors. Back before the elves took the Realm in hand, giving it order and decency, the *custodes* watched over the fae, using their superior strength and speed to keep the beasties away. It was because of this efficiency and brutality in battle that they earned a nickname from the rest of the magical world. They weren't called protectors—they were called warriors.

Steve didn't often listen to Alder's history lessons, but this one had had him in rapt attention. He remembered Charity at what he now referred to as Vlad's impromptu barbecue. She was fierce and intense, ripping through vamps and demons like she was born to it. It had been thrilling. He wanted to know more of her people.

But first, they had to know more about her.

So after the little meet-and-greet with Daddy, they would trek deep into the Realm, hoping to get Charity fixed up. Roger figured Charity could get the pack past the old man and his shotgun without someone getting shot. From what Steve had heard, Charity wasn't so sure.

Barbara stepped through the portal next, her camo

jumpsuit and army boots strange for this detail. The only plants in the area were the brown, scraggly bushes and a few dying trees dotting the sidewalk. She clearly hadn't quite understood the term *urban jungle*.

Despite her dress-code confusion, she was a moderately attractive lady with a good, perky rack. Steve had heard she was a humorless woman with no use for men, but maybe that was because she hadn't gotten tickled just right yet. He wouldn't mind showing her how fun a man could be. They'd have to do something about that intense scowl, though. It was a dick shriveler, for sure.

Cole came through last, all six feet, five inches of him. The guy was massive, with a barrel chest, thick, swinging arms, and a big, flat face. He looked like he'd gotten kicked repeatedly with an ugly boot and left for dead.

Steve had seen the were-yeti in battle a few times, and the dude was fierce. Cole didn't give a damn what the danger was; he ran flat-out at anything the enemy could throw at him. Granted, *flat-out* was more of a slow lumber, but when he eventually got there, he ripped through his opponent no holds barred, vicious and intense.

Steve nearly chuckled.

Three intense fighters, a Rogue Natural who'd earned his stripes by going his own way, a warrior fae losing control of her magic, and a green alpha who intended to lead them all.

Steve would never say it to the alpha's face, because

he didn't want his head ripped off, but this whole situation was a clusterfuck. Roger was crazy for thinking a college kid could lead these rough-and-tumble shifters. They'd walk all over Devon the instant he issued an order one of them didn't like. The discord would likely make the Rogue Natural bugger off back to his crazy old lady and her vampire-loving friend.

If Steve were a smarter man, he never would have volunteered for this detail.

"What's the story with the kid alpha, anyway?" Dale asked as Barbara noticed the condoms not far from her boot. She didn't bother shifting away, just looked on, scouting the area. Nerves of steel, definitely. "Roger didn't give us too much to go on."

"He's an up-and-comer," Steve answered, checking the time on his phone. No word on what was keeping Devon. They must've been close. "He was the head of a pack in charge of extinguishing newbies. Did well there. I hear he took out a couple mid-level vamps on his own, and had a go at Vlad."

"Got his ass handed to him," Barbara said, eyes scanning. "Rookie move, going for Vlad."

"He did it to save the fae," Cole boomed, incapable of volume control. He'd be great at the hiding game, surely. *Good call, Roger.* "I was there. I saw it."

"Still," Barbara said.

Dale spat out a stream of brown liquid. "Vlad is of particular interest to the elves, lately. I got stopped by one of their grunts as I was running through the Realm.

A sprite. She asked what had prompted Roger to try to take Vlad down."

"What'd you say?" Cole boomed.

"He's only a few feet away from you, bro," Steve said, putting some distance between himself and the were-yeti. "You don't need to yell."

Dale shrugged at Cole. "A load of bollocks. That they had a grudge match because Roger got all his newbies…"

"If an elf had stopped you, they would've known you were lying," Barbara said. "They would've hauled you in."

"No shit," Dale said, exasperated. "I would've run like hell from an elf. What do you think I am, stupid?"

"At times," Barbara replied.

Dale scowled—and then scowled harder when he saw Steve's smirk.

"What's the story with Vlad, anyway?" Dale asked. "I heard he hasn't been seen in a while."

"Went underground when Charity barbecued him," Steve said.

"Underground, but not dormant," Barbara replied. "Only a fool would think he wasn't watching that fae from the shadows. He's planning. That's what elders do. They strategize."

"Very insightful." Steve winked at Barbara. "You have a real knack for stating the well known."

"Asshole." Barbara went back to scanning.

"It is true," Cole said. "Both the repeating of information we already know, and that Vlad is still active. I've heard how much interest he showed that girl. I was there when he tried to take her. He showed his determination. He won't let her go easily. He's just waiting for the right moment to strike again."

"Which brings us to why you're here," Steve said.

Cole nodded, his chest puffed out. Where an elder vampire would give most creatures pause, Cole just readied for battle.

"Where's the Rogue Natural, by the way?" he asked, giving Steve some suspicious side-eye. "He was supposed to be here."

"He'll meet us on the other side."

"That right?" Dale continued his sideways stare. "I also heard you wasn't a pack man."

Steve's smile grew at the soft threat. "*Au contraire*—that's French, by the way—I love Pac-Man. I spent a great deal of time playing it as a kid. Oops, here we are now."

Two vans, white and beige, pulled up alongside the crumbling curb, stopping near a pile of trash in front of a sign that said "no dumping." The doors of the vans slid open, ejecting four guys and three gals. Devon, the black-haired lady-killer, glanced Steve's way as Charity stepped up next to him. Her delicate features belied her obvious power. She didn't touch Devon, but Steve knew a lot about body language, and he noticed the way the young alpha leaned into her just a bit, sharing personal space with her. He dropped his head to her, whispering something.

"That's them, huh?" Dale asked before spitting.

"Nailed it," Steve told him.

"He's younger than I remember," Cole boomed.

Steve turned back to glance at the grim-faced snow-giant. "You embarrass yourself a lot, I take it. No wonder Reagan picked on you."

Cole's face crumpled into anger and his hands curled into fists. He'd been the only one brave enough to rise to Reagan's taunting one night in New Orleans. She'd had her hands full with him. He would've ripped her head off if she hadn't set his fur on fire.

"Oops. Sore subject?" Steve grinned.

Devon stalked toward them, power and authority brimming from his athletic frame. In his lesser twenties, he was still filling out, gaining a man's muscle and honing his strength. That didn't diminish the dominance and power that wafted from him like it was his birthright.

He stopped in front of the new pack members, his confidence not the only thing carrying his mantle. Steve's eyes widened as a thick, suffocating wave of magic rolled over him. It was the feeling he got whenever Roger stepped into a room, though not as potent. Not yet, anyway. In just a few months, Devon's power had obviously grown. It was heads and tails more intense than Steve had remembered. That was some fast maturing for this young buck.

"Steve." Devon stuck out his hand.

"Alpha." The handshake was firm and personal. Good politics.

"Emery?"

"Has no interest in seeing the sights of Chicago. He'll meet us on the other side."

Devon nodded as the rest of his pack drifted in behind him, Charity in the lead.

That was interesting. Had Charity naturally assumed the position of beta, or had Devon assigned it to her? Either way, the rest of the pack had acknowledged her status.

Devon's gaze touched on each new person before settling on Dale. Good instincts. Dale was absolutely the one to worry about. Steve had heard rumors regarding Dale's penchant for taking over packs he'd been sent to help, but it would have been obvious regardless. His body language screamed *challenge*, from his tense posture to his slight forward lean. He had no respect for this up-and-comer.

"I'm Cole," the yeti said, and Charity's brow wrinkled. She was probably wondering why he was shouting at everyone. "I took part in the battle on your property."

"Yes, of course," Devon said without skipping a beat, though Steve was certain Roger had kept that detail from him. Devon stepped forward to offer his hand.

Dale spat, the splash landing only a foot from Devon's shoe.

"Gross," Charity said, wrinkling her nose. Apparently no one had told her to look badass and say very little when meeting new shifters. How delightful.

"Barbara." Barbara nodded, not one for touching in any capacity. More's the pity. Devon, picking up on her vibe, nodded in return.

He turned to the side and pointed at a brown-haired guy with a vague sort of face who wouldn't stand out in a lineup. "That's my beta, Dillon."

Steve barely contained his surprise. The pack had a gap in communication where the beta was concerned, that was clear. Titles didn't match how they acted.

"That's Macy, beside him." Devon indicated a short, thin lady with brown hair and a hard expression. She didn't look like much, but Steve bet she was trouble in a pinch. A stunning blonde was next. "Yasmine, and beside her, Rod."

Steve remembered Rod, the linebacker. He'd be a real bruiser someday soon.

"And Andy," Devon finished, motioning at a surfer-looking guy Steve didn't recall. He hadn't gotten friendly with the locals after the skirmish at Devon's house.

Each new pack member nodded in turn, except for Barbara, who stared without blinking.

"We have reason to suspect Charity's dad is in the house," Devon said. "He wasn't too welcoming when Roger's people stopped by a few months ago. Prepare for an altercation upon entering."

"Yeah, but…we have her." Cole motioned at a dour-faced Charity.

"He won't be happy to see me," Charity mumbled. "We had...words before I left for college. He's not expecting me back."

"Getting past one old man isn't a problem." Dale's brown spit splattered the hot cement. "Devon, you take your crew and I'll load up these guys. We'll rendezvous at the address Roger supplied."

Steve grimaced. They'd barely given intros and already Dale was trying to assume control. This whole thing could derail right now. There were two strong leaders in this group, and they wouldn't be satisfied until one submitted to the other. The grapple for power might explode before they even hit the road.

Devon's unwavering stare hardened. Silence rolled through the crowd, only interrupted by Charity scratching the center of her chest.

Don't let him call the shots, bro, Steve thought at Devon. *Don't let him take your power. Make him drop his eyes, or make him challenge you. Don't let this go. Roger wouldn't.*

Steve knew from experience. Roger didn't take kindly to other shifters pushing their weight around, something Steve had learned the hard way.

One by one, Devon's muscles flexed. One by one, Dale's fingers curled into a ball. The air between them sizzled with magic, the two shifters pushed to their limit. Any moment one or both would explode—

Fiery magic tore through the air, biting into Steve's

body with an invisible spray of ghost needles. He jerked backward, startled by the unexpected pain. Dale did the same, bumping into a grunting Cole and throwing a hand up to protect his face.

Devon didn't so much as flinch.

Andy flew sideways, as if Charity were a bomb and the explosion had burst out through her right side. The unlucky sod tumbled through the air like a flailing rag doll, hitting the ground with a thump.

"Oh crap!" Charity exclaimed, slapping her hand over her mouth.

"What the hell, Charity?" Andy hollered when he came to a stop. "What'd I do to you?"

"Sorry!" Charity called over Rod's laughter. She rushed toward Andy, probably to help him up, but Dillon stepped in the way, blocking her. "I was trying to keep my magic in so I didn't blast it out toward the new guys. It accidentally leaked out the side."

"We talked about this, remember?" Andy pushed to standing and dusted himself off. Rod laughed harder. "If you feel one of those surges coming on, you walk away. Remember when we made that deal? Right after you blasted me into the refrigerator? You feel the surge and *you walk away.*"

"I know, I'm sorry! This was just a tiny surge, so I thought I could keep it in." Charity scoffed at Dillon. "Would you move?"

Another surge of power punched Steve. He took a step back with a ladylike gasp. Fire ants of pain crawled along his skin.

The blood drained from his face. This was a *tiny* surge? Steve hadn't even been her target, yet it felt like his face was being sanded off.

For the first time in a long time, Steve's beast did not want to emerge and fight. Unbelievably, he felt like running. Not to mention, elves could sense magical beings. If this magic went haywire anywhere near one of them, even a lesser-powered elf would notice. Traveling off the beaten path didn't matter a whole helluva lot when you were being followed.

They needed to get to the Flush, *pronto*.

"Charity, get in the car." Devon's voice was a whip-crack of command, his alpha magic rattling Steve's bones. The three new people, so damn confused they looked like clowns staring at an empty circus tent, swiveled to look at Devon.

The alpha had arrived.

"It's fine," Charity said. "Honestly, it's mostly under control."

It was a long fucking way from being *mostly* under control.

Devon turned to her. His power struggle was no longer with a slack-jawed Dale, but with a power-oozing warrior fae. His shifter magic boomed, making Steve wonder how he'd blasted that much out without changing shape.

As if she were a dog reacting to a silent whistle, Charity snapped her head toward Devon, staring at him like he was a rival magic holder competing for dominance. A beautiful fluidity took over her lithe body, and a strange glow emanated from her skin. The fingers on her right hand twitched, as if wrapping around an invisible sword.

A flash of brilliant blue eclipsed her focused brown eyes and a lovely smile tickled her lips. A strange music drifted in on the breeze, like cupids singing of battles and death, killing and mayhem. Magic rolled from her in thick, gooey waves.

"Are you done?" Devon asked in a low, rough voice.

How he withstood that onslaught of magic without at least half cowering—like everyone else—Steve had no idea.

Blue flashed over Charity's eyes again. "I'm just beginning. Can't you feel the thrill of it?"

A shiver flash-froze Steve's body, but strangely, his cock hardened. He was man enough to admit that this whole situation scared the shit out of him. Yet, strangely, he'd still take her—or one of her kind—to Pound Town. Exhilarating.

"Enough of this," Devon said, his body brimming with controlled supremacy. "You have to learn to master it until we can get you training. You'll end up hurting yourself or one of your own."

Like a balloon popping, the painful prickles and tiny punching fists dissolved. Her posture lost that breathtakingly lethal edge. She looked like a fallen angel, unsure, worried, and vulnerable. Steve's heart squished.

"Get in the car," Devon said softly, not yet letting go of his magic.

Heaving a sigh as she turned, she muttered, "I hate this weird magic."

Steve let chuckles relieve the tension. Now he understood why the young pup had transformed into such a strong alpha. Devon had needed to gain strength, power, and control to combat the unbalanced and unpredictable magic of the budding warrior fae. Roger had mentioned it, but he couldn't have prepared Steve for the experience. Steve had heard that her kind were mostly gentle and loving, but if roused, they'd rip the world apart. Devon had risked his own safety and well-being to help her control the uncontrollable. He was a good man, but what a trip.

Note to self: bed only trained warrior fae.

"This is the control you have over your pack?" Dale asked as everyone started toward the vans.

"Dave, give it a rest, would ya?" Steve said before Devon could turn around. He ran his fingers through his hair.

"My name is—"

"I agree," Cole intoned. "Give it a rest. At least until the fae has calmed down. That wasn't…pleasant."

"Neither is the volume of your voice," Steve murmured.

"Never enter a library with him," Barbara said, breaking off to go in the front van with Devon and Charity. Steve grinned, mostly because she wasn't kidding. Also because she'd rather ride with an unpredictable fae than Loudmouth Larkin.

"I get the feeling the girl and Daddy dearest don't get along?" Dale whispered as they neared the rear van.

"From what I gather, he was an abusive prick," Steve said, climbing into the van beside Andy. Rod glanced back from the driver's seat, but Macy, in the front passenger side, ignored them.

"A drunk, abusive prick and the reason her mother left her," Andy added as Cole swung into the rear, followed by Dale. Andy nodded at Steve. "Hey. Good to have ya."

"How's your face?" Steve replied.

"Why? Do I have scratches all over it?"

"You can't feel the road rash?"

"Not over the throb in my shoulder, no."

"If she can't control her magic, traveling through the Realm will not be…easy," Cole said.

"Neither will being in confined spaces with you," Macy murmured.

Steve huffed out a laugh while he rubbed his temples. "You're both right. Let's hope Emery is as good as everyone says. Otherwise, we're not going to get very far."

CHAPTER 2

Devon exhaled slowly as he took Charity's hand. His eyes darted up to meet Dillon's in the rear-view mirror. They exchanged the same silent message they'd pinged back and forth on multiple occasions these last couple weeks, waiting to finish the quarter so Charity wouldn't miss any school. *We're running out of time.*

It had initially been agreed that Charity could get through the spring quarter, but Devon worried they'd waited a month or more too long.

The van turned down yet another decrepit street, badly needing roadwork and clearly ignored by the city. This area of town had no end of them. Charity curled up to his side on the seat and dropped her head to his shoulder. Warmth unfurled in his middle, easing the anxiety that threatened to strangle him.

He'd known he would run into dominance issues with the new and more experienced pack members, but he hadn't realized it would come so soon. Dale hadn't even given Devon half a chance to lead before he'd challenged him. Given that Dale was ten times more experienced, Devon wasn't sure he could take the grizzled veteran. He knew for a fact his pack couldn't handle all three if they decided to band together. The new shifters were hardened. Savage. If it hadn't been for Charity, this journey would've taken a bad turn before it had even begun.

"I wouldn't give you this role if you didn't have her by your side."

Roger had said that after the battle with Vlad.

"Fighting is awfully hard when you're being flung through a window."

Devon stroked his thumb across Charity's smooth skin. Roger must've known this would happen. He must've known Charity would be willing to help Devon. Willing, and more than able.

A sudden surge of pride turned immediately to fear. She was wobbling. Hard.

Her power earlier had been sharp and biting. When it hurt even Devon, he knew it was blistering through her, sapping her energy and draining her resources. If the surge had been any stronger, she might've passed out.

He was terrified that one day she wouldn't wake up.

The van slowed to a stop. Charity looked beyond him and out the window, then grimaced. The disgusted expression crumpled into worry. "We're not going to find anything in there related to magic, Devon. I grew up in that house. If there was something as interesting as magic, trust me, I would've known."

He ran his thumb over the small dimple in her chin. "We've been over this. Whether or not we get answers, we're going to the Flush. We're going to get you help."

She sighed and shook her head as Dillon got out of the van. Yasmine joined him before sliding open the side door.

"This is going to be a bad joke if I'm not warrior fae," Charity mumbled, waiting for Devon to get out of the car.

"Vlad has put a lot of effort into trying to capture you," Dillon said, standing beside Yasmine. "If a vampire that old thinks you're warrior fae, then you're warrior fae. He wouldn't make a mistake that big and end up getting barbecued for his efforts." He smiled supportively. "We'll get you help, no problem."

"I have to agree with the boy," Barbara said, climbing out after them.

Dillon scowled at her, clearly not impressed with being called a boy.

The sticky warmth of the humid late afternoon wrapped around them. Garbage littered the cracked and worn cement, and potholes peppered the street. Trees leaned over broken fences and weeds strangled the run-down and forgotten yards.

The tiny, ramshackle house crouched in front of them, its paint peeling. One of the windows was covered with graffiti-scrawled particle board, and another had a ripped screen.

Yasmine picked up her shoe and glanced at the bottom. Her mouth twisted in distaste. She put it back down gingerly, trying to find a patch of cement that wasn't stained or splotched. *Good luck.*

Andy strolled over from the second van, somehow not at all bothered by the tension with the new pack members.

"So this is where you grew up, huh?" he asked Charity, stopping on Devon's other side. He probably didn't want to get tossed again. "A little spot of paradise."

Charity huffed out a laugh. "At least we owned our own home. That was kind of a big deal in this neighborhood."

As Devon took in the crime-riddled surroundings, noticing a used needle on the curb and a discarded little baggie commonly used for drugs up the sidewalk, his stomach twisted for Charity's stolen childhood. There was no playing in these streets, no friends having tea parties or football games on this front yard. Hell, she couldn't have felt safe crouching behind the tiny dwelling's bar-covered windows. The empty bullet casings twinkling in a patch of weeds by the van tires said as much.

He took a deep breath and smoothed over his expression. She'd lose her shit if she thought he was pitying her, and get all kinds of embarrassed if she sensed his disgust for the ramshackle house. This wasn't her fault. She'd had no control over this. And the fact that she'd made it out alive told him she could make it through anything. He was damn proud of her, when it came down to it—something he would tell her when they were away from the broken crack pipes and human feces. At the moment, he didn't trust that sadness wouldn't leak into his words. His childhood had sucked, but compared to this, he'd grown up in Wonka's chocolate factory.

"Is that a chalk outline?" Rod took four steps down the sidewalk and bent down to take a closer look. "It is. Holy shit."

Dillon and Cole both peered at the cement.

"I didn't realize they did chalk outlines—I thought that was only in the movies," Steve said, leaning up against the van with one ankle crossed over the other. His pose said boredom, but his flicking eyes, touching each window in every decrepit home surrounding them, said he was on high alert. He felt the danger of this place, and the lion in him was securing the territory.

Charity's eyes hadn't left the weather-beaten front door. A strange rigidity had crept into her body. "They do it when it's a homicide. If they feel like looking into it, that is."

"Let's get this done." Devon lightly grabbed Charity's arm and directed her along the disheveled walkway toward the blackened front stoop.

"Is it always this quiet?" Cole said.

"Not when you're present," Steve replied.

Charity looked at the sky before letting Devon lead her forward. "At this time of the day it usually was, yes. Later in the afternoon it'll get busier, then the evening and night will see the most action. I was always behind a locked door at that point, not that it would've helped if someone had decided to come in."

Devon barely kept from rubbing her back in support. From the sound of her voice, she didn't need it. This had been her reality, plain and simple. She probably recognized the horror of that, but she clearly hadn't given in to it. His pride rose in tandem with the sadness.

"A couple people looking out their windows," said Barbara, sounding like a SWAT team member.

"They won't bother us. It's the guys loitering or strolling up the street you have to worry about." Charity stopped in front of the door. "I hate being here."

"It's okay," Devon whispered. "A quick chat and we're gone."

Charity's smile held no humor. "I don't think this is going to go how you think it will go." She rapped on the door. "You all will want to clear to the side. He's got shit aim, but that won't stop him from trying."

"This is a level of crazy I wasn't prepared for," Rod said in a wispy voice, stepping off the walkway and onto the mostly dirt yard.

"Real sensitive, dick," Andy muttered.

"This isn't the half of it," Charity said before rapping again with hard, angry pounds. "You haven't met my old man yet."

"What the fuck do you want?" came through the door.

"Open up or I will bust this door down, Walt," she

hollered.

"You don't call your dad 'Dad'?" Andy asked.

"He didn't do a lick of fathering—why should he get the title?" Charity rapped again. "Last chance, Walt."

Tinkling sounded before a deadbolt turned over. The door opened a crack, revealing two long barrels.

"I'll take that." Fast as sin, Charity rammed the door wider with her shoulder, grabbed the end of the gun, and yanked it toward her, wrenching it out of the old man's hands. She kicked the door, catching the side of his face on its trajectory toward the wall.

The man in the doorway had ruddy cheeks from years of drinking and a shiny bald head surrounded by tangled gray hair. His spindly arms and thin, slightly bow-shaped legs didn't match the round gut half hanging out of a stained and ripped white T-shirt. Jeans hung too low, and his fly gaped open.

His bloodshot eyes narrowed when he saw her. He surveyed Devon next, then glanced behind them. "Get off my yard," he rasped.

"Good to see you, too," Charity said. "Now move. I need to get some stuff."

"I ain't got nothin' of yours here," he said with a sneer. "Get outta here, you little whore."

"Someone needs to enter this guy in a Miss Congeniality pageant—he'd clean up," Andy murmured, probably to Rod.

Devon clamped down on his rage. It would rile Charity up, and she didn't need any additional distractions.

"I'll leave when I get what I want, not before," Charity said with fire in her eyes. "Where'd Mom go?"

His lip curled. "You tell me."

"If I knew, I wouldn't need you, now would I? Where'd she go?"

"Get out of here. You don't think I got another gun? I got another gun. Get off my property before I go and get it."

Charity tossed the shotgun into the yard. "Answer me," she said, her voice low, her tone wobbling. A sheen covered her eyes, emotion leaking through her hard exterior.

Walt saw it and laughed, of all things. Rage pulsed hot in Devon's middle despite his desperate attempts to keep it at bay.

"Fuck that bitch, running out on me. She was a worthless whore, just like you."

Charity's jaw clenched. "Did she ever mention anything about magic, or her family?"

Walt stepped into the center of the doorway, staggered, and reached out to steady himself on the doorframe. It was four o'clock in the afternoon and already he was blasted.

"Her *family*?" His lips curled off his brown teeth, a sick smile filled with gaps. "Sure, she mentioned her family. Her deadbeat dad who couldn't kick down a damn dime. Her useless mother without a pot to piss in. Yeah, she mentioned them a time or two. But you know what she never did tell me about? *Your* family. Disgusting whore. She weren't no virgin, I knew that already, but preemies don't come in at nearly eight pounds. I knew something was susp'ious about that. I always did. That asshole who came knocking a couple weeks ago knew it, too. Perfect strangers know you're nothing but a bastard. See? Makes sense why I never did like you none. You were always such a prissy little bitch, just like your mother." He looked at Devon with foggy eyes before pointing at Charity. "You with this little bitch? Because if you are, you better be careful. Her and her mother are just the same; they'll fuck anything—"

Devon's vision went red, and before he knew what happened, he'd stepped forward and smashed his fist into the filthy man's face. Walt went down like a sack of rocks, hitting the floor, bouncing, and staying there.

"Thank God someone did it," Steve said. "I was having a hard time keeping my mouth shut."

Charity stared down at her dad, her back stiff. A tear slid down her cheek.

Devon's heart broke for her. "Don't listen to him," he said softly, this time allowing himself to rub her back. "He was drunk. Drunk and mean. He didn't really mean those things."

"Did you hear what he said?" She blinked her eyes to clear them, sending a few more tears gliding down her cheeks.

"He probably won't remember—"

"He doesn't think I'm his."

"She's smiling," Rod murmured behind them.

"Wouldn't you be with a dad like that?" Andy replied.

"That's a sign of danger in these fraught situations, though, right? I don't want to get blasted. It looks like it hurts."

"Good call."

The sound of shuffling meant everyone was scooting back. Everyone except Devon.

"He thinks I'm someone else's!" She laughed and threw her arms around Devon. "God, I hope he's right."

Devon squeezed her tight, reviewing what Walt had said. One thing stuck out like a sore thumb.

Roger hadn't sent someone out here a couple of weeks ago. Not even a couple of months ago. He'd tried when they'd first found Charity and elected to wait to try again until she could go herself.

So if it wasn't Roger, who was checking up on Charity's past?

CHAPTER 3

Charity shuddered out a breath as she stepped over Walt's foot. She couldn't properly express the hope that this disgusting sack of crap wasn't her flesh and blood. She guessed that was probably sad to say, but there was no use denying it.

"Why wouldn't my mom say anything, though?" she wondered aloud, pausing in the living room to look over the crushed cans and empty whiskey bottles littering the floor. Papers and magazines were strewn across the coffee table and couch. Upon closer inspection, none of them had been sent to this address. "When he was yelling and cursing and we were hiding in the bedroom, or when we escaped for the day to the park, or just when I got older—why didn't she ever mention he wasn't my real dad?"

"Maybe she thought you wouldn't take the news well." Devon stepped in with her before making a gesture to the others. He wanted them to stay outside.

A part of Charity relaxed a little. She wasn't ashamed of her upbringing, but she'd moved past it. With the encouragement of Devon and the pack, she'd blossomed into someone else. To share the horrors of her past now, when she was trying to move forward, would scratch the surface of embarrassment. The only reason she was allowing Devon inside was because he needed to see where her scars had come from.

Not that she'd be able to chase him away. His alpha protectiveness was in overdrive right now. She could tell he wanted to rip her out of this place.

She smiled a little to herself. It felt good to be protected by someone bigger and badder than she was. Not many could fill his shoes.

"The smells in here are…" Devon crinkled his nose.

"What?" she asked, stopping at the entrance to the kitchen. Her heart sank. The faded yellow countertops had felt like her portal into high-dollar kitchens, where culinary magic was just around the corner. Now, they were covered in empty food containers, wrappers, and crumbs. The trash can in the corner was spilling over. Her shoe stuck to the floor, something yellow having been spilled and not cleaned up. More stains covered the faded linoleum at the bottom of the fridge, where a smear of crusty red interrupted the white. "That looks like blood."

"I smell blood, though not much. Urine, something rotting, mold—this place is a petri dish for gross." His hand curved to the swell of her hip. "Are you okay?"

"This was my favorite space. It's where I taught myself how to cook. He never came in here after he started on the whiskey." She took a deep breath and turned away. "I didn't think it would be this hard to see."

Silently, she moved to the two bedrooms at the back of the house. If her mother had wanted to hide anything from her, she would have hidden it in the bedroom she'd shared with Walt. Lord knew there wasn't anywhere else in the tiny house.

Memories accosted her when she stepped inside. Of her mother in the bathroom, doing up her hair. Of the nights she'd snuggled in here with her mother, knowing Walt was passed out on the couch.

Of the day she'd found her mother's goodbye note.

"I asked her once why she'd married Walt—she hated when I didn't call him Dad. She laughed and made an off-handed remark about fortune-tellers and their crystal balls."

Charity's gut pinched, that comment suddenly having a lot more weight than it used to. It hit very close to home, given Charity had received a reading herself not that long ago.

She shook it off. Her mother viewed tarot card readings and fortune-tellers as a means of distraction—as entertainment. If it was anything more, she would've talked about magic through the years, a topic that never came up.

"She said Walt didn't always used to be like this. That the alcohol took over and changed him. So I asked why she stayed. I'll never forget the look on her face. It was the look of a broken woman. A woman beaten down by life. She just shook her head and turned away.

I didn't understand it at the time—I still don't, truth be told, but it was clear that some things were just beyond her. She'd hit a wall in life, and she couldn't figure out how to scale it. I never asked again. Then, a year later, she was gone. It's that look that still haunts me. It's why I finally forgave her."

Emotion rose, unbidden. She bowed where she stood and turned, knowing Devon would be coming up behind her, thankful for it when he wrapped his arms around her and squeezed her close. Sobs racked her body, the pain so fresh it felt like yesterday.

She'd never wanted to come back. Not really. She'd put on a brave face, and even told herself it would be good to see her roots again—a final farewell—but it felt so different now that she was actually here. The horror was sucking her under. The pain was slicing her up a second time.

"Look what you've tied yourself to," she couldn't help but say. "Look what I am. Unwanted. I'm the girl everyone walks away from."

Devon turned her to face him and raised her chin. She looked up into his beautiful brown eyes, dancing with green and gold specks. "There is nothing wrong with you, Charity. Nothing. Do you hear me? You didn't let any of this bring you down. Any of it. You're a fighter. You're a *survivor*. I aspire to be like you. If the others couldn't see that, then it's on them, not you."

She dropped her forehead to his chest, hot tears running down her face.

"If it makes you feel better," he said, rocking her gently, "my mother banned me from my house. I didn't leave—I was forced out. I'm an orphan with living parents, just like you. Except, *unlike* you, it turned me into an asshole. A guy no one could get close to. Then you came along. You make me palatable."

Laughter bubbled up with the pain. She took another deep breath. "I hate this."

"I know."

"I was doing fine, happily ignoring all of this. I finally had my life together."

"And then you met me. See? I'm the real asshole here, not you."

"I love you."

He tipped her face up again and settled his lips onto hers. Despite everything, or maybe because of it, her body wound up. Heat pounded in her core. She wanted to escape into his embrace. To run from this, if only for a moment, and lose herself in the feel of his body.

"I've never had sex in my room," she said against his mouth, feeling down his hard chest. "It seems like a shame."

He groaned, and his arms jerked tighter. He tilted his head so his forehead rested against hers. "I'd love to take you right now, Charity, but your…*Walt* is knocked out in the front room, there's a gun in the front yard, and we're dealing with a few impatient shifters who don't respect me and the ticking time bomb that is your magic. If there was ever a terrible time, this is that time.

But I promise, as soon as it's safe, I'll give you the ride of your life."

She smiled against his lips and took a moment to just hang on for dear life, feeling grounded in the storm. "Party pooper," she whispered.

"It is killing me to be a party pooper, I assure you. I'm hard enough to cut glass. But being an alpha sometimes means saying no, apparently. Who knew?"

She sighed, returning to the moment. "Let's get this done and get out before the man that is hopefully not my father wakes up."

"If he isn't, who is? Roger and Vlad think you come from a royalty line of warrior fae, but they haven't come out of the Flush in…generations. Whoever it was must've had ties to them, except…who could that have been? Don't you wonder—"

"No," she said, searching the drawers. Her mother's clothes were still gone—no surprise there. "I haven't wondered about it yet, no. For two reasons. One, this is the first time Walt has ever implied I'm a bastard. He's yelled every name under the sun at me, but if he had been armed with this ammo, he would've said something before now. Believe me. Even if my mom didn't, he would've." She crossed to the closet.

"And the second?"

She paused in pushing Walt's faded and ratty clothes out of the way. As she contemplated the answer, she fought the tears. She fought the pain. "If Walt isn't my father, then my father had no problem letting me be raised by that incredible asshole in this hellhole. I need to celebrate the possible win before I fall into the loss."

Sadness flickered across Devon's features. Charity felt that same sorrow permeate every fiber of her being. One parent who'd left her was bad enough, but add in a second?

The lid on her emotions wobbled. Tears filled her eyes again.

She pushed them away. She had a job to do here, and Roger was counting on her. She needed to see this through and get the hell out of here. When she was out of this cesspit and wasn't fighting for her life, she could slide into the pain and the rejection. But if she did so now, she risked falling into the strong undertow of magic that was constantly pulling at her. She couldn't afford to black out or go on a killing spree right now.

"If Walt is not blood related, that will have to be good enough for me," she said, checking all the corners and cracks in the closet. As expected, she came up dry.

Devon didn't say anything as she passed in front of him, and she was glad for it.

Her old room was as she'd left it. The twin bed was made, the desktop was bare, and the rickety dresser drawers were empty, as was the closet. She'd taken everything worth having, and had thrown the rest away.

"At least that dick hasn't been loitering in my room. That's something," she said. Her space was still her own, even now. Her corner of the world remained untouched. A small weight lifted from her shoulders.

"The smell in here..." Devon's nose wrinkled near the bed. His brow creased next to the curtains. "It's..." He shook his head. "It's too faint to be certain, but..." His voice drifted away. She didn't have to be told what he was thinking.

"The person who visited Walt..." Charity hadn't missed that little nugget. No doubt the secret visitor was the one who'd convinced him that she wasn't his child. She *had* been large for a preemie—nearly eight pounds. It was why she hadn't ended up in the NICU. Or so her mother had always said.

Who would have come here uninvited to look into her heritage?

"Vlad. It was Vlad, wasn't it?"

His name tasted spicy-sweet on her tongue, which was strange, given the distaste she felt for her would-be kidnapper. But then, vampires were hunters of humans—they wielded seduction as a weapon.

Devon didn't comment. He didn't have to.

"What's he been doing for the last couple weeks, I wonder, besides mucking around in my life?" She took a deep, calming breath to still the sudden flush of anger.

Don't lose your shit, Charity. Gotta stay calm. Keep the magic locked inside.

Her heart sped up as she stepped into her closet. If her mother had snuck in to leave her a message, she would have hidden it in here, in their special hiding place. Those who didn't know about the little hideaway would never find it.

Charity had checked it often throughout her childhood, finding little notes or silly drawings, and just as often after her mom had left.

It had always been empty, then.

She felt above the dusty shelf and reached into the bottom right corner. Her finger traced the little grove and she pushed the flap open. A small package waited inside, wrapped with care. Charity should know—she was the one who had wrapped it.

Tears filled her eyes as a hollow feeling carved out her heart.

She tried to focus on the job at hand. She tried to remind herself that she could fall to pieces later. She tried, but the weight of her suffering dragged down her head. Tears tracked down her face. The fight went out of her.

"What is it?" Devon asked.

Charity shrugged, pocketing the package. "Just some pictures. Of me. When I was a baby. And some other stuff I thought she might want. It was hers. She stashed it in there for safekeeping. In her note, she told me she was leaving it for me. I just thought…" A sob lodged in her throat, making it difficult to swallow. "I'd hoped she'd come back. I'd ho-hoped she'd miss me, and come back." She shrugged, overwhelmed by feelings of inadequacy. "I thought maybe she'd check the little cubby to see if I'd left her my address. I knew she wouldn't want to stay here with Walt, but I thought ma-maybe she would check in on me."

Devon was there in an instant, wrapping her in his arms.

"Why would a mother leave her only daughter?" she begged, her hands limp at her sides, wanting the earth to open up and swallow her whole. The agony pulled at her, dragging her down. "What d-did I do so wrong that she wouldn't want to take me with her? That she would leave me in this hellhole—"

"*Shhh*," Devon cooed, rocking her back and forth. "It wasn't you, Charity, please." His words were filled with pain and rage. "It wasn't you. She wasn't strong enough for this life, and she knew you were. She was probably so broken by the end, like you said, that she couldn't feel at all. Please."

It was the pain in that *please* that snapped all her focus to him. That reeled her in from the pit of raw pain. Because while everyone else might've left, he never had. Even when he hadn't thought much of her, he'd walked into battle right at her side. He'd laid down his life, multiple times, to protect her. Hell, right now he was enduring all this for her.

She'd had crappy luck with people throughout her life, but it had all been worth it to find him.

Without warning, they were tearing at each other's clothes. She grabbed his basketball-style sweats, easy to rip off if he needed to shift, and yanked. Buttons broke free and the fabric came away. He already had her jeans over her hips, reaching between her thighs and kneading her just right. She moaned against his lips, wrapping her fingers around his velvety shaft, desperate to have him inside of her.

"Alpha," Steve yelled down the hall.

Charity barely heard him as Devon pushed aside the crotch of her panties and stroked his fingers up her slit.

"Alpha, we got company, and it ain't human."

Devon shoved forward, trapping Charity against the wall, his kisses wild and desperate. His fingers worked inside her before he stepped back and ripped her around. She braced her palms against the wall and bent, giving him access.

"I want you so bad," she said, her sex swollen and her body on fire. "Devon, please."

"Devon, you back there?" Urgency crept into Steve's voice.

Devon's hand tightened on Charity's shoulder as he held her put. The tip of his cock parted her folds before he paused, breathing heavily.

"Fuck!" he yelled as he stepped back, misery and regret ringing through that one word. The next moment, his fist went through the wall. He pulled back and punched it again before slamming his palm against it a couple of times.

"We can't do this now, Charity," he said in a strangled voice. "I love you more than words can say. I will always do what's best for you. But damn it, as much as I want to, I cannot fuck you right now."

Another wave of heat ripped through her core, and she moaned, still braced against the wall. It took all of her effort not to say the thing she knew would break his resolve: *Please, Devon,* please *fuck me.*

"Boss, you all right?" Steve called. "We got a lower-level demon ambling up the street. We need some direction out here. This old drunk dude is waking up, too. Not sure what you want to do with him. I'd be happy to pull his arms off, if you want."

"Tell them to hold. And leave Walt for now. I'll be right there," Devon yelled, sweat beading on his forehead and his chest heaving. He bent and grabbed up his sweats, his eyes snagging on her nudity. "Being an alpha has never been as hard as it is at this moment," he murmured, turning away.

It was that comment that dragged her out of the fog. That comment that grounded her.

She smiled through the pain of her mother's abandonment, running a finger over the package in her pocket. She'd gotten through this once, and she'd get through it again. This time, though, she had a man by her side who was every bit as strong as she was.

"We can handle a demon in our sleep," she said, pulling up her pants as Devon secured the buttons on his sweats.

"Each of the three new wol—shifters could, too. This is going to be a play for authority." He gritted his teeth and glanced around the room. "We should head out. How much longer do you need?"

She shook her head. "I'll just check my desk and under my bed. That's it. There's nothing here."

He stepped into the hall and glanced around. "Is there a back door?" He glanced at her window. "Will you be okay if I go to the front of the house?"

"I'll be fine. These windows have bars, if you hadn't noticed, and the back door has been swelled shut since before I left. I'm good."

He nodded and took a step before pausing. He put his hand on the frame of the door and grinned. "Don't be too long. I might need a heavy hitter to subdue these new shifters. I'd fight them myself, but I just got my nails polished."

She laughed as she strode over to the bed. A couple of pieces of torn paper lay on the orange carpet under the edge of the mattress. Upon closer inspection, they were from a torn-up photograph. She could make out the leg of a man in one piece, and half a baby's body in the other. Her as a baby and Walt, maybe? She certainly would have left such a picture behind, and she could even understand him ripping it up, but why were two fragments in her room? If he'd ripped it up here, no way would he have cleaned it up. Cleaning wasn't his strong suit.

Although the cleanliness of this room no longer mattered, she stuffed them in her pocket to be thrown away when next she saw a garbage can. That done, she double-checked the dresser—still empty—and moved on to the desk. The long desk drawer where she'd kept her pens and highlighters clunked against the lock when she pulled.

She frowned and tried again, wiggling it a little. She

had never locked this desk. Why would she? She had nothing of value, and Walt had always preferred to scream his curses, not write them down.

The key lay in the first of the small drawers. The lock clicked and she finally pulled it open. Then froze.

A small envelope stared up at her. Her name was scrawled across the center in an elegant hand. Not her mother's handwriting, either, and certainly not Walt's.

She pulled it out and turned it over, revealing a red wax seal.

"Elegant," she said into the hush, feeling a dark foreboding seep into her gut.

The interior of the envelope flashed gold, as did the frame of the cream-colored stationery tucked inside. Written on the paper, in the same delicate scrawl was:

Dearest Charity,

I know where your mother is.

What a surprise, I know, given Roger is still in the dark. But then, few people can hide from me.

To visit her now would certainly mean your demise, given the status of your magic. Have no fear; I will hold the information close to my heart until you are ready to commence the next phase of your life. When you are ready, just let one of my people know. They are always near.

Best wishes,
Your Best Friend Forever

CHAPTER 4

HER VISION PULSED white. Her blood turned to ice.

"Charity?" Dillon called from the front.

She couldn't look away from the note. She couldn't find her voice to answer.

"Charity, do you need help?" Footsteps rang down the hall, the pace urgent. "Oh, there you are. Hey—what's the matter?"

Still Charity couldn't look away from the note clutched in her shaking hand.

Dillon stepped in next to her and peered down at what she was holding. "Your best friend forever?"

"Vlad. It's what I call Vlad. B-F-F."

"Oh sh—" He braced his hands on her upper arms. "Let's show this to Devon. Do you need to get anything else? Hand sanitizer, perhaps? I'd take a squirt, too, if you have some."

Her mouth moved but nothing came out. Her heart pinged around her ribcage.

"Yep, let's get moving. Devon is currently in a standoff with Dale. Cole is siding with Dale, saying we should capture the demon and question it. Which is ridiculous. If the person who summoned it isn't a total idiot, they would've bound the demon from talking. It'll just waste time. There's obviously a reason Dale doesn't have his own pack. Devon can definitely take him, but it'll be a hard fight, and they'll both take a lot of damage. We don't have time to wait for them to heal. Especially now that... Well, Vlad just threatened you, right? His people are always near?"

Vlad hadn't threatened her—he had found her mother.

Vlad knew where her mother was, and while he could be lying...she doubted it. A vampire like him wouldn't need to.

"What do you need from me?" Her voice was hoarse, as though she hadn't used it in decades. She could barely feel her legs. What she *could* feel, however, was her magic. It bubbled and built, rising through her body. Electricity energized her, sizzling through her arms and across her skin.

"Best-case scenario, you quickly end the challenge, delicately if possible, free Devon up to actually lead, and make sure we get the hell out of here. That demon is drawing attention from some interesting characters. Some of those spectators look like they had meth for breakfast. Seeing a real-life demon when you are probably plagued with theoretical demons is not a fun party. Three of the spectators are packing. I don't feel like getting shot today."

"You are awfully chatty."

"It's stress. Stress makes me talk."

Walt sat muttering to himself on the floor next to his recliner, one eye swollen shut.

"We didn't know what to do with him," Dillon said, barely pausing to gesture.

"Leave him." Charity pulled the note tighter to her chest. "If I'm lucky, I'll never see him again."

"We'll make sure you're lucky."

The sun rained down on the strange scene outside. Devon stood opposite Dale, engaged in a silent stare-off. Cole waited behind Dale, his enormous shoulders squared and his eyes hard, standing his ground. Devon's pack waited behind him, their faces grim and their hands flexed. They thought they were about to fight. Barbara stood off to the side with Steve, withdrawn from the scuffle.

Beyond their group, a horned creature ambled toward them from down the street, as though just learning to use its legs. Its misshapen limbs looked like they were covered in dried black tar, with claws instead of hands and hooves instead of feet. Stringy clumps of flesh fell from one thigh, and one huge tooth gaped from its swollen, red, pus-coated lips. Its eyes glowed red.

"That is the ugliest demon I have ever seen," Charity said, her stomach turning.

"It's barely a level-one demon," Barbara said. "A group of uninformed witches can conjure one of those. It can barely function up here."

"Can it speak?" Charity asked.

"No. It probably doesn't even have a tongue. It's in bad shape."

Charity gestured at it in annoyance, noticing a small cluster of men on the other side of the street watching it with wide eyes and slack jaws. "Why the hell haven't you taken it down? Isn't our job to hide magic from non-magical humans?"

"Shifters need one true leader," Dillon murmured close to her ear. "And right now, there are two. They need to sort it out so we can get moving."

Charity stared at Dillon for a beat, her heart in pieces, her nerves shot, her life in upheaval.

I know where your mother is.

Was that how Vlad knew Charity's real father wasn't Walt? And if so, did he have proof of her paternity? He was sure smug as hell—that had come through loud and clear…

Warmth trickled through her middle, then turned into a gush of liquid heat to her limbs. Lava bubbled up from that place deep inside her, followed by a surge of heat so great that she momentarily lost her sight. The day returned, blotchy and overexposed. Her head felt light and electricity sizzled every inch of her flesh.

Devon's face snapped toward her.

"Not this time," Dale growled, springing toward Devon, following through on what must've been a challenge.

The movement seemed so slow.

"Where is my sword?" Charity asked distractedly. Dillon jogged backward.

I don't need a sword.

She shoved a hand through the air. Electricity popped and crackled around her. Green surrounded Dale as he prepared to change, but a spark flared to life next to him and exploded in a silent shock wave of power.

Electric fire scored his skin. His body flew to the side, his limbs windmilling, his eyes as big as the world. He smacked into a tree and fell to the ground in a heap.

Cole had barely turned toward her, violence in his eyes, before she whipped her hand his way.

Magic followed the path set by her hand—a small spark appeared next to the were-yeti's mighty frame, then exploded in a concussion of air so strong it knocked his feet off the ground. Unlike Dale, he didn't move as he soared through the air. He hit one of the vans, dented it, grunted, and landed on his feet. Only his feet weren't prepared to hold him.

His hands slapped the ground, followed by his face and then his body. He groaned loudly.

Charity was already moving.

Fire ate her alive. It scratched across her spine and punched her vital organs. She jogged out to the middle of the street, thrumming with the need for violence. Wanting to blow this whole neighborhood sky-high. A song drifted on the breeze, but it was off-key. Wrong, somehow. Intense agony screamed through her body, making her vision waver again, making her knees weak.

She ignored it.

The demon changed course, ambling toward her.

It had been sent for her. One day, she would find its maker and enact her revenge. For now, she'd take out the messenger.

She turned to face the creature then bent, falling into the depths of her magic. Floating on top of it. Sinking below the surface.

The sky sparkled brighter, and the air filled with a noise like a bug zapper. The power was pounding at her, thrashing her from the inside out, and she'd accidentally called on the wrong magic. Her sun flares only worked on vampires.

She pushed her hands forward. Balls of light condensed in her palms, spitting electricity and fire, and shot toward the demon. They hit it center mass, soaking into its middle before exploding. Body parts flew up and out, arcing through the sky before splatting against the cracked and pockmarked road.

Still her power climbed, an internal explosion blazing across her bones. Her skin felt stretched. Her jaw ached from clenching it against the pain.

"Charity."

Her name sounded distorted, as off and wrong as that loud tune shrieking through the day.

"Charity!"

The urgency in the speaker's voice pulled her out from under the pounding waves of magic. A different sort of magic washed over her, soothing and cool.

"Come back to me, Charity."

The fear in those words hit her first. Then the timbre, so familiar.

The soothing magic pulled her out of the fog. She blinked against the glare of the day, the black receding from her field of vision.

Devon stood five feet from her, his expression one of desperate determination. Pain tightened the skin around his eyes and made a vein jump over his clenched jaw.

"It's over," he said, his next step toward her costing him obvious effort. "Let's calm down. Let's slow it down."

"It hurts, Devon," she admitted, the act of forcing her magic down tearing her apart. "It's hurting you."

"Don't worry about me. This is nothing." His next step came slow, like he was walking through water. "Calm down with me. Let me get to you."

A horn blared behind them.

Without thinking, Charity spun. A blast of magic so potent it crackled like a lightning bolt exploded next to the oncoming vehicle. The metal dented. The car rocked up on two wheels before slamming back down. The driver's eyes rounded as she reached for the glove box. Her door opened and a gun came up.

"Andy," Devon yelled. "Macy."

"On it." Andy raced forward.

"Yup." Macy followed closely behind.

They stood in the line of fire between Charity and the woman who clearly did not plan to take shit, regardless of whether it was magical.

"Come back to me," Devon said to Charity, forcing another step forward.

Something moved in Charity's chest, hot and sharp. It felt like her heart was being cut out. Devon winced and dropped his head, as though walking through a gale-force wind of razor blades.

"We can handle this," he said.

"Ma'am, we'll pay for it, I promise. If you'd just—" Andy's pleas were cut short by the woman's explicit description of what she'd like him to do to his balls.

Charity let the shrieking tune cover it up. She stomped on her magic. Wrestled with it. Forced it down. The effect stole her breath and deadened her legs. Her arms dragged at her shoulders. Her back gave out and bowed. A moment later, she was falling, the blackness coming for her again.

CHAPTER 5

THE PAIN CUT off suddenly, and then Charity fell bonelessly to the ground. Devon barely got there before her head hit the pavement.

"Everyone, load up," Devon shouted, his heart in his throat. That was the most magic he'd ever felt from her. She clearly couldn't handle it anymore. There was too much for her to force into submission. It was like being swept up in a tidal wave. "Dale, give that woman Roger's card. Steve, get on the phone with Roger. We need to get word to Emery. Get him to the portal *now*."

"The plan was to leave at daybreak when—"

"I don't give a shit what the plan was, Dale." Devon hefted Charity and headed toward the closer van. "She has no time. Get your ass in gear, or find yourself a new pack."

"Roger assigned—"

Devon swung around and stared him down. "I don't give a shit about Roger, and I certainly don't give a shit about you. You heard me. Do as I say, or leave. Get in my way when I am trying to save this warrior fae, and I'll kill you."

Dale's chest swelled, and he took a step Devon's way, a dickhead to the last. Before he could get the words out of his open mouth, Steve grabbed him by the shirt, bunched it, and threw, all in one movement. Dale's arms windmilled as he flew through the air for the second time that afternoon.

"I've got Roger's card." Cole reached into his sweats pocket and turned toward the ranting woman still waving her gun. Little did she know that a gun wouldn't keep a shifter down for long, not unless it was a shot directly to the brain. Everything else would heal in time.

"You've won another one," Barbara said softly as Devon passed.

He nearly did a double take, but he didn't have time to dwell on her meaning. Charity's breathing was shallow and her skin felt too hot. This was one of the bad episodes. One of the times when her body struggled to process her magic.

He pumped out more magic to help balance her. His magic always seemed to have a positive reaction— the yang to her yin. Unfortunately, if he did any more, he'd lose himself to his wolf and be forced to change.

"Only those with excellent control in Devon's van," Barbara said, following him and stopping by the door as he got Charity situated in the back.

"Good point," Dillon said, jogging over. "We forgot to mention that. When Charity loses control and Devon has to flood her with power, he'll drive you wild with wanting to change. It's not pleasant."

"I'm fine." Macy jogged over as well, leaving Cole to deal with the irate woman. She seemed perturbed that he wasn't worried about the gun two feet from his chest.

"I'm out." Rod headed to the other van.

Steve paused with a phone to his ear, looking between the vans. Finally, his wild-eyed gaze settled on Devon. His lion clearly felt the call. He shook his head. "I better follow the linebacker kid without two brain cells to rub together."

Andy chortled as he got into the other van.

Cole didn't say a word as he got into the front passenger seat. Barbara filed into the middle bench seat, beside Dillon. Devon couldn't see if Dale picked himself up and headed to the front van. At the moment, he didn't care.

"You guys are coming around, huh?" Dillon said to Barbara and Cole as Macy hopped into the driver's seat.

"That fae needs protection," Cole said, buckling in. "It is our duty, but it's also the smart thing to do. Protect her, and she'll protect the pack. In this instance, I agree with the current alpha."

Cole's words weren't lost on Devon. The *current* alpha. He wasn't offering his allegiance, he was participating *for now*. It was a big distinction.

"Dude." Macy looked at Cole. "Do you always sound like a robot with a broken volume button, or..."

"I hope you grow on me," Cole muttered. Or, at least, it was a mutter for him.

Dillon jolted as the van pulled away. He spun

around, looking down at Charity.

"Stop!" he shouted.

Macy slammed on the brakes, and they all bumped forward.

"We don't have time—" Devon started, but Dillon was already crawling over Barbara to get out of the van.

"She got a note. She must've dropped it." He fumbled with the lock before ripping open the door. A horn blared from behind them.

"What's he talking about?" Devon asked, rocking Charity, terror dripping down his spine. She was burning up and shivering. Something wasn't right. She'd never reacted this badly before.

"He's…" Barbara twisted to try to see.

Macy looked in the rearview mirror. "He grabbed something off the pavement."

"A note, did he say?" Cole tried to turn around in a seat that barely contained him.

Dillon appeared at the van door as the horn blared again. The van in front had stopped down the road.

"She got this." Dillon motioned for Barbara to scoot over. He handed the note back to Devon. "She must've dropped it when she freaked out."

"She did not freak out; she had a magical—"

"Yes, yes, we know," Dillon interrupted Cole.

Devon's gaze snagged on the first line of the note. Then the last. Cold washed through him. "How did Vlad know she calls him her BFF? She only spoke of that around the pack. Didn't she?"

Dillon shrugged.

"The vampires have their spies," Barbara said, looking back. "As do we. What is the nature of that note?"

"Do you also have to be weirdly stilted in your communication to be an elite?" Macy asked her. "Because I'm sensing a pattern."

Barbara showed no signs of having heard.

Devon passed the note forward. "Hang on to that. She'll want it." He hesitated before pressing his hand to her forehead. Still hot. "Did she believe it?"

"She was blindsided," Dillon said. "It threw her for a loop. But yeah, I think she must believe it."

Barbara studied the note before passing it forward to Cole. "It's a trick of some kind," she said authoritatively. "He might know where her mother is, but there is more to it. He hopes to gain something from it."

"Yes. We're not dense. We know that." Dillon shot her a flat look. "Charity must know it too. The problem is, she's still big-time screwed up about her mother leaving. She won't be rational."

"It could be his way of getting Charity back out of the Flush," Devon said, staring out the window. "It's a good lure."

Everyone in the van nodded. There was no arguing with that.

Cole's phone chimed. "Emery has been contacted. He hadn't entered the Realm yet, thankfully. He's heading in now. Roger says to hang tight while he scouts the portal. There's been a lot of activity in the

Realm. Elves are patrolling in record numbers."

Devon gritted his teeth. "She doesn't have a lot of time."

"You'll need to think on what is more important," Barbara said, her eyes softening to something almost human, "her life, or her freedom. The elves would be able to help her."

Words that had been plaguing Devon for months forced themselves into the forefront of his mind.

The time will come when you need to make a choice. A choice that concerns the rest of your life, and more importantly, her life. To save Charity's life—to give her a life—you must take the hard road, sacrifice your heart, and let her go.

Pain knifed through Devon's middle. Karen was an incredible *Seer* who was almost never wrong.

"The longest she's been out is three and a half hours." Devon sucked in a deep breath. "We'll give her that long. If she doesn't wake up…" He swallowed down the words, unable to get them out, and looked down at Charity's beautiful, cherubic face. The alpha in him flared and his arms tightened around her possessively. Protectively. He couldn't imagine leaving her for any reason. He couldn't imagine handing her over to anyone.

But he wouldn't be able to live with himself if he didn't and she died because of it.

CHAPTER 6

Devon stood just outside the open door of the van, staring through the trees at the collection of disgusting creatures in the distance. Like the demon Charity had decimated earlier, these creatures had charred limbs ending in thick claws, glowing eyes, and misshapen heads.

And they were gathered in front of the nearest portal into the Realm.

Devon's pack was a hundred miles from Charity's house on the outskirts of a small town, the entrance point Emery had chosen for their journey. The mage was supposed to be waiting for them on the other side of that portal, which they could only reach through a wall of demons.

Vlad had worked with demons in their last run-in with him. Devon didn't like the implications.

"You're sure this Emery character is on the right side of things?" asked Dale, who had, regrettably, decided to continue on with the journey. Devon suspected his persistence had more to do with not disappointing Roger than any dedication to the cause.

"No, but Roger arranged him as our guide," Devon said, counting thirteen demons in all. That number was probably significant to this situation, but he had no idea how. He wasn't chummy with any witches or mages.

"How would these demons know to show up at the exact portal we'd planned to use, at the exact time we'd planned to use it?" Cole asked, and everyone repeatedly flinched as though his words were machine gun fire.

Devon held up his hand. "Cole, if you can't figure out how to whisper, don't speak at all."

"I am—"

"No." Devon shot Cole a warning glare. "You're not."

Cole frowned, but he shut his trap.

Steve emerged in human form from a bush behind him, his chest heaving from his two quick changes and his body glistening with sweat. Given that were-lions were known for their stealth, and Steve seemed to be on Team Devon for the moment, Devon had sent him to scout out the area.

"Besides, this isn't the exact time we'd planned to use it," Devon said, looking out over the field. The dying sun glinted off the windows of a housing development that overlooked the area. Their adversary was bold—the portal wasn't far enough from civilization that a bunch of inhuman weirdos would escape notice for long. Eventually someone would get curious or suspicious, and walk or drive out to see what had gathered the small crowd. Since there weren't any humans gawking at the monsters, let alone any authorities, these demons couldn't have been here for long. He said as much.

"Good observation," Barbara said, as though she hadn't made that connection. His original pack murmured their assent.

"They also look about the same as the demon in the street near Charity's house," he continued, grabbing his phone. "It wouldn't be a stretch to suspect the same person called them."

"These demons are more advanced," Barbara said. "Lower level three, mostly. A couple of high twos and, if I'm not mistaken, one lower level four. That one might give us some trouble."

"What's the demon scale, again?" Andy asked.

Yasmine shifted her stance next to him, clearly wondering the same thing but not wanting to appear uninformed enough to ask. When she'd first joined them, Yasmine had expressed interest in him—only he'd already started to fall for Charity. Now that he and Charity were openly together, Yasmine seemed to have withdrawn from the pack somewhat, but Devon was confident she'd find her new normal in time. Now was clearly not that time.

"There are levels within the levels, but the overall power scale goes to six," Barbara replied. "Six being Lucifer himself, the most powerful demon in the worlds. He stands alone on his pedestal. So you can see that even a lower level four is reason to bring extra underwear."

Yasmine crinkled her nose.

"And…how do you know this?" Macy asked, not doing a great job of hiding her suspicion.

If Barbara noticed, she made no sign. "I have regularly lent aid to packs combating demons. An *experienced* pack of our size would be facing a tough fight. Healing time would be plentiful. This pack, however, protecting someone unconscious…" She met Devon's eyes. "We'd take losses. Healing time would be extensive."

"Healing time we don't have." Frustration burned through Devon, and he couldn't help flicking his eyes to the van, where Charity lay sprawled out on the seat, her breathing shallow and forehead probably still burning up. "Fine. Dillon, call around and get us rooms. We need to get in contact with Roger and figure out what happens next. We'll probably need to move portals, and to do that, someone needs to alert Emery."

"Shouldn't we—"

Devon took three fast steps and grabbed Dale by the throat. He no longer worried that he didn't have what it took to take the new pack member down. He didn't worry about taking damage, either. For Charity's sake, he needed this troublemaker subdued, and he wouldn't back down until that happened.

Dale's eyes widened as his back hit the van. Devon's power pumped out around them as he leaned into Dale hard, staring into the other shifter's muddy-brown eyes with an intent born of power and authority. An intent demanding submission.

He didn't say a word. He didn't explain his position. He didn't need to.

The silence stretched. A tense moment ticked by. Devon's power beat onto Dale, daring him to turn. Promising him he'd pay if he continued to challenge Devon's authority.

Finally, with a release of breath, Dale dropped his gaze. He bowed submissively.

Devon didn't dwell on it. He didn't have time.

Macy and Rod were already bent over their phones, looking up hotels online.

"Load up," Devon barked, not worried about volume. They'd be gone before the demons ran over to scout them out. "I'll contact Roger on the way downtown. Let's try to get rooms in a populated area. There's less chance of this host, or another, combating us there. I realize the demon earlier walked down the middle of the street, but it was a very bad part of town where I doubt people rushed to call the police. A smaller town in a nice area is a different ballgame."

"We hope," Andy said, now on his phone too.

"We hope," Devon agreed, swinging into the back seat before greatly slowing down, not wanting to disturb Charity's slumber. Hopefully, she was just healing, like shifters did. Hopefully, her body was using this downtime to rejuvenate. Because at this rate, he wouldn't even be able to turn her over to the elves to save her life.

EMERY CROUCHED WITHIN the magical flowers, looking down the cobblestone lane at the Realm side of the portal he'd chosen. More flowers bloomed along the way, a spray of cheerful colors and complementary fragrances. Gold filaments softly tumbled through the air, the perfect temperature for his light green jacket and matching pants. Then again, magic ensured the Realm was the perfect temperature for any attire. Lollipop trees, like a kid might draw in a picture, stood behind three benches off to the side of the portal, along with a magically tended hedge.

It was a lovely, picturesque scene that did not belong in this area of the wilds, with its naturally scraggly bushes, trees with gnarled and reaching branches, and plentiful gray rocks. Not even his dual-mage partner, Penny, could find merit in such stones.

Two months ago, when Emery had scouted this location as a possible entrance point for Charity, before Roger had even approached him to serve as her guide, the portal entrance had been as run-down and decrepit as the rest of the surrounding area. Thieves used this portal. Traffickers selling magic into the Brink. Goblins and other unsavory characters rolled through here, knowing this area, and many like it, were blind spots within the Realm. Places elves couldn't be bothered to have their people patrol.

Emery chewed his lip, his gaze lingering on the tall, thin creature perched on one of the benches. A yellow halo surrounded him.

An actual elf.

Here, in no man's land.

And not just hanging out here, either. This elf had cared enough to fix the place up. That bespoke someone with power. With clout and the exacting eye that went with it.

Why the hell was a powerful elf stationed at this portal?

Emery shook his head and rolled through his options. No way could he attack an elf. They were intelligent and tenacious, and they looked after their own. If he took this sentry down, the elves' retaliation would be swift and brutal. Given their money and influence, nothing was out of the scope of possibility. That would put everyone in danger, including Penny and their crazy friend Reagan, who would stupidly march in here and seek vengeance of their own.

No, he had to get to the Brink so he could use his phone. He had to put Devon and his crew on alert and hold off their crossing until he picked out a new spot. An *empty* one. He might have to get creative, because one thing was infinitely clear—someone had tipped off the elves.

Emery's questions were: who and what specifically were the elves looking for? Was it Charity, or had poor timing thrown them into the middle of something larger?

CHAPTER 7

CHARITY CAME TO consciousness slowly and through a fog of pain. Her temples pounded in time to her heart and her whole body ached. She felt like a wet rag—one that had been trampled on, thrown in the garbage, then buried in a pile of refuse. She'd never had a magical hangover this severe.

Then again, she'd never been flooded with that much power.

Her stomach turned with guilt at the memory of Devon fighting against the gale to get to her. To protect her from herself.

That shouldn't be his job. His job as alpha was to protect his pack against outside forces, not against her magic. She was a dangerous distraction.

A voice rose out of her fog of pain. "When you find your true home, you will know it. And with that home you must stay so that others of your kind will stay with you. The future of all the worlds depends on it."

Karen the *Seer* had said that. She'd alluded to Charity being royalty among the warrior fae, and Devon being destined for greatness in the shifter world. Given that warrior fae lived in the Flush, a place supposedly ass-deep in the Realm, and shifters worked in the Brink, well...it wasn't hard to put two and two together. The *Seer* had been not-so-gently reminding her that while she belonged in the Flush, Devon did not. End of story.

Not for Charity. She'd gotten up and walked away. The worlds could suck it. She'd stay with Devon.

Except now...it was painfully clear that Devon would be better off if he weren't strapped down by a wobbly magical nutcase toting a whole lot of baggage. She hated to think that Karen was onto something, but...

Charity sighed. Now wasn't the time to figure it out. The first step was figuring out where she was.

She pushed up to sitting against the ache in her joints and the throbbing of her head. A dingy sort of room crowded in around her. She lay on a bed with a mustard-yellow bedspread and sharp corners that advertised, correctly, how old and hard the mattress was. A dingy white sliding door had been shoved to one side of the empty closet, revealing an open safe at the bottom corner. The inlet to the bathroom ended in a slightly ajar door she couldn't see past, and there were two sets of drapes for the small window on the other side—a heavy gray one to keep out the sun, and a faded and ripped yellow one to cheer up the room. Only one was working. The glowing red numbers on the nightstand clock read 8:43.

It was clearly a hotel room, and judging by the

murmuring behind the slightly cracked open door in front of her, it was a suite.

She hastened off the bed despite her protesting body. A room this small in a suite this dingy was very cheap and probably filthy. She wondered if someone had checked for bedbugs.

Devon looked up as she opened the suite door, and a look of such supreme relief crossed his face that she felt guilty all over again. Insecurity and guilt, two pastimes she wished she could quit. While Devon stood at the door leading to the hotel hallway, the rest of the pack, old and new, sat or stood around the equally cramped space, their expressions leaving little doubt that something had gone badly wrong. Well, something else.

Her magic felt like a leaf on the forest floor, stirred by the breeze. Even now, it was ready to go again. There had to be something she could do differently to make these surges feel normal. Or at least less painful.

"What happened?" she asked.

For a wonder, Dale glanced at Devon before lowering his gaze to the floor. The dynamic between them had shifted.

"We have a small arsenal of demons blocking the portal," Devon said. "Roger has someone to help us break through them, but there's an elf on the other side. Even if we got through, we'd be nabbed almost immediately."

Charity smoothed the hair away from her aching

skull and leaned against the doorframe. Rod jumped up out of his seat.

"Here, Charity, sit," Rod said, ushering her over to his spot on the dingy love seat against flowery wallpaper.

"No, it's fine—"

"Emery has checked out the backup location," Devon said over her protests. She relented with an eye roll. "That one is guarded, as well. But he's lined up three other options for us."

"Who did he tell about the portals?" Charity asked, the note from Vlad suddenly surfacing in her mind.

In a sudden panic, she patted her chest and then dug her hands into her jeans pockets.

"Wait... Where's..." She stiffly stood and checked her back pockets.

Devon slipped his hand into his sweats pocket and pulled out the gold-rimmed note. "Dillon noticed you'd dropped this and grabbed it off the street."

Heart pounding, Charity clutched it close to her chest before sitting down.

"That's what we've been asking ourselves. Who else could've known about the portals?" Devon said, his eyes on the note. "I don't think you've ever mentioned your nickname for Vlad around a vampire. Yet he knows it. But I'm sure he's got spies, and you've said that nickname often enough among mixed company, so fine. And logic would've told him that you'd eventually check in with your dad. If he kept someone close by, and that person could hastily summon a lackluster demon, then I could see all that making sense. But the portals? He must have heard about our plan from someone on the inside."

"I mean...if I had to guess..." Charity pointed at Dale.

He glowered, and Andy and Rod both smirked.

"I still don't understand why Vlad would try to keep Charity out of the Realm," Cole said, and Charity palmed her pounding head. She wished he came with volume control.

"I agree," Macy said, sitting in a wooden chair in front of a desk with a very suspicious hack mark on the side, like someone had lost control of their axe. "Vlad's note said she should check in after her training. Whether he actually knows Charity's mother's location or not, it is a strong lure to bring her back out of the Flush. It's *intended* to be a strong lure. When she returns, she'll be an even more enticing target, and his game of cat and mouse can recommence. But none of that is possible if she dies before she gets her magic sorted out."

Charity's hand shook around the note, the ache of hope burning in her chest. "Vlad has a lot of resources at his disposal, right? And it isn't like my mom disappeared into thin air. He could know."

Macy's eyes softened. Andy, sitting next to Charity, patted her knee.

"It's likely he does know," Macy said. "Vlad is a collector of information. All elder vampires are. He would want to trace your ancestry to figure this whole thing out. Why else would he visit your dad and charm information out of him? He must know by now."

"Charm? More like use his vampire compulsion to wrestle the information out," Rod said.

"He said his people were watching her," Yasmine added from her position in the corner. "He isn't taking an active role. That doesn't seem like him. Before the battle at the alpha's house, he was very hands-on."

"Understatement," Andy murmured. Rod nodded.

Silence fell around the room, interrupted by Charity's hand spasming and accidentally crinkling the note.

"Why couldn't Vlad use his people to escort her to the Realm?" Dillon asked. "He's good at tiptoeing around the elves, he's got a ton of people on his payroll, he clearly has spies in our organization. There's no reason for him to take a back seat and depend on a hope and a prayer to draw her out."

"Yeah," Andy said, his brow lowered. "That's a good point. Given what we know of him, if he thought she *had* to go to the Flush, he'd want to get the credit for taking her himself, wouldn't he?"

"*Stupid,*" Devon said softly, threading around the others to cross the cramped room. "The hotels downtown said they were booked because of a convention, but did any of you see people wandering around with nametags, looking out of place? I sure as hell didn't. If anyone has the money to buy out all the rooms in a small town like this—in any town—it's Vlad."

Dale rose slowly with a scowl. A knowing gleam lit Macy's and Dillon's eyes, followed by their brows creasing.

"Vlad might've put that note in Charity's desk as a fail-safe," Devon said, "but yes, he's always been hands-on. And he's always been one step ahead."

"A couple of hotels on the outskirts of town had vacancies," Dale argued. "He couldn't possibly pinpoint which we would choose."

"Who cares?" Devon reached the window. Cole stepped up next to him. "Vampires move fast, and all the hotels we had to choose from had plenty of dead space around them. Right now, we're easy pickin's."

The air left Devon's body and Cole swore under his breath. Or he probably thought it was under his breath.

They were looking at something—no, someone—in the parking lot.

"It's just one, though," Cole said as Dillon joined them. "And it isn't Vlad."

A feeling of unease tingled across Charity's skin, and not just because the vampires were again trying to nab her. For one heart-stopping moment, she'd hoped it *was* Vlad. She was desperate to ask him about her mother. If her mom was nearby, surely Charity could spare a day or two to visit her. See her face again. Hear her voice.

Ask her why she'd left her daughter behind.

"Awful cheeky, standing there in the light, looking up at this window," Cole said. "Aw-ful cheeky."

"It's Vlad's underling," Devon growled. "I remember its face from the grocery store parking lot where they tried to grab Charity."

"Vlad doesn't want to get barbecued again," Andy said. "He's probably around here somewhere, though, running the show from the shadows."

"Most likely." Devon turned from the window, and his gaze burned into Charity. He yanked his phone from his pocket and tapped the screen. "Everyone, get ready to move. Prepare to fight your way out of here."

CHAPTER 8

"ROGER, WE HAVE a problem," Devon said into the phone as a metallic click caught Charity's attention. Barbara, standing closest to the door, cocked her head. She must've heard it as well, but didn't know the origin.

Charity did.

"The door." She pushed herself to standing amid a wave of dizziness. "The lock on the door!"

Barbara darted forward as the handle turned. She cranked the deadbolt back over but didn't bother with the chain. Why would she? A vampire could shoulder through that in a moment.

"What's the ETA?" Devon shouted into the phone, darting into the connected bedroom. A moment later, Charity's long black bag came flying into the room. Metal clanked within it, her weapons riding atop her clothes.

"Time to get angry, Charity." Andy hurried to the duffel and pulled back the zipper. He extracted a finely wrought sword with a deep crimson blade. "I realize you're not feeling your best, but being tired has got to be better than being a vampire's food source."

The lock clicked over again, and Barbara flicked it back. "What's the plan?" she yelled.

"Come out, come out, wherever you are," came a musical voice through the door.

"Well, you know where we are." Andy brought the sword to Charity. "Take a hint."

"Smells like an upper-mid-level," Barbara said. Still not Vlad.

Charity hated the small twinge of disappointment. She squeezed the familiar handle of her sword. Strength seeped into her, though not enough to counteract the fatigue.

Devon reentered nude with a pile of clothes between his hands and anxiety pooling in his eyes. His bare chest rippled with muscle as he dropped the items into Charity's duffel before zipping it up. He met Charity's eyes. "Stay safe. I need you to take my change of clothes to the van. I don't want to meet your people naked."

She huffed out an unexpected laugh.

Devon looked around the room as the shifters peeled off their clothes. "Roger has help on the way. She's nearly at the portal site now. We've had a stroke of luck with timing."

"Or Vlad realized he was running out of time and had to engage quickly," Cole replied.

"Or that." Andy pulled off his shirt. "But seriously, can we have someone round up the clothes? Because

Devon's not the only one who'd rather not meet Charity's people naked."

"I've got it," Yasmine said.

"I can help," Rod replied. He glanced at Yasmine. "You'll need someone to guard your six."

She nodded, and Devon did the same. He stepped closer to Charity, who had her sword in her weaker left hand, the note in her right hand.

"I know the pull to see your mother again is strong," he said softly. The lock clicked over. Barbara flicked it back. "And I want nothing more than to escort you to her. In fact, I *promise* to escort you to her...when you're no longer in danger from your magic. But right now, we have to get you to the Flush. We have no choice in that. *You* have no choice in that. Can you accept that?"

"We've got demons," Cole yelled from the window, his voice filling every inch of the room. He stripped off his sweats, and Charity got an eyeful. The man had size everywhere.

She squeezed her eyes shut and tried to ignore her throbbing head. Her body still felt like it had been scraped hollow and filled with Silly Putty. Her heart still ached.

"If Vlad knows where she is today, he'll know where she is a week from now," Devon urged, his hands tightening on her upper arms. "I need you to get angry, Charity. I need you to want to fight. To ignore the pull of Vlad."

Her head whipped up of its own accord and her

eyes widened. It was like he had read her secrets, the feelings she was desperately trying to ignore. She tightened her hand around the note.

A tiny smile ghosted his lips. "You've never been able to hide things from me. Now is no different." The smile disappeared. "We need you—*I* need you—to stay safe. To protect yourself. Will you do that?"

She searched for her inner fire, hoping it would incinerate her emotions. It didn't. She nodded anyway. She desperately wanted to see her mom, but Devon was right. More, he and his pack were risking their lives for her. She couldn't ask them for any more than what they were already giving.

This time, the nod came more easily. Determination hardened her resolve.

"Hopefully you won't have to save my life, again," he said, and grinned, the heaviness in his tone easing a little. He believed in her. Now it was time for her to believe in herself. To the room, he said, "Our goal is to get to the vans and then the portal. This will all come down to timing. We're fighting and running on this one. Maim and move on, kill only if it's convenient. Yasmine and Rod, you're driving. Get the gear and get out. Shouldn't be hard—it's mostly all dumped in Dillon's room."

The lock clicked over again. Barbara was on it.

A fierce look crossed Devon's face. "That's the last time. Next time, we run out to meet them. Charity, are you set?"

She slid the note into her jeans pocket and sucked in a deep breath. She'd never tried to access her magic so soon after a power dump, and truth be told, she was more than a little afraid to do so. She had very few resources to stop her power from taking over. That was if it even came at all.

"I'll do my best," she said, pulling for rage to help get things moving. Hell, she'd settle for mild disappointment.

Devon squeezed her arms, and his eyes delved into hers for a beat. Warmth blossomed in her chest, deep and intense and heartfelt. He was saying *I love you* without the words.

She smiled and put a palm over his heart, knowing now wasn't the time for soggy declarations and fervent PDA (not that it had stopped them before).

"Let's roll. Change form." Devon stepped back from Charity. "Barbara, wait for that lock to click over before—"

"I'll do it," Charity said, shifting her sword to her right hand and immediately feeling a small vibration in her grip. Like shaking hands with an old friend. Some of the fatigue cleared, sapped from her strung-out muscles, but she was still running on fumes.

Magic flared through the room. It flirted with that spark deep inside of her, the one that never went out. It felt comforting and refreshing. It felt *right*.

Almost immediately, however, the spark turned to heat. Her fear rose as the heat turned into a molten gush of magic, then a torrent. She tried to temper the flow. To float on top of it instead of being sucked under, but she didn't have any resources left.

"Point me at the enemy," she said, her voice wispy. "If I lose myself, just point me at the enemy and back—"

A cool breeze, foreign to the stuffy hotel room, danced across her face. The smell of mud and horses tickled her nose. Light flared from above and the hotel ceiling peeled away into the strange orange sky she remembered from the Realm.

"What's…happening?" Her voice echoed in her ears. Sleek mail covered her body, decorated with intricate scrolls and designs like the blade of her sword.

"Charity?"

Devon's voice drifted on the breeze. His large black wolf form waited beside her, his hackles raised and his teeth bared. He shouldn't be able to call her name like that when he was in wolf form. To the other side of Devon waited an equally large gray wolf, a growl deep in its throat. Without seeing its dual-colored eyes, she knew it was Roger.

"That doesn't make sense…" Her voice still didn't sound quite right. Something told her it didn't belong in the moment she was witnessing—the words didn't fit. "He isn't here right now."

"Charity!"

Mud and grass stretched out in front of her, and a voice in the back of her mind whispered, "This is a field of battle."

She heard Devon say, "Hurry, everyone change. *Change!* Yasmine and Rod, as soon as we clear the door, get moving. She's not in control."

But she was. Charity was in control, just not exactly in the present. She felt so damn good. So light and carefree. The blood song called to her, winding through the air. Pulling her *home.*

Across the battlefield, she saw the perfect face of Vlad smiling at her sadly. She'd picked the wrong side, and he'd be loath to kill her, she knew. Beside him stood a man with black, slicked-back hair and a face made by angels. He wore formfitting jeans and a crisp white button-up shirt, completely inappropriate for the battlefield, yet somehow not out of place. Behind them stood row after row of vampires in monster form, demons, goblins, and other large, lumbering beasts.

She glanced to the left, her hand tightening on the hilt of her sword. A man who looked familiar nodded in acknowledgment, love and pride in his eyes. Fanning out beside and behind him were men and women dressed in the same battle gear she wore. They oozed magic like a wound oozes blood, but it comforted rather than frightened her. Her kindred. They nodded to her.

"Battle is a part of us," she said, loud and clear. These words did not seem hollow and out of place. They clearly belonged in the scene she was witnessing. "We have the blood of warriors. We will decide the victor."

Three figures stood between the two groups, pushed

off to the side and standing close together, their formation something of a pyramid. Charity couldn't make out their features. Opposite them, halfway between Charity's and Vlad's groups, waited a breathtaking man who could only be a vampire.

Expectation rose. The song of battle intensified. But still they waited.

They waited for *her*.

A blink and it was all gone. The light faded and the colors muted into the dingy yellows and beiges of the run-down hotel suite. Furry bodies launched past her, heading for the open door. A huge, snarling wolf stepped into the doorframe and blocked the others from leaving.

Devon tore his lupine gaze from her, and a growl rumbled deep in his chest. If she had to guess, Dale was challenging him, even now. He probably didn't think they should rush out with Charity in this state.

But for the first time since the battle at Devon's house, she felt strong and capable. Ready to kick some ass.

"Let's go," she yelled, noticing Steve and Cole were still in human form. "What's the hold-up?"

Steve winked. "Too many wolves in here. Not enough space for the big guns."

Devon rushed forward, pushing through the furry bodies to get to Dale. In front of the mutinous wolf stood two vampires, their eyes hard and their claws extended from human hands. Only higher-level vamps could partially transform like that.

Didn't matter. They were blocking her way.

"Move!" Charity pumped a pulse of power in front of her, clearing the wolves to the side (a little more forcefully than she'd planned). The vampires' eyes found her immediately. One grinned.

She lifted her hand to send bursts of power after them, but they dashed down the hallway, one in each direction. They were trying to split Devon's pack.

"Filthy buggers," she grumbled, pausing just outside the door. Wolves filed out around her, spreading out but not following the vampires.

A bone-shaking roar ripped through the hotel, followed by a different, but no less heart-stopping, cry.

"The lion, the yeti, and the dingy hotel suite," Charity said as Devon ran right. "One wonders why that never became a beloved children's book."

Doors opened down the hall. A curious man, a confused woman, and a delighted kid all poked their heads out of their respective rooms.

"The wildlife exhibit has run amok," Charity yelled, belatedly realizing that excuse wouldn't explain her sword. "Just kidding…it's cosplay! These are dogs!"

Andy growled at her side.

She laughed as they turned the corner, closing in on the stairs.

"You guys would be screwed if you didn't have someone around with opposable thumbs, huh?" Charity ran through the sudden parting in the furry crowd and ripped the stairwell door open. They caught a flash of their prey's back as he headed down the steps.

Considering the speed at which vampires could run, it was clear this one had waited for them. He wanted to keep the pack right on his heels.

Charity gritted her teeth as they thundered down the stairs, nearly barreling into a random woman who'd picked an unfortunate time for her trip to the ice machine. She screamed as she ducked out of the stairwell, her eyes riveted on the wolves.

"Call the pound," Charity yelled, hoping the woman wouldn't call the cops.

At the bottom of the stairwell, not even winded, Charity stopped with her hand on the newly shut door. The vampire had just run through. There was no telling what waited for them outside.

Devon yipped, and Charity had a feeling he was trying to express something to her. Wolves filed in around her, their large bodies stuffed into the small space. The rest waited on the stairs, Steve with his huge body and bushy mane in front of an even larger form, the snowy-white yeti. As a human, Cole was faintly ridiculous, but as a yeti he was fearsome, arms pushed out to the sides and wicked fangs dripping drool.

"I would not want to be the enemy," Charity said as she felt Devon's nose on her thigh, shoving.

Time to go.

She yanked open the door and then staggered and nearly fell as the wolves pushed out ahead of her. They'd spread out into a circle around her by the time she was able to get through the door into the warm, humid night.

Few cars sat in the spaces, leaving the battlefield mostly bare. Bare, except for the enemy vampire host emerging from the surrounding trees and hedges. There were only a handful, but they ran over with easy, liquid grace, denoting their age and therefore their dangerousness.

"Could be worse—"

A smoldering humanoid form walked from around the corner of the property, its eyes pits of fire, its arms too long, and its chest covered in molting, burned skin.

"The fae will come with us," one of the nearest vampires said.

"Maybe not," Charity said.

CHAPTER 9

Charity's power throbbed within her, hot and ready. Sweet and light. Music, on key this time, curled within the breeze.

The door behind them opened. Yasmine and Rod ran out of the hotel, each laden with bags. Devon launched himself toward the vampire who had spoken. The others were right behind him. More demons poured from around the corner up ahead, all of them burned-looking, and one with actual flames dancing from its arms.

Charity's sword glowed from her magic. She wasn't sure if she should slash and run, light up the parking lot and run, or go after the demons…

Steve answered the question for her. He loped forward, each movement telegraphing the incredible strength and power of his massive body. He slammed into the closest demon, crunching his teeth into its neck before shaking his head. He ripped the neck right out of the creature. The head tore off and flew away. The body slumped to the ground.

Cole was right behind him, running with an arm-swinging lumber that was no less powerful for its awkwardness. When he reached the next demon, he batted it in the face with one great arm. The blow threw it to the ground, its head flopping loosely.

"Holy—" Charity danced after them, light on her feet and fueled with adrenaline. The song of battle blazed through her blood, quickening her heart and bringing a smile to her face. She'd almost forgotten her magic could feel good. That using it could feel as joyful as playing with fuzzy puppies.

She slashed into a spindly sort of demon, opening up a gaping hole in its chest. Fire danced down its arms and fumed from its mouth.

Charity rolled away, sliding her magic across its front. Her magic electrified the air and the demon's body, counteracting the fire spewing from its mouth, but not totally stopping it.

Pain kissed her skin and raced along her arm as the demon howled out his agony. She stepped back, brought up her sword, and then slashed down, severing its right arm. The left swung around, and she dodged before thrusting her blade up into its armpit.

"Head," grunted Cole as he lumbered by. "Head."

Charity stepped, spun, and swung, all in one clean, graceful movement that felt so incredibly right that she couldn't help laughing as she lopped off his head. Probably a bad sign, her taking joy in this kind of carnage.

We have the blood of warriors.

Oh good, and now she was quoting her hallucination back to herself. When it rained, it poured.

The vans screeched out from the corner behind the demons, the leader mowing one demon down. The demon flew up into the air, flame dancing along its limbs. An orange-red burst flew after the vans, but the fire didn't last, fading into the night.

The vans skidded near Charity, the back ends whipping around before stopping, the movements almost in sync, as if they were wolves. The sliding doors opened, and Rod leaned out of the leading van with Yasmine looking out from the one behind. Rod motioned Charity toward him.

A wolf yelped, drawing Charity's attention to the opposite end of the parking lot. Wetness sparkled in the parking lot lights, four gashes in its gray coat. The vampire that had wounded it darted in for another attack, faster than thought.

Devon, who'd been dashing toward her, wheeled around to go back for his pack mate. Another vampire, pasty white in its monster form, cut him off. More of them rushed in from the sides, trapping the wolves in a widespread circle.

The vampires didn't seem to be interested in Charity at all, however, apparently satisfied to leave her to the demons. What sense was there in that?

Steve's roar boomed through the parking lot, pain threading through the sound of a challenge. Flame flickered on his thick fur even as he ripped into another demon. An explosion of flame rose behind the vans. She glanced in that direction and saw Cole's thick, furry arm swing down at the thing attacking him.

A demon reached for her. She ducked under its charred limb and thrust upward, cutting a thick slice deep into the demon's stomach. Black blood dribbled out, down its legs. The creature bellowed, and smoke came from its maw of a mouth. It swung at her again, anger making it forget it wasn't supposed to harm her. Vlad wouldn't want her spoiled. She slashed and danced away, finishing off the thing's leg with her blade. The demon dropped to the ground, but when she looked up, she saw another set of claws slicing toward her. She twisted, avoiding the blow, and a burst of power from her hand had the creature flying skyward and back before its body exploded, flinging wet globs everywhere.

"Gross."

Sirens sounded in the distance. The vampires charged toward the snarling wolves, and the demons slashed their way toward Rod and Yasmine in the vans.

Time to go.

Charity thrust her left palm skyward.

The sun lit up the sky, pulsing in wattage, sounding like a bug zapper. Vampires screeched and twisted, throwing their hands in front of their faces to ward off the attack.

"Run!" Charity shouted, feeling her energy drain the longer she held that magical sunlight in the sky. She released it as she turned, slashing through a roaring demon and sprinting as fast as she could for the lead van.

"How the hell did they organize so many so quickly?" Rod asked as she stopped just beside the open door, looking through the far window. Cole's white fur was patchy black and red from being burned. Two demons advanced on him, one nearly as big as he was, its arms and legs as thick as tree trunks.

"Vlad's an elder vampire—he probably has this many on call," Charity said.

"I meant the demons," Rod yelled over the din. "I've always heard demons are hard to control, but he has them moving around pretty handily."

The first wolf reached the van and dove in, changing shape as it did so. Andy. He pulled a duffel out from under the seat, hauled it onto his lap, and started digging through it. He was probably looking for weapons.

Charity ran to the back of the van as another wolf jumped into it behind them, changing as she did so. Barbara. The shifter twisted toward the back window to check on Cole, but Charity was already on it. She sent a pulse of power at the were-yeti's larger attacker, blasting it in half.

Cole roared and slashed at his other attacker, tearing out the demon's stomach with his sharp claws, and then turned and lumbered toward the vans.

He might be powerful, but he was not fast.

"Hurry up, you bastard," Andy yelled, clearly seeing

the problem.

A lesser-looking demon moved to intercept Cole, and Charity hit it with another pulse of power. The spark blew the thing sky-high. Nothing was left. The creatures behind it weren't dead, having enough juice left to keep going.

"Charity, behind you!" Andy yelled, pushing out of the first van, gun in hand.

Vampires zipped toward the wolves, Devon and someone else flanking a limping gray wolf that was moving at half speed. Charity gritted her teeth and turned on the sun. The loud buzzing competed with the wailing of the approaching sirens. The vampires shrieked, the whole scene suddenly overpowered by Cole's pained bellow.

"Load up," Andy said, falling in at Charity's side and squeezing out a handful of bullets. They fell true, tearing into the side of the demon who'd just slashed at Cole's back. The creature barely bumped backward.

"Damn it," Andy swore as the other shifters piled into the vans. Cole was the only one left.

"Leave him," Barbara shouted. "He knew the risks. Protect the fae. Leave him!" She slung the van door shut. Something hit the vehicle from the other side, shattering the window. The van lurched forward, Yasmine doing as Barbara had said.

Dread spread through Charity. "Like hell I'm leaving him!"

Gunshots blew up the night. The moving van's

wheel rolled over a demon's arm.

Charity sprinted around, straight for the nearest demon. She slashed with her sword before slapping a palm into the center of its chest, the feeling of its sludgy skin making her grimace. A shock of power and the creature flew backward, but two more were already coming, blocking Cole from sight.

"Crap, there are too many—"

Steve lunged in front of her, ramming into the two demons and sending them flying. His mane lit on fire, but he didn't stop. He chomped down on the nearest before shaking his mighty head, ending its movement. Another came at her from the side. Charity spun, her sword up and ready, but it belched fire before it got to her. This would require her magic, not her sword. The flame kissed her face before she could switch gears, the pain searing, and the demon kept on coming. She swallowed down fear and braced for the blistering impact.

The fire dried up, like it had been sucked away.

Charity had barely drawn in a surprised breath before the demon went flying, but not from her doing.

"Why the hell does no one ever invite me to their parties?"

Reagan, the fierce and possibly insane woman Charity had met after the attack at Devon's house, ran into the scene with her sword flashing.

"Is it because I'm screwing a vampire?" She slashed down at a demon flailing on the ground. "Go home,

Harry, you're drunk."

Reagan reached out her hand in Cole's direction, her eyes raging with the fire of battle despite her flippant comments, and squeezed her fingers into a fist.

Amid shrieks and howls of surprise, the demons froze. Every last one of them.

If not for the wailing of sirens and Devon's shouts to give Dillon space, Charity would've thought this was another hallucination.

"Hey, guys," Reagan said, her body language nonchalant but her tone wary. Something she saw here disturbed her, and Charity didn't want to know what would discomfit someone like her. "Looks like this neighborhood has gone to hell—Nope, you don't get to turn around, Fred." Reagan's eyes narrowed. One of the demons squished, as though from an invisible vise squeezing it. "You chose your side. You all did. Surprise! It was the wrong side."

"You know their names?" Charity asked stupidly.

Reagan cracked a smile that didn't reach her eyes. "No, and to keep them from telling me themselves, I'll just assign them. Oops. The yeti seems to have wandered away from his snow."

Cole emerged from behind the frozen demons, a loud growl in his throat. His furious gaze locked on Reagan, his fur a mess of black and red. He'd taken some serious hits, but they didn't seem to matter as much to him as his clear dislike of Reagan.

"This has got to be awkward," Reagan said as Cole

passed her, his growl deepening. The demons still hadn't moved. "You said you were going to kill me when next you saw me, and instead, you got saved by me. How embarrassing."

"The vampires took off. Get back to the van—let's go," Devon yelled, striding toward them quickly. "Steve, change."

The lion, who'd been rolling on the ground, trying to put out the last of the flames, shifted form before patting his head and chest profusely. He pushed himself up to standing, burn marks over half of his body.

Devon nodded hello at Reagan as he reached them. "Thanks for coming." He spared a glance at the frozen demons as he slipped his arm around Charity. "What magic is that?"

"The icy kind. Smells weird, right?" Reagan waggled her eyebrows, and it was clear from the crease between Devon's brow he didn't understand her either.

"You have those demons under your control?" he asked, his hand resting on the small of Charity's back.

"Yup. I was just communicating with one or two before squeezing them into nothing."

It wasn't nothing. It was a squish of goop and globs that erupted from the tops and bottoms of those invisible grips.

Charity didn't get a chance to ask Reagan how she communicated with demons without speaking, let alone why Roger or Devon would trust someone who *could* communicate with demons without speaking, because

Steve was making his way over. The sirens blared louder.

"Reagan, good to see you." Steve's nude saunter was, amazingly, not ruined by his pronounced limp. "Did you dump that vampire yet? I want to show you what real passion feels like."

"Let's talk and walk, Steve," Reagan said. "You can still walk, right?"

"I'd rather be lying down and letting you do all the work."

"Of course you would. You're a shifter." She smirked at him and jerked her head toward the vans. "I'm still with him, yes. Sex is always amazing, thanks for asking. He's rich as hell, too. Good observation. Don't you worry, though—just as soon as things fizzle out, I'll go for a ride on that big dong of yours."

Despite the urgency of the situation, Steve's smile pulled a chuckle from Charity's lips.

"So you noticed," Steve said, his eyes twinkling.

"Hard not to. It swings when you walk." Reagan got into the van.

Steve winked at Charity before he followed her.

"I'm not sure what's worse," Charity said, looking in at the sea of skin. "My magic, which I can't control, or your magic, which forces you to brave seatbelts when you're naked."

"You better not buckle those seatbelts," Rod hollered back as Devon pushed in after Charity and shut the door. "I don't want your junk all over everything."

"This is why you're single," Andy said, fatigue lining his words.

Charity knew how he felt. With the adrenaline from the battle wearing away, she had nothing left. Her eyes drooped as she sat there, barely able to hold up her head.

"Don't fall asleep yet, fae." Reagan's tone was laced with warning, more serious than Charity had ever heard from the woman. "Your journey has just begun, and from here on out, it's only going to get harder."

CHAPTER 10

STEVE WANTED TO lean his head back and get a little shut-eye himself. He'd taken some serious hits from those demons, which hadn't acted like the demons he was used to battling. These were sturdier, somehow. And what was with all the fire? One or two usually had some sort of smoke or fire, sure—it came with the territory—but not a whole fleet of the assholes. It had made for some very annoying and frustratingly painful burns. One of those things had nearly singed his balls off! That was foul play.

"What kind of read are you getting on this situation?" Devon asked. Steve had to admit that the kid was really coming into his own. Protecting that fae was bringing out the true alpha in him, something Roger had apparently seen from the beginning. And strangely, Steve was cool with following the kid's lead. He hadn't once wanted to push back. Imagine that.

Reagan shook her head while staring out the window, strangely quiet.

"I don't know," she said, and if Steve wasn't mistaken, he heard a little worry in her tone. "Something about those demons seemed…ancient. Different. Their burned skin, for one thing—I've never seen that before, and I've seen a good few demons in the last year or so."

"I concur," Steve said, his voice gruffer than usual. Pain had a way of doing that to a person.

"It made them…hardier, somehow. Tougher in battle than they should have been." She shook her head.

"I concur," Steve repeated, leaning his head back on the headrest and closing his eyes. "It's like we're sharing the same brain."

"Better than the same bed."

"I do not concur."

"I'm sure the effect of those demons can be achieved through a circle and blood offering," Reagan went on, "but I've never heard of it or seen it written. They were bound to their maker. I couldn't easily will them to give up information, which is abnormal. I need to capture one and spend a little more…effort on it."

Fabric rustled, and Steve's eyes drifted open to see her sitting forward, a crease between her shapely brows and a worried expression on her beautiful face. The woman was a looker, that was for sure. She was a permanent resident in his spank bank.

He let his eyes droop again. She was also intelligent, highly competent, and delightfully brutal. Steve could afford a reprieve while she did the heavy lifting in this annoying situation.

"Just up here… What's your name again?" Reagan asked the linebacker kid behind the wheel.

"It's Rod," Devon answered, "and this portal is blocked. Even if we can get through the demons—which might be easier than expected with you around—your buddy Emery says there's an elf on the other side."

"I know." Her voice was flat. "I spoke to Roger more times today than a non-shifter really wants to."

Steve chuckled, and spears of agony drilled into his left side. The chuckles turned to coughs, creating more spears of pain.

"Are you okay?" The voice was light. Musical. Extremely pleasing.

He opened his eyes to see Charity in the seat in front of him, exhaustion dragging at her features and dark circles under her eyes. Something within him snapped to attention, and a protectiveness he hadn't expected stole over him. He struggled to sit up a little straighter within her kind eyes. A leader's eyes, looking after her people.

Royalty.

The thought came out of nowhere, and nothing in him rebelled against it. Another first. What was the world coming to?

"Yeah. I'll heal up right quick. It's just shitty in the meantime," he said, much softer than he'd intended.

She analyzed him for another moment before facing front again. The pressure of her notice gone, he melted back down into the seat. Eyes beat into the side of his face.

Reagan was looking at him with a smirk.

"What?" he asked.

A knowing gleam lit her eyes. She'd caught that little show, just then, of him accepting someone else's dominance. Someone who wasn't pack, no less.

He shrugged, and the movement made him wince. "Sometimes you just gotta ride the waves and see what happens."

"I mean...you know what'll happen. You'll hit the beach or drown," Andy muttered.

"Exactly," Steve replied.

"So if the way is blocked, why are we heading there?" Devon asked. "We don't have time for you to play *capture the demon*."

Reagan huffed out a laugh. "You're much more fun than Roger, I'll give you that. And I'll play that game once you're in the Realm, don't you worry. But the elf won't be a problem by the time you get through the portal. Penny is on the job."

"Ah. The little witch." Steve grinned. "She still with the Rogue Natural?"

"You need to get laid, bud," Reagan murmured.

"Always."

"And yes," Reagan said. "Right now, actually. Emery knows how to fool the elves—so much so that he was kicked out of the Realm for it—and Penny knows how to make anything Emery does better. You'll be good to go."

"Roger knows about this?" Devon asked Reagan, turning in his seat to look at her. He was suspicious. As well he should be. This was a ludicrously half-baked plan. Steve thought about sitting up straighter to be a part of the discussion. Instead, he just looked on from his slouched position.

"Yes." Her tone was flat and eyes serious. "Roger gave Darius a list of Charity's symptoms. Darius, being an incredible nerd when it comes to trivia, did some calculations. He doesn't think we should risk taking a longer route. He thinks the shorter the better. And then he clammed up, because he decided his involvement was getting dangerously close to stepping on Vlad's toes. He's freaked out Vlad will…return the favor. Regardless, one thing is very clear—if we want Charity to live, we need to get through this portal, and we need to get through it now."

"I felt okay this last time, though," Charity said, her voice weak. "I was in control. Except for the hallucination before the battle started."

Reagan laughed as Devon whipped around to study Charity.

"Fantastic," Reagan said. "I always manage to find magical nut jobs." She wasn't being sarcastic—she was the queen of magical nut jobs. "You look like shit, though. I don't know crap about your magic, but I know magical poisoning when I see it. You need to get to your people."

"If they even are my people," Charity muttered.

"Okay, here we go," Reagan said as the linebacker slowed the van. She pushed into the empty space between Devon and the door. "Given how fast the vampires split when I came on scene at that fleabag hotel, we'll either face a shitload of them right now or none at all."

"Is that because you're...with a vampire who has a deal with Vlad?" Charity asked, her suspicion obvious. Steve chuckled again; he couldn't help it. This situation was such a clusterfuck that it was comical.

The linebacker had stopped in nearly the place they'd parked before, well away from the portal site, hidden behind a line of trees beside the road.

"The creatures at that hotel weren't Vlad's," Reagan said, and the smile wilted from Steve's face.

CHAPTER 11

DEVON WATCHED REAGAN'S face for signs of lying. Her bonded partner was a vampire—an elder to boot—and everyone knew not to trust vampires.

"What do you mean they weren't his?" Charity asked.

"I recognized one of them as Vlad's," Devon said.

"Yeah. So did I. I'm wondering if he knows he's got a traitor on his hands." Reagan chewed her lip. "Regardless, the rest were not. I know his upper-tier minions, and those weren't them. He doesn't trust easily, especially not with something as valuable as Charity."

"If the rest weren't his, whose were they?" Devon asked, motioning for her to get out of the van.

Reagan complied quickly and gracefully, waiting for him to climb out after her before continuing in a whisper.

"I knew all but two, and they all belong to different vampires. This was a team of spies, basically." Reagan's eyes narrowed, and she stared off at nothing, obviously thinking through the implications.

"Spies..." Charity lost her balance as she got out of

the van, falling against Devon. He threaded an arm around her back, taking her weight so she could stand. Her body trembled against him. Devon didn't completely trust Reagan, but she was definitely right about Charity—they didn't have much time left.

"If someone has spies in the vampire community, they have spies with us," Devon said. Of course, they knew that already. The portal had been compromised.

"Yup." Reagan made her way down the small, grassy ditch and climbed the other side. Devon swung Charity up into his arms and followed her. The rest of Devon's pack hurried to get out of the vans and fall in behind them. "I could hazard a guess of who it is, but that's all it would be. A guess. And guesses won't do you a helluva lot of good."

"Is this another play for Charity, do you think?" Devon asked, stopping beside a reaching branch and looking at the scene across the way in the field. The moonlight shone down on the stationary creatures. Flame flickered here and there, crawling across their bodies.

"I have no idea, and that's the honest truth. If it was just a bunch of vampires, sure, maybe. But the demons? No. Somehow…it feels like they're a message. Their presence here kept you from walking smack into the elf on the other side. In a messed-up way, their presence saved you. It also brought me here. It's possible the person who sent them did it to help you, and challenge…someone."

"Challenge who?" Devon asked.

Reagan turned to him, her eyes lost to the shadow, but her focus no less acute. "Me."

"Why is a message for you mixed up with us?"

"That's the million-dollar question. One Darius will have to sort out. For now, let's get that fae through that portal, shall we?"

"What's the plan, boss?" Steve asked, stopping beside them.

Devon looked at Reagan. He might be alpha of this pack, but she was clearly running the show. Even Roger had stepped out of the way when she'd come barreling into the battle outside of his house. She had some kind of magic that trumped everyone in this field, not to mention the experience to complement it—he needed to allow her to choose the best approach.

She nodded at Devon, a show that she recognized his status. She might not like dealing with Roger, but she'd learned how to cooperate with an alpha. And she was extending that same courtesy to him.

"There's a real strong demon milling around in that field, and a whole bunch of magic blocking their ugly mugs from non-magical view. I've never seen that spell before, but it's as ancient as the spells used to call those demons. A few wicked spells have been layered in that would've blasted your faces off if you'd run in by yourselves." Reagan shifted her stance, popping out a leather-clad hip supporting a scratched and beat-up leather fanny pack. "Yeah, someone was extending me an invite. Someone who knows I will eventually tell Penny and Emery that one of their best—whoever that might be—is working for one bad mammajamma. But in the meantime, I'll capture that demon, break it down, and steal all its secrets. The rest I will turn inside out and make them rue the day they wandered into my home."

"She is not right in the head, alpha," Cole said, and everyone startled from the shotgun blast of sound. Three demons across the field moved, their bodies turning toward the pack.

"Quiet, snow-tits, or I'll slap you around a second time," Reagan murmured. She clapped and started forward. "Let's do this. I'll need a few of you to change and take down the lesser demons. I'm going to have my hands full with the more powerful one."

"What about the spells?" Devon asked, shooting the shifters who needed to change a quick look. Barbara, Macy, Yasmine, Dale, and Rod dropped whatever they were carrying and shifted on the spot.

Cole grunted, clearly not happy about being left out, but didn't protest. Devon wasn't sure if that was because of him or Reagan. Dillon winced as he grabbed a duffel, as did Steve when he grabbed another.

"The spells are nothing. I'll take those down," Reagan said, walking fast.

"I can fight," Charity said, struggling in Devon's arms. "I'm okay. I'll rally."

What Reagan had said ripped through Devon's

mind.

Magical poisoning.

"No," Devon said, a little too forcefully. He didn't know much about magical poisoning, although he'd heard the words before. Didn't matter. One simply needed to look at Charity's face to know Reagan was absolutely right. Charity looked terrible. Worse than she ever had after a bad episode, almost like she was in the last stages of cancer. "We don't need you." Harsh words he softened by squeezing her in his arms.

A few poignant looks and his wolves fell in step, flanking him and Charity. Steve and Cole took the back, ready to change at a moment's notice. They had a good unit. A strong unit.

But as they got closer to the waiting demons, Devon's heart started to pound. He didn't know squat about demons, but he knew these creatures were much more powerful than the ones in the parking lot. Their fire flared brighter, they were larger in stature, and their movements were more fluid and natural.

"You sure you got this?" Devon asked, Charity's weight in his arms like a warning. Without shifting, he couldn't protect her from those things. Hell, he couldn't even fight them in human form with her cradled in his arms. Neither could he put her down. She could barely hold her head up, let alone hurry through a portal crossing. He'd need his pack to carry them through.

"One more shifter," Reagan said without hesitation, her head high and her sword out. "The yeti. He's an ornery bastard. He's perfect for the job."

Cole grunted, but again he didn't protest. The bag he carried hit the ground. A roar rumbled through the field a moment later.

"Jesus, man, do you need to wake the neighbors?" Reagan murmured, jogging at the enemy now.

Another thought struck Devon. "Is she going to make the crossing like this?"

"I'm okay," Charity said, her head lolling on Devon's shoulder. "Anyone have a Red Bull?"

"She's a fighter," Dillon said, worry tracing his words. "She'll make it."

"She will," Andy said, shouldering most of the luggage. "She'll make it."

"Seriously, you guys, I'm fine. Just tired." One of Charity's arms slid off Devon's shoulder. "Slippery when wet." She sighed and dragged it back up.

"She just needs a nap," Andy said. "Like earlier. She got a nap and was ready for another battle."

She hadn't been ready—she'd had no choice. Hence the frightening new development of her hallucinations.

"You can sleep on the other side," Reagan said, and a pulse of power rocked through Devon's middle.

He staggered, not expecting it, although he'd felt her power before. She was going in hot, using everything she had.

"You're going to make it, love," Devon said in Charity's ear, increasing his pace to match Reagan's. "No one is going to stop you. Not me, not Roger, and certainly not some meddling vampire. We'll find your people, get you well, then find your mom."

Her arms squeezed a little tighter. "I love you."

"Here we go." Reagan slashed with her sword, barely slowing to do so. Fire crawled through the air to either side of her sword strike, burning away an invisible wall. She flung her left hand out and something like dry ice rolled across the ground, fizzling and sparking as it did so. "As always, you didn't see any of this."

"Any of what?" Charity asked, straining to lift her head and look.

"The fireworks, babe," Steve said from behind them, laughter trailing the words. "Reagan has the best fireworks. I'm good to change, boss, if you need me." The thrill of battle rang in his voice. "I don't need clothes on the journey. I'm more impressive without."

"Your ego is a wonder," Andy said, "but you're carrying my bag. I want clothes. Keep hold of that thing."

Devon cocooned himself and Charity within his pack as they kept pace with Reagan. "Hold, Steve. Stay on two feet for now."

As the demons watched their approach, they spread out into three short horizontal lines.

"Organized," Reagan said, as though to herself.

"Someone's watching us," Charity murmured, before coughing. She pointed to the left. "I feel someone watching us."

"I agree with her." Reagan glanced in the direction of Charity's finger, even though she couldn't possibly have seen it.

Devon scanned the tree line as they neared the demons, the creatures not even fidgeting with anticipation.

"Great control," Reagan said. "What's to the left?"

Shadows loomed within the trees, thick and syrupy. He looked for an odd shape. Movement in the branches caused by something other than wind. Nothing stuck out. But then, if it were a vampire, nothing would. They could give a stone a run for its money on patience and stillness. He said as much.

Reagan just grunted.

"Shifters, fan out," she said a moment later. "Hit them from the sides and work in behind them. I'll take the middle. Man, I wish Penny were here. I'd make her go in first."

Yasmine slammed into the first demon, ripping and tearing through it, its blood spattering her white coat. Reagan hit dead center, as promised, her sword flashing faster than Devon's eye could track. She sliced through one's middle before moving on to the next, a wound that shouldn't have had much effect. Yet the demon howled, garbling words that Devon couldn't understand as it shook and spasmed, falling to the ground.

Rather than launch into another demon, Yasmine fell back to make sure his flank was covered. Macy, to her other side, took up the pursuit immediately, tearing into the one Yasmine would've gone for. The two women often had their problems, but in battle, they were a strong unit.

"We're good from behind," Steve called up. "Much as I hate to admit it."

Flame blossomed into the sky, like an explosion. The fire spread across the ground, crawling toward the pack. Charity stirred against Devon, her eyes wide as she looked ahead of them. Reagan swore before plunging her sword into the center of the demon that was the source of the fire.

"My bad," Reagan called. The flames died. "Didn't see that one coming. Nearly got my eyebrows, the bastard."

The portal loomed just ahead, a shimmering, glowing white line visible only to those with the magic to see it. Power throbbed from around it, pulling at Devon's energy.

Charity's arms jerked tighter around Devon's neck, her eyes rooted to that line. Her body trembled, and Devon wondered if she was losing her nerve. She had to recognize how weak she was—how low on energy—and wonder if she'd make it. A person needed power to make it through the portal, and plenty of it, but that wasn't the only requirement. There was a certain mental component to it. A strong mind could overcome a weak body.

"You were unconscious the first time we brought you through," Devon said, latching on to facts. "You'd worn yourself out by using your magic for the first time, but you still made it through."

A sob bubbled up. "Devon, I was lying before. I'm not fine. It feels like something is…draining me. I can't explain it. I was good for that last battle. I felt in control and powerful. But then the adrenaline died away, and when it was gone, it was like…it just kept sucking energy from me. I keep getting weaker, and I feel like I can barely lift my head."

"I know," he said, dodging a reaching, fiery limb. The body kept coming, though, right for them.

Steve pushed forward, into harm's way. He swung the pack in his hand, hitting the demon across the face, before ripping into the demon's chest with a bare hand. He growled out a curse but didn't relent, dragging his hand through burned, gooey flesh.

An enormous clawed mitt batted the demon's head, ripping it off in a fast, hard strike. Cole flung the body aside with a ferocious growl before turning back to the fray.

"Little late on that one, mate," Steve said with annoyance. He fell back a little.

"In the past, you've always been able to sleep it off," Devon said into Charity's ear. A disembodied demon arm flew overhead. A jet of cold washed up over Devon's face, nearly punching him. He shook his head, confused, but the feeling cleared. Reagan, probably. He'd learned that all unexplained magic generally originated from her. "You just need that nap, like Andy said. We'll get through, and then you can rest for a second."

"What's magical poisoning?" she asked in a tiny voice.

Devon gritted his teeth and squeezed her closer. "It's so rare that I don't even know. You don't have that. You just need sleep."

She blew out a breath and burrowed her face into his neck.

"You're a terrible liar," she said.

CHAPTER 12

"LET'S GO, LET'S GO!" Devon kicked a falling demon out of his way. Another came out of nowhere, stepping on its comrade to roar fire at Devon's face. He spun so his back would take the hit, but he needn't have bothered. Dale rammed into the creature from the side and knocked it away. The fire blasting from its maw did nothing more than splash heat across Devon's shoulder.

"Order them back," Reagan yelled, her voice rising above the din. Rod jumped, grabbing a smaller demon around the neck and ripping its head from side to side before he'd even hit the ground. The demon didn't have a chance with the weight and strength tearing at it. "Order them back!"

A strange, wet sort of cackle filled the air. "Order who back?"

The raspy voice belonged to a demon standing in front of the portal, massive and grotesque, its burned limbs covered in sores oozing pus or slime.

Cole finished with a demon and roared his victory. Macy and Yasmine ended one together before falling in beside Devon. The field slowed of activity. Reagan stood in front of the last demon standing.

"Hello, gorgeous," she said, acid dripping from her voice. She cocked her head. "You know I'm being ironic, right? You're one of the ugliest I've seen to date, and that's saying something."

"What?" The demon cocked its head to match her.

"Get it out of the way. We need to get through," Devon commanded.

"I don't think that's wise," Charity said. Reagan glanced back, her brow lowered, and determination flared in her eyes that Devon felt down to his core. He didn't know why she would have a vested interest in helping them—maybe she was just the sort of person who devoted herself to whatever cause she'd chosen—but whatever her motivation, he was grateful she was on their team.

"My body aches," Charity said. "Well, hurts more than aches. It feels like dull razor blades are slicing through my middle. I'm not sure I'll make it."

"Magic will fix you right up. Penny's on the other side. She can handle this, trust me. If it has to do with magic, that chick can figure it out." Reagan nodded with confidence, raised her hand, and fisted the air. "But yes, I will get this disease out of the way. And soon, I will find its maker."

"Not even you can scrape that out of me, Heir," the demon rasped, frothy drool sliding down its fangs. "We are bonded, my maker and I. She called me with her body. I have planted my seed within her, as the circle demanded. I could not tell you if I tried."

Reagan jerked as if struck. "Good God, that is gross. Luckily, I know a guy that is great at messing around with bonds. Transferring them, forcing them—what have you. I wonder if he knows that your master has a spy in his fold, eh? I wonder what he'll do to you when he finds out."

"Reagan," Devon said. Roger would want to hear about this conversation, but interesting though it was, Devon couldn't wait around to listen.

"Yup, sorry." Reagan braced, her whole body tense.

The demon grinned around its fangs. "You will be great one day, Heir. Or you will die."

"Yeah, yeah. Let's go." Reagan jerked her fist, and the demon haltingly moved out of the way. Reagan stepped aside, but before Devon could go through the portal, she put up her other hand to stop him. Her sword nearly sliced off his nose.

"Oops, sorry," she said, sheathing the blade. "Listen to Emery. That guy is about as tough as anyone you'll meet, and he's been through hell in the Realm. He has no stake in this game besides paying it forward. You can trust him as your guide." She nodded, and her gaze fell on Charity. "I hope to meet the rest of the warrior fae one day. I hear they were feared back in the day—they didn't bow to anyone. My kinda people." Reagan scanned the tree line where she and Charity had sensed a silent observer. "Now to find the Peeping Tom and force it to a tea party with my new friend here."

Devon didn't watch her march the demon away, nor did he stop to wonder how the hell she could control it. He faced down the portal and took a deep breath.

"This is probably going to hurt, Charity," he said. "It might hurt a lot. But just hold on, okay? I'm right here. Once we get through the portal, we'll be fine. Okay?"

"Okay," she said, her voice quavering.

He held her tightly, refusing to notice the weak grip she had on his neck. Refusing to notice her lack of fire in the face of danger.

Refusing to notice that the natural inner glow that usually shone so brightly within her was fading.

"Let's go," he said, terror riding high in his chest. "Hurry!"

CHARITY COULD BARELY think through the fog. She could barely see past the haze over her eyes. The weight of her limbs, once so heavy and hard to manage, barely registered. They were nearly completely numb.

Without warning, or maybe there had been warning, an incredible flash of heat boiled her blood and blistered her skin. Hot needles stabbed her eyes. Sharp points dug into her ears. The strange suck of energy that had been continuous since the battle in the parking lot intensified, sapping what few reserves she had left. Stealing it, and her life force with it.

She screamed against the onslaught, struggling to get away. Trying to break free.

"Easy now," Devon said, his voice miles away. "Push through it. You can get through it."

Agony clawed at her insides, fierce and hot. It yanked at her limbs, threatening to pull them out of their joints. Her guts twisted, and then felt like they were being pulled from her body. Acid dribbled across her bones, eating them away.

"I can't make it," she yelled. She didn't have any strength, not compared to the iron wrapped around her body. "Please, stop. I can't make it!"

Devon gritted his teeth against her cries of pain. Her words ripped at his heart, but he pushed through the pain.

"I can't make it!" She thrashed against him, as weak as a kitten. "It's killing me!"

Tears blinded his eyes and fear pushed against his chest, but he kept walking. Kept going. If he didn't, she would die anyway.

CHAPTER 13

CHARITY FLUTTERED HER eyes, trying to get them open, to see past this darkness. She couldn't feel her body. She couldn't feel *anything*. She floated in a blank, featureless space that part of her realized was the holding room between the living and the dead. The place for those who were too obstinate to move on.

She didn't want to go.

A sob tore through her, but it didn't manifest. Because crying was only for bodies. Tears only existed with eyes. She didn't have either of those anymore.

"Honky-tonk crusted toilets," she heard, as though through a wind tunnel. A woman's voice. Familiar, but she couldn't place it. "She's in bad shape. Hurry! Run her this way. That goofy-eyed elf might not be able to see us, but if it can feel even half the magic I can, it knows something's here."

"It knows," a man said, echoing through the darkness. "It just doesn't know what. They keep their composure until the moment before they strike. It won't be able to tear through our magic by itself, but if it figures out someone is messing with its eyes, it'll start searching for us. We need to get out of here."

"You sound like you have experience with this."

"I have a lot of experience with this. Don't ask about it—it'll give you hives," the man said.

"Move. *Go.*"

Devon!

Charity wanted to cry out to him, to beg him to save her, as he always seemed to. Her heart ached, the pain of losing him filling her whole world.

No, not her heart. Not even her person. She didn't have any of those anymore.

Her soul.

The thought of saying goodbye to him now, so soon after they'd found each other, made it feel like her soul was on fire. She couldn't bear the pain of it. She couldn't bear to move on to a place he couldn't follow.

"Help me," she cried into the darkness. "Help me! I'm still here! I can hear you. Please!"

"Crying babies holding lollipops, I can't—" There were tears behind the woman's words. "I can't bear it. Emery, it feels like distress. Intense distress and suffering. Can you feel that?"

"No, babe. I can't feel the magic, remember? She's alive, though. She hasn't given up. Where there's a will, there's a way."

"Clichés, yes. You and my mother love clichés." The woman fell silent, and Charity felt a pulling within her being. Then a pushing. Which should have been impossible without a body. Right? "She needs... She's lacking…"

"Words, babe. We need words."

"Energy. She needs… She has so much magic. *So* much magic. More than the last time I met her. It's like a wildfire raging within her. But she doesn't have enough energy to sustain it. Reagan had something like this, I think. She suppressed half her magic until she could handle it. This lady—Charity—can't possibly do that. There is no half. There is just the whole. And that whole is like a fire needing oxygen."

"Tell us something we don't know."

Steve!

Charity tried to take a deep breath, forgetting the separation from her body.

"There—did you see?" the woman said excitedly. "She is present. She just needs a little help to blossom."

"How do we help?" Devon asked, the desperation clear in his voice. Charity felt a deep pang of longing. She missed him. She hadn't been herself these past few months, forcing him to be better. *More.* The easy banter they'd enjoyed from the beginning had fallen to the wayside recently. He was always worried she'd randomly explode.

She was always worried she'd randomly explode.

She wanted her life back.

"Help me!" she cried out in the darkness, reaching. Straining to get back. To open her eyes and see the light. "Please!"

CHAPTER 14

Devon knelt next to Penny as she looked down on a pale and lifeless Charity.

"What can I do?" he asked, trying to keep his voice hard and in control. He could barely think for the fear of losing her. Until Charity had slammed into his life, he'd shunned meaningful relationships outside of the pack. He'd invited bitterness to creep inside and stay. She'd woken him up, like a breath of fresh air in a stagnant room. She'd helped him become a better alpha. Her magic, even when painful, felt like a natural part of him. He couldn't imagine walking through life without her.

"Okay." Penny lifted one of her hands, waving fingers in the air, and stared sightlessly down at Charity. Emery watched Penny from the other side of Charity, poised as though ready to move at a moment's notice. The rest of the pack fanned out in the thick trees, watching for passersby.

They were a quarter of a mile from the portal, having run as fast as they could to get clear of whatever invisibility magic the dual-mages had erected. Any closer and they'd be too close to that elf sentry if he started to piece things together and went looking for the source of the magic.

"What are you…" Emery's eyes flicked from Penny to Devon. "How much do you want her to live?"

"What kind of a stupid question is that?"

Devon ignored Steve's outburst, mostly because he was thinking the same thing. "With everything I have and am."

Penny's luminous eyes lifted, latching on to Devon's. "You would give your life for hers?"

"Yes," he answered immediately. "I've tried twice. She keeps saving me."

Penny cocked her head, studying Devon. "Interesting. You are driven to rescue each other. I can mimic that in magic, I think." She looked down at Charity. "If I just…"

"But should you do that?" Emery hastened to say, putting out his hands to stall Penny.

"Yes," Devon said in a tone that brooked no argument. "You should do that. Do whatever it takes. She needs to live."

Penny looked up again. "It'll be a hard road for you."

"My life has always been a hard road. Charity makes it worthwhile."

A sweet smile crossed Penny's face. "Let's hope this isn't the biggest mistake of your life."

Her fingers started to move, weaving something

Devon couldn't see. Emery's brow furrowed and his eyes roamed the air before returning to Devon. "This will be permanent, what she's doing. What I'm about to help her do. It's an energy exchange. If one of you needs energy, you will take from the other. If one of you is dying, and the other doesn't have the resources to help, you will die together."

"She is dying," Penny said, her hands still moving in a lovely, silent dance. "If I don't do this, that's it. It's over. We all go home and listen to my mother bicker with vampires over how many guests at one time is prudent."

"We really shouldn't be bringing our own lives into his decision, babe," Emery murmured. Even so, he reached out his hands and started weaving his fingers through the empty air.

"Do it," Devon said without hesitation. "Do whatever needs to be done."

"His magic is a bonfire among sparks," Penny mused, as though to herself. "It is so deliciously wild. It's the song of the forest. The thrill of the hunt. It complements hers perfectly. It's part of the reason hers has exploded. Why *his* has exploded. They are greater together than the sum of their parts. Dual-mages…"

"Don't try to make sense of it," Emery told Devon, focused on things Devon couldn't see, hands still moving. "She's just figuring it out aloud."

Penny smiled, and something warm twinkled in her eyes. She barely flicked her gaze up to Emery. "And he's making this into a masterpiece."

"It's usually the other way around," Emery murmured. "But it just so happens I know exactly what she means to him. This is how I pay it forward."

Something grabbed Devon by the vitals, way down deep in his person. He clutched at his sternum without thinking.

"Yes, that's the spark that ignites your magic," Penny said. "Take that out, and you can't change into your animal. You are no longer a shifter. But connect it to Charity's spark, and no one can take away your ability to change unless they use her magic to do so. *But* she has the same fail-safe, because of the energy exchange, so it'll go back and forth until the end of time."

"Unless one of you is dying," Steve said from the sidelines.

"Yup. Unless that. Then who cares if you shift, am I right?" Penny said.

"Bedside manner, love," Emery whispered.

"Sorry," she responded, just as softly. "Reagan has grown on me."

"We got something coming this way," Macy called out. "It's a long way off, but it's tall and slim and…like…swishing when it walks. It might not be the same elf, but—"

"It's the same elf. They would have chosen someone smart for this duty," Emery said. "Good at solving riddles. We should've had Reagan come through. She would've been good at figuring out how to hide a body."

"You're thinking of Dizzy and Callie," Penny said. Devon vaguely remembered those two from the mage battle. A trickle of sweat ran down the side of Penny's forehead. An invisible fist reached into the very center of Devon, a primal place directly linked with his wolf.

He gasped or snarled, he couldn't be sure which, and doubled over, trying to protect his middle. Straining to keep his defensive magic from forcing out his wolf.

"Yes, right there," Penny said softly.

"We gotta go," Steve said. "It's definitely the same elf."

"Almost…" Penny's hands moved faster. Emery matched her pace, his face breaking into a sweat as well. "Just about… *Yes*, Emery. Perfect—"

Searing pain sliced through Devon before settling into that primal place deep inside of him. His wolf thrashed toward the surface, threatening to take over. His magic blossomed outward, only to pull back inward as energy drained from his body.

He swayed with dizziness and felt Emery's large hand on his shoulder.

"This is really going to suck for you, bro," Emery said. "But we're out of time. Those elves can move fast when they want to. Welcome to that hard road Penny talked about."

Devon nodded as his energy kept draining. He scooped Charity up into his arms and stood. The blood rushed from his head and his vision swam.

"Steve, take her," Devon said, just barely preventing himself from staggering. He should've asked Dillon, his beta, or maybe one of the girls, but were-lions excelled at protection and defense turned offense. Steve was Charity's best bet, even still recovering from his previous injuries. "I'll need to change. The energy is sapping out of me too quickly."

"You got it, boss," Steve said, leaving the lookout point next to Macy.

Emery took Steve's place at the edge of their grouping of trees, looking down the long, wide path toward the portal. He swore. "Yup, it's onto us. It must be higher up in the chain of command than I'd thought. What the hell has gotten the elves so riled up that they'd send someone important way out here to no man's land? It doesn't make sense."

Devon bowed, his arms suddenly so tired that he wasn't sure he could hold Charity up while Steve covered the short distance to take her. But before they could make the exchange, she jolted and sucked in a breath. Her eyes fluttered open. Her gaze found his immediately and filled with tears.

"Devon!" She struggled to wrap her arms around his neck. "Thank God, Devon! I was… You brought me back."

"Penny did," he said, falling to a knee, barely keeping her off the ground. He kissed her, relief filling his whole being. "Penny and Emery did," he said against her lips. "You're going to be okay. You'll be okay now."

His limbs gave out. He half lowered, half dumped Charity onto the ground.

CHAPTER 15

"I GOT IT, boss." Steve bent quickly and scooped her up, flaring Devon's possessiveness. He pushed the primal reaction away and wasted no time changing into his wolf. He'd be stronger in his animal form, both physically and in magic.

Sights and sounds filled in around him, so much sharper than they'd been. The smell of pine mixed with the sweetness of flowers. The crunch of grass rode the scuff of Emery's shoe on a rock. An animal in the distance screeched out a warning, alerting others of a stranger in its midst.

If that stranger was the elf, it wasn't far away. Emery was right: they needed to get a move on.

He checked in with his pack, all in human form. They smelled of blood and sweat, most of them still healing and hiding their pain. If they could hide it, they could endure it. They were good to move.

Through body posturing and a few minimal movements, he got them up on their feet, picking up packs and preparing to go.

"What's happening? What's this…this feeling?

It's..." Charity said, and a surge of her magic slammed into Devon.

"Devon let me set up a sort of energy share between you two," Penny explained, but Devon lost the string of words immediately.

He wobbled where he stood and lowered his head, digesting the changes wrought by the energy share. Her magic didn't flirt with his like it had in the past—the two were intertwined, his power boosting hers, and hers boosting his. His senses had taken on a keener edge. He could pick out more layers to the smells, hear nuances in that animal's warning, and feel the fatigue and battle wariness of his pack.

He could also feel danger winding toward them, finding its way and picking up its pace. And Charity's magic was pushing against him, too. Impossibly strong and spicy and *not right*.

Urgency prompted him to push past his tiredness. He could rest when he was dead.

He regained his footing, instinctively shoving his magic at Charity, infusing it with the thrill of the hunt, the serenity of silently cutting through the forest, and the victory of a fresh kill.

"Oh! That's..." Charity closed her eyes and sighed. "*Hmmm*, Devon. I feel you. I feel... It's like you and the good side of my magic pumping through me together. Hmm, God, it feels *so good*."

Steve's eyes widened and his face turned red. He faced Devon. "I'm good with being a mule for a beautiful woman, but if she's going to make sounds like that, things might get hairy."

"Didn't need to say it, brother." Rod's gaze flicked below Steve's bared belt line. "You're showing it."

"A few of us are showing it." Andy covered himself. "This is why I said we needed clothes."

Devon emitted a low growl, desperately pushing away his possessive urge to rip into Steve's jugular. Instead, he passed through the brush while sending his magic back to Charity, feeling his own energy build from the exchange. Good news.

"Amazing," Penny said as Devon dodged back out, cataloging the various smells in the area. "Their magic is similar to a dual-mage bond. Emery, that was your addition. How'd you know it would work like that? I was just thinking they'd share energy, not actual magic. You had your finger on the pulse of the situation."

"We can talk about my genius later." Emery strode over, all business. "Penny, you need to get out of here." He slung a backpack over his shoulders. "That elf is going to follow our group until we can give it the slip, so no one should be guarding the portal from this side. But you have to go now. Do not, under any circumstances, let an elf stop you. It'll want to question you, and that'll lead to torture. Do you understand—What are you doing?"

Penny's hands were moving, clearly working magic. "I'm putting up a screen to deaden the trail Charity's magic is making. Right now, I bet that elf is making use of it. Oh, also, I'm not going back."

"Yes you are." Emery grabbed her upper arms and turned her to the left. "You *are* going back. It's too dangerous to stay with us."

"It is safer to be in danger with you, where you and all these fine shifters will take lead, than in supposed safety with Reagan, who creates trouble and then shoves me in front of her while laughing. Besides, you need me. Without me, you'll have no idea when Charity's magic is seeping out of her, calling anyone who can feel it—"

"My magic is a low hum now," Charity said, her voice cutting through the dual-mage's argument. It reeled in Devon's focus. Her glow, which had been absent moments before, pulsed within her, breathtakingly beautiful. "It feels better." Her words were almost a whisper, sultry and sensual. So much stronger. "Everything feels better. *You* feel better."

Steve tensed, tightening his lips, and shook his head. His body was still responding to her sensuality and probably her proximity.

Devon couldn't take it anymore. He was standing on human legs before he'd thought to change. Breathing heavily, weak from the effort and the energy exchange, he nonetheless stalked over to Charity as the dual-mages finished their argument, and took her from Steve's arms.

Her smile was just for him. The love in her eyes increased the speed at which their energy and magic pinged back and forth until it seemed like they were sharing all of it. Like they were one.

"Am I too heavy?" she asked him, curling up in his arms as Devon followed Emery and Penny through the brush.

He hugged her close, feeling the reassurance of her magic curling around and within his. He'd almost lost her. She was alive because of the dual-mages, a debt Devon would repay if it was the last thing he did.

"You're light as a feather," he whispered, hiding the strain from his aching and energy-starved arms. The small hairs on the back of his neck rose to attention. Danger was drawing closer. "Faster, Emery. That elf has gained speed."

Emery glanced back with a furrowed brow. "Shifters can sense predators on their tail?"

"It seems that shifters with the help of fae magic can." He gave Charity a squeeze. "Thanks for arranging that boost in my effectiveness."

"Good," Emery said. "Keep me updated. Powerful elves can run as fast as elder vampires, and they are every bit as vicious and cunning. In fact, aside from what they eat and the fact that one is born, the other created, there isn't a whole lot of difference between the two."

"Can they track?" Charity asked.

"They bring in other magical species to track for them," Emery said, emerging from the brush onto a thin dirt path. He took a left, heading toward a thick wood with moss weeping from branches and vines draping between the trees. Light reduced down to murky shadows and pools of black, emanating a forbidding feeling that urged Devon to turn away. "If we see one of those on our trail, we'll need to kill it. They're better than any dog. Better even than a hellhound on a blood trail."

"A hellhound...on a blood trail?" Penny asked, looking behind them with wide eyes. "That's a real thing?"

"You don't know much about the magical world either?" Charity asked her.

"Not really. I didn't know about magic growing up. I'm still learn—" Penny stubbed her toe and fell face-first into Emery's back. He slowed as she clutched his shoulders to pull herself back to her feet. Once there, they walked on without saying a word. They'd learned to rely on each other, to share their strength.

Much like Devon and Charity were doing.

He couldn't help but squeeze her again, and when she turned his way to see why, he stole a quick kiss. He'd be relieved when this was all over and they could get back to their lives.

"The time will come when you need to make a choice. A choice that concerns the rest of your life and, more importantly, her life. I cannot see when this choice will come, but you will know when it is before you. The choice you must make will be against your heart. Against everything you've always wanted. Against your very being. To save Charity's life—to give her a life—you must

take the hard road, sacrifice your heart, and let her go."

Devon's heart stopped. Had he just committed the error he was supposed to avoid? Had he doomed her?

But no, that couldn't be—the *Seer* had said he'd know when the time came. Besides, if he hadn't agreed to share his life force and magic with her, she would have died. He'd saved her, not doomed her.

"Soon I'll be able to walk," Charity murmured, cutting into his reverie.

He gave her a confused look, his mind still swirling.

"I can feel you shaking," she explained in a whisper before leaning in and running her lips down the shell of his ear and sucking in his earlobe.

A delicious shiver ran the length of his body. He leaned into her hot mouth, wanting her with a desperation that was inopportune for entering a spooky magical wood with a powerful elf hot on their trail.

"By the by," Penny said, thankfully pulling Charity's focus away from her ministrations. "What is it with shifters and wandering around for long periods without clothes? That happened after the Guild battle, too. Dicks just swinging everywhere. And don't get me started on the number of nipples staring at me. Don't you guys have pull-away sweats for when you need to change?"

Charity huffed out a laugh.

"Some of us like to show off the goods," Steve called up.

"None of us like to be poked with those goods,

though. Keep your distance," Andy replied.

"What can I say, when I get hard, I stay hard until the job is done."

"That isn't making me feel any better about this particular situation, bro. Stay back."

Penny laughed, her hand on Emery's shoulder to keep from face-planting into him again.

"We might need to change at a moment's notice right now," Devon explained, wishing he had the strength and energy to hold Charity away from his body so her proximity and pleasing aroma weren't such a distraction. "In the Brink, there are usually a plethora of clothing options nearby, so if we have to discard a pair of sweats, we can grab another when we need it. But we don't have those options out here, and I'd rather not have my pack meet Charity's people in the buff."

"Huh." Penny turned back around. "All good points."

"Get used to looking at the sky, babe," Emery said as he reached the tree line. He stopped and turned around, his blue eyes lacking any sparkle from the joke he'd made moments before. Reagan had been right—their guide knew his business. "Listen up. There is a reason most people try to avoid this wood. It's filled with bogles, doppelgangers, exiled gnomes, ghouls, you name it. The worst of the worst gather in this wood, intending harm. Most have a tendency to confuse their victims before killing them. This is, by far, the most dangerous leg of our journey. I'd intended to get a good night's sleep before braving this wood, but with that elf on our heels, that's no longer an option." He took a breath, his gaze touching on Charity, then Devon, then the others waiting behind them in a single file line. "I know you're tired. I know you've had a long day. But to let down your guard in this place is to suffer a fate worse than death. Penny and I can run interference, but we'll need to walk in pairs or single file, and we can't guard all of you. Those at the back are in the most danger. A wendigo can sneak up on you from behind, melt into your body, and take control, using you to attack and eat the person in front of you. That's you dead. That's your friend dead or bloody and very grossed out. So watch yourselves. Stay alert." He paused. "Who's excited?"

CHAPTER 16

"Who's excited?" Charity said, pulling her arms from around Devon's neck. "What kind of stupid question is that?"

She fought the aches in her joints and the overall exhaustion dragging her down and struggled out of Devon's grasp. Whatever the dual-mages had done to them had literally brought her back from the dead, but it hadn't completely repaired her. Only food, time, and sleep could do that. Hopefully.

Given Devon's inability to hold her steady, he was just as low on fuel. They were sharing the energy of one person. She'd pulled him down enough—there was no way she would tie up his hands so he couldn't even defend himself. She was done being a leech. Done crying about her past and worrying about her future. These people were making this trip because of her, putting themselves in danger, and she was damned if she'd send them to their graves.

Emery didn't answer her. He didn't need to. A strange, hollow sort of laugh drifted out of the trees.

"Welcome," a disembodied voice said, the tone

taunting.

"I got the back," Steve said, savageness ringing through his words. "They can try to sneak up behind me."

"I'll take the back," Cole said. "I am already here."

"I got it—"

"I'm in the back," Devon said, cutting Dale off. Command and assurance rang in his voice. Dale and Cole both opened their mouths to argue, but a burst of magic thundered out of Devon, thicker and more potent than Charity had ever felt. A wave of it washed through her body, tightening her core and shortening her breath. "Charity will be in the center. Steve, you stick to her back. Cole, you're in front of her. Protect the fae at all costs."

Cole's mouth clicked shut. Dale glowered, but didn't comment about being left out. Both men and Barbara crisply responded, "Yes, alpha."

Steve said, "I'm your huckleberry," making Charity grin despite the anxiety rolling through her body.

Devon's original pack said nothing at all. They didn't waste time with formality. Instead, they filed in quickly, nudging and bumping Charity into position before divvying up the duffel bags, making it so everyone had an equal load and a good range of motion.

"It's nice working with shifters," Penny mused, her gaze pointed upward at a diagonal to the right. "No arguing, no pushback, just everyone working together to get the job done. My mother and the Bankses should take a lesson."

"Your mother and the Bankses push shifters around, or don't you remember the battle with the Mages' Guild?" Emery waited until Cole and Steve filed in before turning.

"Wishful thinking, then. We've got company." Penny's fingers were moving as Emery started forward. She didn't keep pace with him, waiting on the sidelines until Charity reached her. Only then did Penny start walking. "It's targeting the fae—Charity. It's targeting Charity."

"Can you read minds?" Charity whispered, not wanting to disturb Penny, but not able to keep from asking.

"No," Penny said. "I read magic. I can feel magical intent. And that fork-tongued tea toter is whipping up something nasty."

"That sure is helpful," Emery murmured, walking into the brush beside the path. His hands moved in front of him as if they were shaping a ball. He flung out his palms. A moment later, a scream rent the quiet of the wood. A small shape tumbled through the space between trees before low-hanging branches covered its fall. "It would've been nice to have you with me the last few times I came through this wood."

A dead silence descended as they moved forward. Their shoes didn't even make scuffing sounds against the dirt.

Charity caught movement from the corner of her eye. A feeling of danger scratched at her from the same direction.

"No, don't worry about that thing, whatever it is," Penny said. "It's trying to form a confusion spell of some sort, but its efforts are rudimentary at best. Emery will take care of it."

An agonized wail throbbed around them before ending abruptly. This time, Charity didn't see the creature fall.

"Incoming! Something like magical acid. Your direction, Devon." Penny spun, her hands out.

Without warning, Charity's magic surged, scraping through her painfully. Almost immediately, a wave of Devon's magic soothed the angry sting. A euphoric, somewhat erotic feeling flowered in its wake.

"Got it," Devon said, his voice strong and sure.

"Where's my sword?" Charity asked, flexing her hand, ignoring the ache in her knuckles. She tried to thread her way around Steve, wanting to help Devon, to hold up her position in the pack. But Steve and Cole both pressed in closer, trapping her between them. Penny stopped her from going around them.

Frustrated with her inability to do her part, she gritted her teeth. She should be fighting, leading the charge. She felt it in her bones. The role of precious cargo didn't suit her.

"Do we change, boss?" Steve called.

A grunt sounded from behind. A tug at her middle urged her to take her place beside Devon. Her magic surged again. Just like before, Devon's magic blended with it, purified it, and when it washed back through her, it carried the sweet song she kept hearing when her magic was working properly. Maybe it wasn't her song at all—maybe it was theirs.

"He needs help," Charity said, shoving Steve to get him moving.

"That kid does not need help," Steve said, respect in his voice. "He can work a blade as good as he can work his wolf."

"Yes, Steve, change. You too, Cole and Yasmine," Devon called. "The rest of you, take the packs. Get moving, Emery."

The line started moving again, Emery taking orders without a problem.

"You are shedding your distress," Penny said urgently, plucking at Charity's sleeve. An itch between Charity's shoulder blades said they were being watched. "It's calling to the creatures in this wood. You're basically advertising your vulnerability. That can't possibly be the way your power's designed to work—"

"It's probably supposed to do the opposite and I'm doing something wrong," Charity said in frustration.

"Can you do something about that, Turdswallop?" Emery called back.

Charity frowned, wondering if he was talking to her, when Penny answered. "Working on it."

"Turdswallop?" Charity asked.

Penny shrugged one shoulder. "He finds strange things funny. Anyway, don't stress about your magic. I didn't have a clue at first. Thank pearl-clutching hobos that I met Emery when I did, or I would've been lost. You'll get it, don't worry. As soon as someone gives you direction, you'll take to it like a duck takes to water. I can tell. Now…" Penny patted her arm, which was nice, then slid her palm into Charity's personal space—down her elbow to her lower back, over her butt, and down the back of her thigh.

"That's… Why—"

"Sorry. Just pasting a spell to you without asking permission. It's faster that way." Penny moved to the other side. "It'll help us all."

A flickering light caught Charity's eye just beyond the tree to their right. Steve growled, a sound like an earthquake. The light flicked off.

"We got company," Emery called.

Another light flared to life deeper into the wood, flickering happily. It called to Charity, beckoning her closer.

"Nasty buggers," Penny murmured, her hands working.

A silent purple explosion lit up the trees, illuminating the wood in violet light. A crowd of humanlike creatures, no more than two feet tall, screeched within the brush that only partially concealed them. Pointed teeth filled their mouths, and huge, pale blue eyes blinked in their leathery faces. They ran from the light, two clattering into each other and falling down.

More light explosions flared brightly, making

Charity squint. The feeling of danger throbbed from her other side.

She turned in time to see one of those creatures launch itself at her, its wide mouth full of teeth, its arms out to wrap around her neck.

She staggered back and thrust out a palm, eyes wide. A spark ignited next to the creature's chest, and her magic exploded in a violent surge of electricity. The thing was shoved backward before its entrails splattered across the leaves and brush behind it.

Charity's head swam and her knees weakened, but she pushed on as another creature jumped toward her. She punched it in the face with her magic. The back of its head blew off. She ran forward on wobbly legs and kicked one of the leathery things like a football. It tried to latch on to her leg, but it couldn't get purchase. Its little claws ripped her jeans and scraped along her skin before it was airborne.

"I need my sword," she yelled.

"You need to conserve your energy or you'll kill the alpha of this pack," Penny shouted, her hands dancing through the air.

The end of her words were drowned out by Cole's roar. He lumbered in front of Charity, swinging his big arms at the growling and spitting little creatures. He was too slow, though. They dodged his claws and raced between his legs, chittering laughter all the time.

Charity kicked another, barely stopping herself from using her magic. It wasn't her only defense. She'd taken martial arts lessons since she was twelve. She moved through her fighting styles, punching and kicking the small creatures with ease. They were fast, but she was faster, fueled by adrenaline and nearly a lifetime of practice.

One launched into Steve's mane. He roared and shook his great head, flinging it off, but another dropped onto his back from God knew where. Andy lunged forward and punched it off before stomping on its head.

Another violet explosion lit up the wood to Charity's right. A second, larger explosion flared to her left before zinging out in all directions, sending sparks directly at a handful of creatures. Those sparks detonated as they hit their targets.

"Your magic is insanely good for attacking," Penny murmured, at Charity's side. A strange thing for her to say, given that she was the one who'd created the second, more impressive spell.

The area to the right of them lit up with an even brighter spell. It almost seemed like they were one-upping each other. Their blasts of electrified light zapped ten or more creatures on each round.

A wolf snarled, followed by a creature howling. Steve caught one of the things between his teeth. Blood squirted in all directions.

Another explosion went off. Squeals crowded the air. That did it. The creatures took off, scattering back into the wood, beaten.

Like a bubble popping, suddenly the full spectrum of sound rushed back. Leaves rustled and feet crunched the dirt.

"First ambush down, who knows how many to go," Emery said into the following hush.

CHAPTER 17

By the time the murky orange glow filtering through trees lightened, reminding Charity that they'd technically been traveling at night even though the entire time her eyes and brain had said it was day (common in the Realm, she remembered), the edge of the wood loomed within sight.

Their party had been deathly quiet the last couple of hours, traversing the danger with keen eyes and exhausted bodies. Strangely, though, they'd only encountered one other group of hostile creatures—a group of exiled gnomes who clearly didn't give a fuck, and were intent on fighting regardless of the odds.

They were now deceased exiled gnomes.

"I thought you said this wood was the most dangerous you'd come across," Penny said, her voice soft to match the false tranquility of the wood. Her eyes continually scanned their surroundings and her hands stayed near her chest, ready to work magic.

"It is," answered Emery, who'd drifted closer to her and stayed there. "This trip has been unnaturally quiet."

"Is it because we have a larger crew?" Penny startled

and her hands jerked. A strange sheen spread through the trees before winking out. "Oops. I thought I saw something."

"I saw it too. And maybe the size of our party has scared some attackers away, though from the stories I've heard, a large party is usually an invitation for the wood's more cunning inhabitants. They take it as a challenge."

Penny looked back through the line. "Everyone is still here, right?"

"Still here. No one has eaten anyone else," Andy replied.

Emery leaned around Charity to see her side of the wood. "It doesn't make sense." His brow furrowed before he scanned his side again.

"The elves?" Charity guessed. "It seems everyone in this place is terrified of them."

"For good reason." Emery scratched his face. "But if they'd taken over the wood, someone would have stopped us by now."

Penny tensed as they crossed the tree line, the path opening up as it led up a gradual incline toward a small mountain. Trees and brush still dotted the way, but the early morning glow bathed them in soft light, chasing away any dark shadows or easy hiding places for predators.

Charity sighed softly, giving in a little to the tremors racking her body and the fatigue that made each stop arduous.

"We're almost to a secluded resting spot," Emery said, and if it wasn't for the comforting smile Penny gave her, Charity wouldn't have known he was talking to her.

"I'll be okay," she assured them, wondering how Devon was faring. He probably wasn't showing his fatigue, trudging on with the confidence that befitted an alpha, but he was just as tired; she could feel it.

Emery was true to his word. Not even an hour's trudge later, he held up a fist and slowed. Everyone slowed with him. Well, almost everyone. Charity, having shut off her brain to try to ignore the throbbing in her shaking legs, bumped into the back of a yeti built of what felt like bricks.

"Sorry," she murmured, backing up.

A small outcropping flanked by brambles ended in a bench broken down the middle, each end sticking into the air. Scraggly bushes and spindly flowers—or weeds?—pushed in around it, the least inviting resting spot Charity had ever seen, and that was saying something, given where she'd grown up.

"This isn't going to fit all of us," Penny whispered.

Emery walked into the gardener's nightmare anyway, looking deeper into the brambles and kicking at the skeleton flora around the bench. Apparently satisfied, he went right—and disappeared.

"But...I don't sense magic." Penny rushed forward. Charity moved to follow, but Cole lumbered into her way and Steve pushed in behind, blocking her.

She gritted her teeth. What she wouldn't give for full health.

Penny got to the bench and turned, looking the way Emery went. A big smile lit up her face. "It's an illusion."

Emery reappeared. "No, it's just a little path you can't see from the main road."

"This is a road?" Rod looked ahead before glancing behind.

"Thieves' highway, road, whatever." Emery gestured them closer.

"How many people know about this little outcropping?" Devon asked. As Charity expected, he didn't look tired at all. In fact, to the undiscerning eye, he might be gearing up for a marathon. What a faker.

"Enough to ensure I put up a good ward." Emery motioned everyone in again. "It's safe enough for us to rest. We need it."

Devon scanned his people. "Choose whatever form you want. Let's get settled and get some shut-eye."

When Charity neared him, he took her hand and peered into her eyes.

"How are you?" she asked to get the jump on the conversation.

A grin ghosted his lips. "Right as rain. Ready to do acrobatics. You?"

"Wondering how fast I can get to sleep."

He nodded and stood by as his people followed Emery and Penny beyond the bench, disappearing one by one. "I caught a whiff of vampire in that wood," he said quietly. As soon as he and Charity were alone together, he turned away from the bench, peering through the trees to the wild land beyond. "Yasmine didn't smell it, though. Neither did Rod. But since Penny..." He slid his hand across the top of her butt and hooked it low on her hip. "My senses are boosted, somehow. The scent was faint—I couldn't tell the level—but I'd swear it was vampire."

"Is that unusual?" She leaned against his solid chest.

"I don't know. I'll ask Emery about it. It could be nothing. Vampires haunt the dark places like any other creature in the Realm. But here, within the elves' jurisdiction, they usually mind their manners."

"So it seems, because it—or they—didn't attack."

"So it seems," he repeated, that grin ghosting his lips again. "I am so fucking tired, I can barely think straight."

She burst out laughing, not expecting that admission, and especially not with the grin making his eyes twinkle.

"Me too," she said, turning into him and trailing her fingers down his sides, flitting across his skin. "At one point, I had to stop myself from asking Steve if I could get a lift."

He cupped her butt and pulled her closer. "I'd be good with finding a secluded corner, lying on my back, and letting you go to town."

She closed her eyes as his lips trailed down her neck.

"I'd be good with finding a secluded corner, lying on my back, spreading my legs, and letting *you* go to town."

He growled against her neck, sucking on her skin. "I think I have just enough left in the tank to make that happen."

"No big deal, boss, but I don't think it's the best place for that," Steve said, just out of sight.

Charity felt Devon's release of breath. "We can't get to the Flush fast enough," he murmured.

"Is this the part where you're thinking about yourself and not me?" She pushed away from him with a smile, taking his hand.

His eyes were on fire as he stared at her, refusing to budge and head to the campsite. "Yes. I need to pound my love into you."

"Pound it in? And here I didn't think you were a hopeless romantic."

"Pound it, bang it, fuck it—whatever you want to call it, it's going to be hard and fast, and you will love every minute of it."

Charity laughed delightedly, and thankfully, she was too low on energy for her magic to surge and ruin the moment. Small miracles.

The area Emery had led them to wasn't large, but it was big enough to fit everyone comfortably. Devon found a patch of green weeds, laid down, and waited just long enough for Charity to push up beside him before he fell asleep. Charity followed soon after.

"Devon, wake up!"

Charity startled at the urgent whisper. Devon stirred beside her.

Penny leaned over him, her brown hair falling around her anxious face.

"Wake up," she said again, shoving him.

His eyes snapped open and he sat up so fast that Charity rolled away.

"Nice," she said.

"We've got company." Penny motioned Devon to stand.

Charity was up a moment after him, noticing the tightness in his eyes, his shoulders bowed and his muscles tight before he could school his face into that mask of alpha confidence. Charity wondered if Roger always did the same thing.

Steve and Cole were waiting to the sides, and the rest of the shifters were rousing, most still in animal form. The big yeti tried to step in Charity's way.

She slapped her palm to his chest and let loose a small surge of magic. No way was she letting him stop her. Cole staggered backward as though shoved by a four-hundred-pound man. Magic leaked out of Charity's well, but Devon's magic rushed in, light and clean and comforting, to smooth things out.

The dual-mages were geniuses, that was the bottom

line. Charity only wished they'd done their trick sooner.

As Charity rounded the brambles near the broken bench, she heard, "I merely wish to speak with her. She'll come to no harm, I can assure you."

Fireworks went off in Charity's middle. Hope flooded her.

Vlad had come, and he better have answers.

CHAPTER 18

"SECOND, WE HAVE news."

Romulus hesitated in glancing up from the architectural plans spread across his workstation. Soft light from the morning sun splashed onto his design. Spun-glass ornaments threw colored splotches around his desk, lending beauty to the chaos.

He breathed in fresh air from the many open windows before lifting his gaze. There was never a reason to rush when nature was offering up such a bounty.

Halvor, his assistant, stood in the doorway, his head tilted to the side, awaiting acknowledgement from a superior. His regal bearing displayed his excellent lineage and advanced training. Unlike normal, however, his right shoulder was raised ever so slightly, a tell that he was hard-pressed to disguise whenever troubling news conflicted his duties.

"What is it, Halvor? Is the First not pleased with her garden?"

"Not at all, Second. She expressed her immense pleasure."

Romulus couldn't help a smile. He sat back into his

raised seat. Other than the High Elves, his mother was quite possibly the hardest to please in the entire Realm.

"Then what is this news that has you so out of sorts? Or did you have another fight with Jauni?"

Halvor's head drooped slightly with embarrassment. The week before, he and his mate had had a truly exhilarating domestic squabble in the public park. Most of the community had enjoyed watching them, wondering who would force the other to submit, never a sure bet with two such masters. But they'd let the fight get out of control, destroying the tables for the communal cook-off. They'd had to reschedule the whole affair! Romulus had been forced to order Halvor to a week's worth of plowing, a pastime his assistant detested.

"No, Second. Jauni and I have resolved our differences. We've had word from the office of the Red Prophet. Her latest prediction involves most of the Realm. The elves, mages, vampires, demons...and fae." Halvor waited for a nod to continue. "It seems a half-human, half-guardian will be integral in deciding the victor of a power struggle between the elves and vampires. Representatives from the underworld were also mentioned in the reading, though the nature of their involvement was not clear."

As if one drop of acid had plopped onto the top of his head and started burning its way down, Romulus felt his muscles tensing one by one.

"A half-human, half-guardian, you said? Half *custodes*?"

"Yes, Second. The outcome of this battle will decide who rules the Realm."

"I see. And this halvsie creature is integral to the outcome?"

"Yes, Second, though the winner remains unclear. This is largely because of the role the underworld plays, a component that is too blurred for the Red Prophet to interpret. It is clear, however, that both sides of this battle will seek to enlist the aid of the half-human, half-guardian."

"Of course they would. That is common sense."

Romulus's brow crumpled in contemplation of this news. He brought his elbows up to the armrests of his chair and clasped his fingers in front of his face, rolling through the short list of half-human, half-guardians in his acquaintance. A few had trickled in from the human lands over time. Halvsies were simple, in his experience. Easily pleased. Many of them had inherited the fae's long life span, but the ones he'd met were all incompetent fighters. Battle one of them, and all your focus went to not killing them. It was no sport at all.

Given that they also lacked skills that would improve the Flush in any real way, they weren't regarded or esteemed favorably. Their status was low, and their options limited. They had all, so far, found their way to the outskirts of the Realm, living their lives with the lesser fae and probably getting along swimmingly.

How any of them could hope to lead the guardian into battle, Romulus could not imagine.

"Can this prophecy be believed?" he asked. "Is the Red Prophet dabbing in the hallucinogens again?"

"She was sober when she relayed her discovery. I believe it came to her yesterday evening. She spent last night meditating with her people about it, then she hastened to her rendering machine. The scroll was shown to me. The seal was intact."

Romulus's eyes widened. "Well, that is news. And were we given a means with which to narrow down the candidate? Leading a battle of this magnitude will be a great honor! I almost wish I had been named. This will elevate the family of the guardian greatly."

Three fingers on Halvor's sword hand twitched. Based on all the highly unusual fidgeting, he was clearly flustered. Or possibly excited. He was practically dancing in his skin!

"Speak plainly, Halvor. Out with it."

"The Red Prophet saw a young woman."

Romulus stared dumbly for a moment. "A young woman?" He thought back to all the female halvsies he had met over the years. Only a very few had possessed any sort of fighting experience. Most were shocked it was considered normal for males and females to fight each other. "Has someone left our lands that I was not aware of, Halvor?"

"You were the last, Second."

Acid leached into his blood. "The Red Prophet is sure it was a woman?"

"Yes, Second."

"I've often wondered if she has some way to cheat. And are you absolutely positive she was of clear mind? Sometimes she drops mind relaxants in her morning tea. Remember when she lit the tree on fire and claimed it was possessed?"

"I was thorough, Second. This battle is coming—she gets the feeling it has been building for decades. Now the key players are being named. This young woman is one of them, and the Red Prophet is nearly sure her quest has already manifested. She believes what she saw was an echo."

A quest was a magical coming of age for a guardian, manifesting when the time was right. The quest holder was to stop at nothing to fulfill the obligation to the best of their ability. A great range of quests was possible, but the more complex ones tended to garner the fae higher status within the community.

If the halvsie woman was fated to lead a battle of this magnitude, she would earn a place among the elite. She was a woman to know, and to watch, which was troubling, since they didn't know who she was.

A little surge of adrenaline fueled Romulus's bloodstream as he thought of a battle to come. It had been a while since he'd torn himself away from his gardens and visited the battlegrounds, where they practiced sword work and hand-to-hand combat. He should see to it soon. Focusing solely on one form of his magic—the natural—would leave him out of balance. Fighting was every bit as important as the gardens in this community, especially if there was one on the horizon.

"An echo?" Romulus leaned against his worktable, accidentally crushing a papier-mâché garden.

Halvor's hand flexed, and Romulus braced himself for the news to come.

"She said the echo was so powerful, it knocked her from her chair, making her spill tea on her book. She mentioned she'll be seeing you for the damages. It was her favorite book."

"What does an echo have to do with me?" Romulus asked, the acid spreading through his stomach.

"An echo of that caliber can only manifest from the result of a successful quest. She did not say it outright, Second—forgive me if I've misunderstood—but she indicated this young woman's quest is a result of your successful quest to sire her. Your quest was essentially leading toward this all along, which has compounded the impact of both quests."

Romulus shook his head, unable to stop his hands from fisting and his fingers turning white with the pressure. "It is impossible, Halvor. I've been gone from the human world for…"

"Over twenty-one years, Second. Making any child you sired not yet twenty-one."

"When I left, my beloved wasn't with child. I would not have left if that were the case. I never would have abandoned a fae child, mine or someone else's. I would've ignored the call of our people; you must know that."

"Of course, Second. No one would doubt it. But women can be pregnant for some time before it shows."

The chair creaked as Romulus rose. "I sent people back to check. To make sure."

"As you recall, Second, the men were unable to find your beloved. They surmised that she must've changed her name. They did not feel the fae influence in the area and returned home."

"Could the infant have been missed?"

"Sometimes, when the mother is human, the child's fae blood is masked for some time. Diluted. It isn't until the magic starts to manifest that it presents itself. Often a large event of great stress and pressure will bring about the change. Of course, most children of mixed lineage have weak magic. A few do get lucky and lean heavily toward the fae. Their magic and skills are mostly salvageable, though still not exemplary. Very rarely will a half-fae child develop strength and power that propels them beyond that which is their birthright. Given that your quest was to merge the human and fae blood, it stands to reason your child would be a diamond in the rough, called forth by fate and prophecy."

"It seems you have done your research, Halvor, before bringing this to me. I can only assume you have more information to offer."

The regal man bowed, ever so slightly. The harness of his sword, wrapped around his torso, issued a soft clink. He'd unconsciously flexed his chest. More disturbing news was coming.

"The elves have gotten various disturbing reports centered on a young woman. Now, I must warn you, they don't seem to know if they are looking for one woman or two. The first has been whispered about for some time, apparently. She and a vampire are linked to a large disturbance in the underworld. After great contemplation, Lucifer is sure he glimpsed this woman from a distance—in the middle of a demon battle, of all places. He has requested a meeting with the elf king and queen to discuss the matter in more detail. Although few people have been informed of the reason for this meeting, those in the know have to wonder if he's suspicious of the elves' interference. How else would a non-demon woman get past his magical barricade? Given Lucifer is a mighty adversary, on par with the elf king in power and magical finesse, the elves are stopping at nothing to find this woman and question her.

"It could, then, be the same woman and vampire who have inspired the new rumors. We have heard reports that a young woman chased Vlad off a battlefield. For someone to do such a thing, she would need to be great in power. Vlad is a worthy foe."

"I have heard many reports of him over the years, yes," Romulus said, calling up a picture of the vampire in his mind. "He has as much presence in the human lands as he does in the Realm, I believe."

"He has a foothold in the underworld, as well, I hear. Apparently, he has called this young woman an Arcana. He has judged this by her magical smell as well as her skill set. If these rumors are about the same woman, it's possible they could merely be having a spat, as guardians are wont to do. It is dangerous to be in league with a vampire. That would be a black mark on her status."

The room swirled. Memories flashed—of the quest illusion that had overcome Romulus one night after a Gathering. Of the excitement of embarking on his quest. When he'd first stepped through the portal, the sky had been so clear and blue, and the sun was almost hot on his face. He'd soon met a smiling beauty who'd transfixed him, placing him under the sweetest of spells.

He remembered, still so fresh, his time with her. The connection he'd felt with her, the bliss, the earth-moving desperation to be near her always. He hadn't realized love like that could exist. It had ruined him for all other females.

He'd thought it must be divine, that feeling. That the Fates were entwining the two of them as part of a larger plan. But then he'd woken up one morning and felt the call of the Flush, a pull so hard, so intense, that he could barely think for needing to get back. It was like his oxygen was drying up, and he could no longer breathe within the Brink.

He'd tried to bring his love with him. He'd tried to show her the portal to the Realm, but she hadn't seen it. She'd thought he was crazy. Eventually, he had to let her go. It had broken him to leave, and he'd longed for her every day since, but had left her anyway. By herself.

Crying all alone as he walked away.

That he might've left her to fend for herself with an infant—*his* child—

The windows spun around him, the floor racing up to meet him.

"Second!"

Halvor's concerned face appeared in his vision.

"It cannot be true," Romulus muttered.

Halvor did not attempt to lift him. He'd been the one to receive Romulus as he stumbled back to his home those twenty-something years ago.

"The elves were able to find a shifter that had taken part in the battle Vlad was chased from. A werewarthog. After days, he finally succumbed to their magic. Apparently, not only is this young woman able to blossom the sun in the night sky, she can summon the *pulse*."

Romulus stared up at Halvor, not comprehending.

Summoning the *pulse*, a bundling of electrical energy that could concuss the air and magically blow the skies apart, was a rare gift graced to the worthiest of the Arcana family line—*his* family line. His grandmother was the last to have been bestowed with the mighty gift, and she was largely favored as the strongest and fairest First in the history of their race.

Air couldn't get past the constrictions in Romulus's throat. All he could do was shake his head and flutter his eyes. This was impossible. He might have a child he'd never met, one who'd grown up without their kind to guide, train, and protect her...

"If she is mine, and what you say is true..." His voice could barely be understood, it was so raspy. "She is in grave danger. I came into my full power at twenty-one, as did my mother, as did her mother and father before her. My father's hit at twenty. She won't understand what is happening. She won't be able to control it, and certainly won't be able to contain it. I'm sure she's already having problems with the surges—how is she surviving? She will kill herself and probably everyone within her immediate reach and range. It would almost be a blessing if Vlad were to capture her. As an elder, he must be strong enough to counteract most of her magic."

"But would he know how, Second?" Halvor asked.

It was a good point. Likely not. Fae largely did not trust vampires, and few, if any, would have taught the elder such a valuable lesson. But if the elves were able to intercept...

"If what I understand is true," Halvor went on, "Vlad is attempting just that. To capture her, I mean. Or was, until she burned him so badly he was forced to go underground."

Romulus allowed himself one more moment of absolute shock. Allowed the acid to drip to the soles of his feet. After that, he let the guilt wash over him, sucking him under and dragging him down. He opened up to the intense suffering for his lost love and their infant, to the impossible situation he had unknowingly put his daughter in. He let the guilt corrode him, eating away like a maggot. And finally, he allowed himself to push all that aside. He possibly had a little girl out there who needed to join her family. She needed guidance, but first, she needed saving.

Romulus lunged up, swiping his hair from his face. Halvor stepped back to the door, firm and resolute once more. The situation had been laid bare, at last, and now they needed a solution and a path.

"What are my orders?" he asked.

"Find the girl and bring her here. Send someone who's strong in both magic and fighting. Her most immediate danger is herself. Beyond that, keep her away from the elves and vampires—we must not let her become a pawn. If she is truly an Arcana, and my daughter, she must be steeped in our culture before we allow the elves access to her. They are our benefactors, but they may have to be reminded it is a contract, not an obligation. Finally, get our people training harder. Stage mock battles. Create a community competition. If this is a quest, the battle the prophet has foreseen will surely come to pass. We must be ready. No guardian will be left to stand on her own. We will be behind her when the Fates call."

CHAPTER 19

THE MOST HANDSOME and dangerous creature Charity had ever seen in her life stood two feet away, separated only by an invisible ward the dual-mages had erected. The last time she had stood this close to this vampire, he'd lunged forward to grab her, and she'd retaliated by beaming fake sunlight down on him. This time, however, her magic wasn't up to par.

"It is so good to see you again," Vlad said. His tailored suit, somehow not out of place despite the fact that they were in the middle of a forest, highlighted his perfect body. Even the guy's hair was perfect. It was just too much for any one individual. It was annoying that he made it work. "I have missed our dealings."

"You miss being barbecued?" Penny asked, and she was entirely serious. A point that brought bubbles of laughter from Charity's middle.

A smile turned up Vlad's lips. "I see our illustrious Arcana keeps the very best of company. Tell me, how is the mage game going for you, Miss Bristol?"

"Great," Penny replied. "The Guild structure is really coming along. Our training is churning out some of the very best mages."

"Yes, I know. I've purchased many of their spells—and their silence. Loyalty is so hard to come by these days, don't you find?"

"Hello, pot," she replied.

His smile didn't seem to change, but suddenly it sent chills up Charity's spine. "Yes, it does seem I have my own issues with loyalty. Quite the surprise." He resumed his focus on Charity, so intense that it almost seemed like those around them dropped away. "You have my deepest apologies on your struggles to get this far. I never intended for you to come into harm's way. I will not layer the issue in pretty words and lackluster excuses. Quite simply, I was outmaneuvered. My attention was elsewhere, and you were left exposed at the worst possible time. Trust me when I say that it will not happen again."

His suave demeanor lifted, for just a second, and the exposed viciousness made her want to take a step back. Or blast him with her magic. His calm and collected mask settled on his handsome features once again.

"But let us talk of other things," he said, his musical voice filling the tense moment. "Did you get my note?"

Her heart hammered and her palms started to sweat. "You mean…the one—"

"In your desk, yes. I'm glad you found it. I dared not leave it out for your father to find. It would've been ripped to shreds, along with all the pictures he must've found within the house. Your room was in a state. I figured that if I locked the drawer, it would deter his interest. I'm glad I was correct."

"But…" She narrowed her eyes at him. "My room was like I left it."

"Yes. I hope you don't mind my tidying up. Your father is certainly a character. I didn't think you'd want evidence of that in your personal space."

"You…" Charity remembered the torn photograph that had been forgotten under her bed. No, not forgotten. Missed. "You cleaned my room?"

A small smile graced his face, but he didn't comment. Obviously that was a yes.

What sort of person broke into someone's room and cleaned it? Had he done it out of arrogance, to show her he could do what he pleased, or actual concern for her well-being? She couldn't decide.

"You convinced my father that I wasn't his," she said, needing to lay out all the facts. If he lied here, she could better determine if he'd lied in the note.

"I did not convince him, no." Vlad clasped his hands behind his back. "I laid out a timeline, highlighted some facts, and he put it together. It was a wonder he hadn't figured it out before now. Although, I have to own—and I don't think this will hurt your feelings, given his nature and the fact that he's not blood related—he isn't very bright."

"Do you know where my mom is?"

"Yes," he said, and she didn't miss a tiny sparkle of cunning deep in his eyes. "And when you are safely at ease with your magic, I would be happy to take you there."

"She isn't going anywhere with you," Devon said, his voice low and rough. He stood beside and a little behind her, letting her handle the situation but showing his support.

"Little puppy, nice to see you again." Vlad's smile widened, and Charity's small hairs stood on end. "Rest assured, Charity will be in no danger from me. In fact, as a token of my good faith, I have taken the liberty of clearing your way. I could not get here in time to completely clear your path through the wood, unfortunately, but I trust your journey went smoothly after your skirmish with the gnomes?"

Emery shifted his stance. He'd just gotten his answer as to why it had been so quiet. Vlad clearly had more power and influence than they'd realized.

Vlad's smile said he knew it.

"Your way ahead is clear as well," he continued. "You will run into no danger. Except from the elves, of course. Their minions are under my control, but I have no power over them, merely spies among them." A cunning gleam shone in his eyes. "At present."

"Why are you doing all this?" Devon asked. "Speaking to her father, the note about her mother, making it easy to get to the Flush…"

"Simple." Vlad took a step back. "She is a blooming flower among the decay of this world. She is a beacon of hope. Do you small-minded little puppies not see the shining radiance that surrounds her? That is not because she is fae—it is because she is *important*. The Fates have their hands on her in some way. I wish to know why and, if necessary, help her cause."

"You mean, you wish to bend her to your cause," Emery stated in a flat voice.

Vlad studied Emery for a long moment. "Your past has made you cautious. Darius must be taxed greatly trying to keep you in line."

"I hope so," Emery replied.

Vlad squinted, but that cunning gleam was back. This vampire was forever plotting.

His attention swung back to Charity. The world seemed to drop away again. "I admit, I would certainly like to bend her to my cause. But do you not realize the elves are no better? One is stalking you as we speak, working through the shadow wood. He has called for aid. To hunt you. Once they have you, they will stop at nothing to get the information they seek, not even torture. One of your shifters recently learned this the hard way. They will claim they are doing what's necessary for the safety of the Realm. What a lofty cause, no? They will deem this treatment *just*, because one of their own, whom they placed in charge without the consent of their constituents, made the…arrest, we'll call it. Some would call it an abduction, of course. Is this the sort of authority the people of this land deserve? Brutality without consequences? Heavy-handedness without accountability? Half the land lives in fear, scared to cross those in power." He tilted his head to the side. "That is hardly the mark of a properly run nation. I simply want to even the power balance between the people and the leadership."

A humorless smile spread across Emery's face, but Charity spoke first, the words spitting out of her like acid.

"You took my friends' lives without consent. You changed them into monsters without consulting them. Without telling their families. Where is the balance in power there? Where is the accountability?"

Vlad *tsk*ed. "I did not take their lives; you and your shifter friends did that. I merely opened up a new world for them. I altered them for the better."

Guilt, then rage, tore through Charity. Her magic spiked; eating through her. Devon's calming influence settled her a little, but not enough. Red tinged the edges of her vision.

"*You* did that," she ground out. "Don't you dare try to put that on me. And let's not forget, you tried to kidnap me. You're only being magnanimous now because your other approaches failed. I'm not fooled by you, Vlad."

"No, you are not. And you are better for it. I only ask that you do not be fooled by the elves, either. As you see, I am open to change. I wonder if you can say the same for them." He paused for a moment. "Emery can attest to the danger you are all in, I am sure. The elves might spare some of you, but they might not. Your best bet is not to get caught." He reached into his pocket and extracted a glass vial filled with red liquid. "Given your current state, you don't have a chance. You are too weak, Charity, drained by your ill-functioning magic. The little puppy isn't much better, though he is doing a miraculous job of hiding it. If you continue on in this fashion, you and your friends will be overtaken."

"And let me guess, you are offering yourself as my savior?" Charity said dryly, the note forgotten. The only thing on her mind right now was survival, because he was absolutely right. Her reserves were nearly empty, and if she didn't have time to rest and regain her strength, her condition would only deteriorate. "You'll whisk me away and run me to safety?"

"That is very tempting, but impossible, I am afraid," Vlad said, and Emery frowned, clearly surprised by his answer. Charity's gut churned. "If the elves capture even one of you, they will crack you open like an egg and extract all the information you are trying to guard. All the information I would like you to guard. So, with deep regret, I must leave you in the hands of your watchdog and his friends. It pains me to admit they are your best bet now. Given this is partially my fault for being waylaid by...an intriguing new adversary, I have brought something to aid you."

He pushed his hand forward, his fingertips nearly touching the ward. Somehow he knew exactly where it existed. The vial lay on his palm.

"This is a vampire's best kept secret. I cannot tell

you what it is, but I can tell you that it is your only hope. It will restore your energy and then some. It is like a drug, however, and it will not last forever. You will crash at some point, but hopefully you will find your people before that happens."

"We're still days away," Emery said.

Vlad shook his head, analyzing Charity. "You don't have days. Take the fastest route."

"But—"

Vlad held up his other hand to silence Emery. "The elves are following you. They have not guessed your destination yet, dimwitted and uninformed about the wilds as they are. If you take the fastest route, by the time they realize their error, you will be in the Flush. I will clear the way, have no fear about that."

"What are you, the godfather of the Realm?" Penny asked. "You can't have everyone in your pocket."

He laughed. "Those who don't want trouble will find somewhere else to be. Those who are more audacious are either in my employ, or are too stupid to realize their position on the food chain. I will simply…educate them."

"And if they are minions of the elves?" Emery asked.

Vlad's eyes sparkled with malice. "I will kill them, as they would me."

Charity shook her head and took a step back, her eyes on that vial. "How can I possibly believe you?"

Vlad's hand swung in Emery's direction. "I trust you would believe him?" He raised his eyebrows. "He has no doubt heard certain rumors, and is wondering if one of those rumors could possibly allude to what is in this vial. Let him convince you. But do not dawdle. You have precious little time before that elf will break up this camp. You had best be on your way. Oh, and one more thing…"

He bent to place the vial on the ground next to the ward and extracted a piece of paper from his pocket.

No, not a piece of paper. A picture.

Charity's stomach flip-flopped as he held it out.

"How did you find that?" she asked, nearly charging through the ward to get it.

"What is it?" Devon asked.

Vlad placed the picture next to the vial.

"A picture of a man," Penny said, squinting down at it.

"It's my mom's. Her first love," Charity murmured, staring at her BFF in blind rage. "She never spoke of him—I think he broke her heart—but she always kept his picture. It was in the package I left for her in the little cubby in the closet. How did you even find the cubby? Did you go through that whole package?"

"I do apologize," Vlad said, taking a step away. "When it became evident your stepfather would not be very helpful, I had to investigate further. That picture struck a particular interest for me, so I needed to borrow it to ascertain the man's identity."

Charity gritted her teeth, the intense need to piece more of her mother's life together fighting her outrage at the incredible breach of privacy. The feeling of longing won out. If Walt wasn't her father, then maybe her father hadn't been some anonymous fae passing through the Brink. Maybe her mother had actually loved him.

She wasn't sure if that made his decision to leave better or worse, but she wanted to know more. Besides, she recognized him. How could she not? He'd been standing right next to her in her hallucination, wearing battle gear with pride sparkling in his eyes.

"And did you?" she asked, centering her weight, unconsciously preparing to fight out her feelings. "Did you find out who he was?"

"Of course I did." Vlad's smile was serene. "He is your biological father."

Charity stared after Vlad with a slack jaw, watching him saunter away like he hadn't just dropped a bunch of bombs. Once he made it across the path and between two leafy trees, he turned on the jets, giving the illusion that he had vanished.

The man sure knew how to make an exit.

Charity stared down at the photograph. She'd wondered why her mother had left the photo behind. Charity hadn't known the man, after all—the photograph wasn't sentimental to her. Now, it struck her that it had been her mom's way of telling her about her real father.

It had taken a nosy, arrogant vampire to solve the riddle.

"He didn't say who your father was," Penny said, anger hot in her voice.

"Her father is exactly who Vlad always thought he was, or did you miss his smugness?" Emery waved his hand through the air and quickly bent to collect the vial and photograph. Even as he was straightening back up with them, Penny was working magic, probably putting the ward back in place. "Her father is Arcana, he's warrior fae, and the elves are coming. We gotta move. Devon, get your people ready. Rest time is over."

Emery handed the vial to Charity.

"We'll talk about this on the road," he said. "It could be a trap. But…"

"But what?" Charity said, searching Emery's incredulous expression.

He laughed and shook his head. "But…it could be unicorn blood."

CHAPTER 20

"Wait, unicorns are real?" Charity asked as Emery headed back to the camping site.

"Unicorns are real?" Penny echoed, hurrying after him.

"I don't know." Emery stuffed his thin bedroll back into his backpack. Devon stepped away for a moment to talk to Dillon. A couple of other shifters changed back to human and started grabbing up packs. From the way they were eyeing Emery, she suspected they'd heard the exchange with Vlad.

"In the years I spent wandering the Realm, I heard a million rumors," Emery said. "Most turned out false, as you might expect, but a year or so ago I heard from a reliable source that the vampires were hunting someone who was smuggling unicorn blood from under their noses and selling it in the Brink. The blood acts as a sort of magical booster, I guess. It was turning witches into mages, and they were organizing. Or trying to. I heard whisperings about them...until I didn't."

Devon returned to Charity's side and slipped an arm around her waist as Emery continued. "The vampires must have taken out the culprits and all of their followers. My source disappeared not long afterward, which suggests they didn't just go after the people directly involved—they went after everyone who might know their secret. Now, here we are, with an elder vampire handing us a little red vial to help boost Charity's magic and energy. I'm guessing there's some truth to it."

"So, if that's what Vlad left for Charity…then we can expect to be hunted and killed by Vlad and his minions to keep their secret?" Penny asked.

Emery laughed, and Charity had no idea what was so funny. Sure, the vampires were unlikely to go after her, but Charity wasn't sure Roger could protect Devon's pack from being picked off one by one. Not from a vampire like Vlad.

"When he's done with us?" Emery waved his hand near the ward and walked through without looking back to make sure everyone was following him. "Probably. Those he deems useless, at least. The rest will probably be given an offer they can't refuse."

"That dirty cheat," Penny said, her fists balled up. "He can't just throw a big secret at us and then blame us for knowing it."

"It's Vlad," Emery said as though it was reason enough. He was probably right.

"Look—" Charity struggled to keep up with Emery's fast pace. Devon kept by her side, clearly thinking this information exchange was more important than taking rear, a task that had been silently assigned to Dillon. "This doesn't make any sense. Why would Vlad help me? I mean, he's basically rolling out the red carpet to get me to the Flush. This is the same guy that tried, on several occasions, to kidnap me and kill the man I love."

"He told you why." Emery peered through the trees on his right. A slip of movement caught Charity's notice, but when she looked that way, only empty trees and still bushes dotted the landscape.

The path rose steadily up an incline. The rocks on the side of the path got bigger, the plant life sparser. They were heading up the mountain.

"He thinks Fate has plans for you, and he wants to bend your journey to fit his own design." Emery veered to the edge of the path to look behind them.

"We're being followed," Devon said, clearly reading Emery's movements. "Vampires. I smell them."

Emery nodded. "I figured." He turned to the front again. "He tried to snatch you and force Fate's hand, Charity, but that didn't work, so now he is trying to work his way into your life so he can manipulate you. This approach is infinitely more dangerous for you. And if this vial holds what I think it does, and what I've heard is true, then he'll have one more hook in you."

"Knowing his secret won't change my situation," Charity said.

"Unicorn blood is said to be ten times more addictive than heroin. He's got the lure of your mother, and now the hook of a highly addictive drug. Not to mention the drop on all your friends. Vampires have no problem killing—it wouldn't be a stretch to think he'll blackmail you with their lives."

"Vampires have always tried to kill us," Devon growled. "This is no different."

"Vampires have tried to kill you when you got in their way," Emery countered. "But if what I've heard is true, they'll kill for this secret. Unless Charity plays along, they'll *all* target you. He's backing you into a corner."

"Jesus, babe, you *have* been studying vampire politics," Penny said with wide eyes.

"I promised I'd keep us at arm's length from the vampires, Turdswallop," he said softly, and took her hand. "I keep my promises."

"Can I see that vial?" Charity held out her hand.

Emery must've been curious, and possession was nine-tenths of the law, but he handed it to her at once. Whatever else he was, he was honest and trustworthy.

She wound up and threw the vial down the small incline off the path. "Whatever it is, we don't want it," she yelled out, knowing that vampires would be able to hear. "I guess we'll never know if the rumors are true, or if it was a trap."

A rustle sounded not far off. Someone had just given their presence away. Not that it mattered. Emery didn't slow or alter course.

Devon stared at her silently, his face blank. It wasn't hard to guess what he was thinking.

Charity looked straight ahead, ignoring her aching body. And she'd keep on ignoring it until she trudged her way to the Flush and got a real cure. "I will not save myself at your pack's expense, Devon. You must know that by now."

"Sometimes I hope you'll learn some sense," he replied.

Emery huffed out a laugh. "That woman right there has rock-solid sense, are you kidding?" He glanced back at Devon. "You oughta try dealing with Reagan and her older dual-mage sidekicks for a week. Talk about no sense. Then mix in Penny's mother—trust me, brother, you've got it good. Hold on for dear life and hope she doesn't leave you."

"See?" Charity said, raising her chin.

"The problem is, we have a trek ahead of us, and we don't have the gas for it," Devon said.

"We're switching routes," Emery said. "It'll take us away from the cover of the wilds, but it's easier to travel. We can move faster while still staying to the sidelines. Mostly. Hopefully the elves only have minions patrolling, and those have been cleared."

"We're trusting that Vlad has taken care of the danger?" Penny asked, aghast.

"We don't have much choice," Emery murmured.

CHAPTER 21

THE REST OF the day and into the night passed in a blur of fatigue for Devon. His limbs felt like they had weights tied to them, and his wolf kept struggling to break free. Charity's magic was buffeting them both in faster and stronger waves, building up even though she had absolutely no energy to help it flower. Even so, Devon suspected the energy link between them wasn't as open as they'd originally thought. That, or Charity had figured out (possibly unconsciously) how to keep more of the pain for herself and spare Devon, because they'd had to stop repeatedly for her to clamp down on a power surge that he didn't feel as much as he should've.

"We should be able to get some rest up here a ways," Emery said, leading them along a narrow path between bent and twisted trees and straggly, reaching bushes. The area was a no man's land. Nothing seemed to be stirring on the periphery. No winged creatures flew overhead.

Devon counted his blessings. A few times on the trek, they'd seen creatures staring out of the trees at them, silent and watchful, keeping at bay when normally they would attack, or so Emery had murmured as they passed.

They still didn't know why Vlad had cleared their path—was he being true to his word, or was he leading them into an elaborate trap? Only time would tell.

The soft pounding of danger thrummed in Devon's middle. He had no way of knowing if he was right, but it felt like the elf or elves were catching up. He nearly said as much, but what choice did they have but to rest? Charity was staggering like a drunk with a pale, sweaty face and weak, useless limbs. She was in a bad way. Any farther, and they'd have to carry her.

Any farther, and they might have to carry Devon.

"We can drape an invisibility spell over the cave," Emery murmured to Penny. "Any higher-powered elves would be able to sense the magic, so we'll...have to get creative."

"How much farther until the Flush?" Penny asked.

"At this pace and after a rest?" He paused for a moment. "A day, probably."

A surge of Charity's magic rushed into Devon, making his eyes water. She bumped into him before putting her hand to her sternum, slowing. A moment later, she bent at the waist and squeezed her arms around her middle.

"You okay?" Penny asked, turning to Charity with a concerned expression.

"The Realm..." Charity struggled for breath, coughing into her fist. "It's boosting my magic."

"This surge is more powerful," Emery said, concern screwing up his features. "It feels like lava needles."

"It feels like she is getting ready to blast us with something nasty," Penny murmured, her hand on Emery's arm.

"I'm good," Charity said through clenched teeth. "It's good."

Devon could barely stand upright. He pumped out his shifter magic, the effort nearly taking him to his knees, counteracting the stinging pain of her magic. His pack backed off, probably a survival mechanism, except for Steve in his lion form.

Steve pushed in close, his strong shifter magic swirling around and within Charity's and Devon's magic. Helping them fight back the tide.

"More," Devon said between clenched teeth. "More shifter magic."

"Oh, I see," Penny said. "Yes, that's smart." Her fingers started moving. Emery watched for a moment before he reached in between her hands, his fingers dancing.

Devon held on, working with Charity's magic, using everyone else's power to help balance it. To back it down.

"I'm good," Charity said again, her fists balled up and her eyes shut. "I'm good."

"More magic," he said, his head getting light from the effort of calling up his magic.

Andy bumped Steve to make room and pushed in. Dillon and Macy crowded in behind him, the others behind them. Penny pushed her hands toward the group.

Charity sucked in a breath. Thankfully, the surge calmed. The tide turned.

"Almost there," Devon said, taking a breath with her, pushing the hot agony of her magic away. "Almost there."

Charity took deep, ragged breaths. She nodded and straightened up slowly, her whole body shaking. "It's okay. We're okay."

This time, Devon thought to himself. This time they were okay, but it had taken the whole pack and two natural dual-mages. If these surges got any stronger, he didn't know if they'd be able to pull her back.

***

DEVON, IN HIS human form, awoke with a start in the dim cave they'd chosen to hunker down in. A rock poked into his back and water dripped on his head from the cave ceiling. His pack fanned out around him, one and all in their animal forms, making the most of their rest. Deep breaths said they were still deep in their slumber.

Two shapes stood at the mouth of the cave, shadows against the glow of the coming day. Their hands worked together, the movements urgent.

That was when he felt it—danger, deep and intense. It thrummed through him, a warning he couldn't possibly ignore.

He straightened up quickly, careful not to rouse Charity beside him. Dillon, who lay on his other side, snapped his eyes open and lifted his head to see what was wrong, quickly noticing the dual-mages at the front of the cave.

After pushing to his feet and stepping over the furry bodies of his pack members, who woke up one by one, Devon stopped at the mouth of the cave beside the dual-mages. His bones practically rattled with the pulse of warning just outside.

"The wards have been tripped," Penny said quietly, her hands still moving. "We're trying to invert our magic so a magical person can't see or feel it. I think what we're doing is going to work."

"It'll work," Emery said, barely loud enough for even Devon to hear.

"What creature, do you know?" Devon asked as the pack roused.

Penny shook her head. "Being that there are a lot of magical creatures in this neck, and I don't know the feel of any of them, I couldn't build any sort of identifier into the spell."

"This far into the wilds, it could be a handful of creatures, most of them not looking for trouble," Emery said.

"I sense danger." Devon peered out into the thick

trees and brush directly in front of them before trying to see to the sides. The small, overgrown path they'd used to get to the cave curved off to the left. If someone was on it, they were excellent at stealth, because even with improved shifter senses, Devon couldn't hear or smell anything out of the ordinary.

"How do you feel?" Penny asked.

Devon took stock of himself. His feet ached and sleep dragged at his eyes, but he wasn't as tired as before. This was manageable. Although he wasn't in his wolf form, he was healing up at his usual rapid rate.

Which meant…

He dashed to Charity's side and pressed two fingers to her neck. Her pulse thumped like a jackrabbit. He felt her forehead and sucked in a breath. She was burning up.

"She's cutting me off, somehow," Devon whispered. "I don't feel the gush of her magic."

"I can't…" Penny sounded frustrated. "I have to finish this before I can help."

"Yasmine, change," Devon commanded softly, knowing Yasmine's mom worked as a nurse in the Brink.

Yasmine met Devon at Charity's side. Her eyes widened as she pressed a hand to Charity's forehead.

"Did we bring any ibuprofen?" she asked. Devon shook his head. Shifters never needed it—he hadn't thought Charity might. "Bring her some water. She needs to stay hydrated. If we have a cold compress, that would help, too."

"Go," Emery said to Penny. "I can finish this."

A twig snapped outside of the cave. Everyone froze, turning that way.

A soft rustle, so quiet that Devon wondered if his ears were playing tricks, sounded to the right. After a brief pause, he heard it again. Adrenaline coursed through his body. Magic drifted around him, everything in him saying he needed to change. Danger was right outside. But if he did that, he couldn't communicate with Charity or the mages.

Charity moaned and thrashed her head to the side. Devon grimaced and gently shook her awake. She moaned again and rolled her head the other way. Her eyes fluttered.

He shook a little harder. Her eyes fluttered again, but she didn't rouse.

Fear punched him.

"Penny," he said, barely able to keep his voice low.

"I'm here." Penny wove through the furry shifters. All of them were standing now, their hackles rising. She lowered to her knees beside Charity and closed her eyes. A crease formed between her eyebrows. "It feels like…" She hesitated.

Emery's hands continued to weave through invisible air as he held his position near the cave mouth. A footfall, closer, ran a tingle up Devon's spine.

"It feels like a bomb." Penny's eyes blinked open, and her worried gaze churned Devon's stomach. "It feels like her magic is getting ready to explode."

"Fix that energy-sharing link," Devon said.

"*Shhhh!*" Emery pushed his hands outward, then acted like he was smearing butter across the cave opening. "That should help deaden our sound, but something's out there."

Devon didn't waste time looking over his shoulder. He stared hard at Penny. "Fix the link," he whispered, the sound barely riding his breath.

The lack of volume didn't matter one bit. She felt his alpha magic and jerked back as if slapped. She bent immediately, her hands hovering over Charity.

"If she closed down that link somehow, she did it to protect you," Yasmine said softly.

"I know," he responded. "She's an idiot."

"I feel…" Penny began, and Devon felt an internal prod deep within him. "That's you, and… She's, like…walling herself away. How interesting. Ugh, her magic feels like acid. Like poison. It's really tumultuous. She really does feel like a bomb. But just here—Ah. Here. Yes…"

A gush of agony seared through Devon. Black clouded his vision. Fire melted his bones. He sank to his hands and knees, his fingers clawing the cave floor.

Shifter magic rose around him, stuffing the air full to bursting, everyone offering up their magic without being asked. Good. He couldn't have asked if he'd tried. Devon's energy sapped from him, but he'd been here before. He knew what to do.

With an assist from Penny, he grabbed hold of Charity's magic. He yanked it to him, buffering it with his pack's magic, forcing the balance he knew she needed. Like before, breathing became easier. Less painful. The balance pushed his head above water.

But she still didn't open her eyes.

"She's on borrowed time," Penny said, pushing to her feet. "Emery, can we fight whatever is out there? Surely the fae can smooth it over for us. Aren't they treasured or something—Buck-toothed doppelgangers!"

A form skulked by, hunched and sneaking, with leathery skin and big eyes. Devon let out a breath. A goblin, not something to worry about. And yet that thrum of danger still vibrated through him. The elves weren't far.

"What happens if we meet an elf along the way?" Devon asked Emery. "What sort of fighters are they? Can we overcome them?"

Emery looked between everyone, as though putting what he saw on a scale. His gaze finally landed on Devon. "One? Easily. A crowd?" He shrugged. "Let's see, shall we? Bring only what is essential. The fae are bound to have clothes. Fight in whatever form is strongest."

"Who's going to carry Charity?" Penny asked.

Yasmine raised her hand. "I can. I'm already in human form. No point in wasting energy with another change." When Devon hesitated, Yasmine lifted her chin defiantly. "We haven't always gotten along, but she's pack. I will protect her with my life."

Devon nodded and let his wolf finally surge out, stronger physically and in magic. Sights and smell intensified. Danger still throbbed in his middle. He waited while Yasmine and Penny quickly rifled through packs. Those on two feet pulled on clothes and grabbed the bags that were deemed necessary. Yasmine gently lifted Charity and slung her over her shoulder, fireman style.

Vlad's words came back to Devon: *If the elves capture even one of you, they will crack you open like an egg.*

CHAPTER 22

EMERY TORE DOWN the magic ward, and Penny ran through at once, peeling off to the side with her hands up and ready.

"I should've gone first," Emery said through clenched teeth as he quickly followed her out.

"Oh, sorry—with Reagan I'm used to being the fall guy," she replied as Devon emerged from the darkened cave into the glow of early morning. The goblin turned to look at them, its brown eyes enormous in its thin, bony face.

Without warning, it took off into the trees.

Devon tensed and pointed with his nose. Andy, Dillon, and Macy took off immediately, Dillon in the lead. They couldn't risk that goblin getting away and telling people where they were. Skulking around like it was, it was probably a spy, and it was doubtful it was Vlad's.

Which raised the question, why hadn't it been dealt with sooner?

At Devon's glance, Steve and Cole fell in around Yasmine and Charity. Devon hurried to the front of the group, picking a pace he knew Yasmine could handle.

When she tired, Devon would switch out Charity's chariot. According to their guide, they had less than a day's travel left. If they could bear down and keep the elves from catching them, they'd make it. They had to.

It wasn't long before Dillon and his team returned. A look and Devon knew the threat had been neutralized. His beta hadn't had a problem.

"This way," Emery said, jogging beside Devon. Penny fell in next to Yasmine and Charity. "If we see an elf, we'll pretend not to notice it at first. They are cautious. They don't rush in unless they have assessed the risk. It'll buy us time to figure out a strategy. If they do attack, aim to disable, not kill."

They rounded a bend, and a whiff of funk rolled over Devon. He didn't recognize the smell, but he could tell it was a creature that ate flesh and didn't bother to wash up after.

Luckily for it, it stayed hidden as the pack ran by.

The sense of danger thrummed heavily in Devon's middle. He barely kept from looking behind them, wondering if something was dogging their heels, if a trap lay just ahead.

In no time, they found a larger path that led down to the flatlands. They ran as fast as their two-legged companions' legs could go, wary and always scanning. Senses on full alert.

It wasn't until they neared a wide road lined with fragrant, blooming flowers and fruit-laden trees that danger presented itself, though it wasn't in the form they'd anticipated.

"What the hell are demons doing in the Realm?" Emery said, followed by a string of curses.

"What? What's happening?" Penny asked, pulling up beside him.

A crowd of creatures stood in front of the intersection leading to the thoroughfare they wanted to use. Each was a different although equally horrific nightmare—a goat head atop a naked human body, a beautiful woman with horns and furry limbs, and so on. While one or two smoked from internal fire, a couple looked like they wielded glimmering weapons of ice.

"Is this Vlad's interference, or whoever recently outmaneuvered Vlad?" Penny asked. "And if Vlad's not involved, how did they know we'd be coming this way? Even if we have a spy among us, there are no phones. There has been no way to relay our whereabouts."

Emery shook his head slowly. "I don't know. Regardless, why are they allowed to hang out around here? The elves don't allow creatures from the underworld into the Realm without strict permission, and that permission comes with a certain…dress code, if you will. No way would they have let this go. Those demons are breaking the treaty."

"You think Lucifer might've sent them?" Penny asked.

Emery just shook his head. He had no answers.

Devon huffed to get their attention before pointedly looking away to the right. Three figures, lean and fair, sauntered along the path. Their arms practically swished from side to side with a graceful flair. Though the elves were too far away for their eyes to be seen, it was clear their focus was on the group of demons blocking Devon and his pack. That could be a good thing—

The first demon noticed Devon's pack, its clawed hand coming up to point. The rest turned, and as one they started running, charging directly toward Devon and crew.

Time to go.

He dodged left and pushed through a green hedge, creating a hole that Yasmine wouldn't have a hard time following. The hole was made bigger as Cole tore one section up by the roots, roared, and threw it. Stealth was not in his wheelhouse, not that it mattered at the moment.

They took off across the short grass, the appearance green and soft but the feel hard and scratchy. It was a magical illusion.

The demons leapt over the hedge and the elves surged forward, hurrying to catch up. The elves were outnumbered three to one, but clearly that didn't trouble them. Good news.

"I'm following your lead," Emery said to Devon. "Let me know when to unleash hell."

Devon cut across the field at a diagonal, aiming to meet up with the thoroughfare, hoping the elves would reach the demons before the demons reached his pack.

No such luck.

The first demon came within five feet of them, its large arm thrown back in preparation to swipe at Cole. Devon changed direction on a dime, darting between Emery and Cole, and launched himself at the demon. He tore through its chest with his paws before ripping through its throat, the element of surprise on his side.

The rest of the shifters engaged, slamming into the larger creatures. Strange roars and a goat's bleat filled the field. Devon rode the demon to the ground, waiting for it to convulse and go still.

A wolf hit the ground with an incredible *smack*. Dillon. He bayed in pain. Hard air slammed down on top of him. Bones cracked, his crying cut off, knocked out by the invisible impact that must've been solid air.

Shock ripped through Devon. He'd never seen Dillon go down so quickly. Macy whined, frenzied, dodging a demon reaching for her and getting to Dillon's side. She nudged him with her nose. He didn't move, out cold. It would take him a while to heal from this one.

Sorrow and desperation soaked into Devon. It filled his body and ate away at his coherent thought. He ripped through the next demon, feeling fire lick his hindquarters and ignoring it. A blow clocked him behind his ear, knocking him into the brittle grass.

He caught a glimpse of Barbara, surrounded by a ring of fire growing into a bonfire. She howled in pain, trying to break free, but something held her in place.

A zip of blue magic cut into the fire, dimming the flames somewhat. Emery swore, his and Penny's hands moving. Their magic wasn't counteracting the demon fire as they'd planned.

These demons were more powerful than any they'd seen so far. They were mighty in a way his pack wasn't, in a way that only Roger's strongest shifters could combat.

They were outranked. As much as he hated the thought, they needed the help of those elves.

Devon struggled up, running to help Barbara.

The demon closest to Barbara blew up. Its head flew in an arc and parts sprayed everywhere. The fire surrounding her winked out, leaving her lying on her side, a bloodied, charred mess of flesh and fur.

Devon looked back in surprise. Charity stood straight and tall, dark bags under eyes the color of a bright blue crayon. This time, the strange color didn't roll over her irises and disappear. This time, it stayed.

Fear squeezed Devon's middle. He hoped to God that was normal for a fae.

"Sword," she said, her voice scratchy, damaged.

Yasmine dropped her pack and started digging through it.

The next demon reached them before her hand was filled. Steve surged forward, but he was too late. Charity rose her hand in the air. Sunlight sparkled overhead. For a moment, Devon thought her power had misfired—that the light would do nothing to combat the demons—until sparks started to spit from false sunlight. Miniature lightning bolts rained down, striking the demons and sizzling through their bodies. They shook and screeched, arms out and bodies convulsing. The second the magic wore off, the wolves were there, perfectly synchronized, tearing them down.

The elves slowed in their advance, fifty yards away, watching Devon's pack with obvious interest.

"Devon!"

Devon glanced back at Yasmine, seeing her pointed finger.

A crew of six vaulted over the hedge behind them, lithe and graceful, with swords in their hands and sleek chain mail to match. Blond or brown hair blew out behind them, and their swords flashed as they descended on Devon's pack.

Devon turned, his teeth bared, ready to meet the assault head-on, but their magic reached him first. His own magic was boosted by its soothing yet immensely powerful waves. His heart leapt.

The warrior fae had come.

They ran past him, straight at the demons. Their swords flashed, perfectly complementing their fighting movements in a deadly dance.

Hand newly filled with her sword, Charity fell in among them, not even seeming to notice they were strangers. One of them hesitated a moment before skewering a demon with his sword, as though this was the first foe he had properly fought. Charity wasted no time in helping him out, lopping off the creature's head and turning for the next efficiently. Another fae slashed at a demon's leg. An electric hole blasted through the demon's middle, although this time Charity wasn't the one who'd put it there. Penny was replicating Charity's magic. Steve fell onto the demon a moment afterward, ripping through its neck.

Two fae working seamlessly together rushed a squat demon with fire curling out of its mouth. The first slashed as the other waited just behind him. The demon dodged and struck. The second fae stepped forward and swung, severing one of the creature's limbs. The demon roared and struck again, only to be blocked by the first fae, while the second danced around and plunged its sword through the demon's side.

Cole swung his great arm and smacked the head clean off the demon as he passed, aiming for another of the creatures.

The two warrior fae jumped back as the creature fell, eyes wide, following Cole with their gazes. It seemed like this was the first time they'd seen a shifter of Cole's caliber in action. Maybe he was the first shifter they'd fought beside, full stop.

Everyone knew the warrior fae no longer left the Flush.

The elves watched it all from a safe distance.

Charity slashed through another demon, and Devon fell in beside her, carrying it to the ground and ending its struggles. A burst of fire shot at Devon, but before it could land, Charity blew the demon who'd attacked him sky-high. Her magic felt ragged and raw, but she wasn't stopping. Maybe she couldn't.

The tide had turned after the warrior fae had joined them. Soon, only one demon remained standing, its great horned head and small black eyes homed in on Charity.

"Lucifer wishes to see you," the creature managed through a mouthful of pointed teeth.

"Lucifer can kiss my ass." Charity slashed down on its reaching hand, severing it at the elbow. It screeched, but she didn't slow. She lunged forward, sword swinging, and sliced its side. She reached out with her palm, pumping out a surge of magic that brought Devon to his knees. The demon flew backward, somersaulting in the air. Before hitting the ground ten feet from the elves, it exploded, spraying the silent observers in blood and guts.

The warrior fae all cowered, their hands thrown up, but not to ward off the guts. To ward off the debilitating sting of Charity's magic. They straightened, wide-eyed. They clearly didn't recognize her magic.

Charity dropped her sword, stared at the remnants of the demon for a moment, then fell bonelessly to the ground.

"Charity!" Devon hadn't even meant to change. But the next thing he knew, he was lifting her into his arms. "Charity." He bent over her and squeezed his eyes shut, drawing her pain into himself. Cocooning her with his magic.

"Don't just stand there, help her!" Cole boomed, having also changed.

A wave of magic rolled over Devon, sweet and blissful. A song rose into the air and was carried on the breeze, playful and exciting, the call of the hunt.

"What is this strange magic that flirts with ours?" a man said, stopping beside Devon and Charity and looking down on them.

"How about you talk less and help more?" Steve strode up, nude, bloody, and ready to keep fighting.

The man, barely older than twenty yet arrogant as a king, turned to Steve. He didn't say a word, and even so, his sentiment was clearly conveyed. *Your opinion is not warranted here. Be gone, ingrate.*

Steve's response was just as clear, and he didn't need to raise his middle finger to convey it.

"Stand down," Devon ordered him, soaking in the light and fresh magic of the warrior fae and funneling it to Charity. Her heartbeat, a moment ago sporadic and weak, increased. Her ragged breathing eased slightly. But she was a long way from safe.

"She's..." Devon stood with her in his arms. He faced the man, ignoring his people fanning out behind him, ignoring the elves walking up slowly, taking it all in. One of these groups of people was going to help Charity, and they were going to do it now. "She's one of yours, we think. She doesn't have control of her magic, and I can barely keep her from succumbing to it."

"She's the spitting image of the First," a fae woman said from just behind the man, her long hair braided down the side of her cherubic face, offsetting the hot violence in her light eyes. "Is she the one we seek?"

The elves picked their way around the carnage, ever closer.

"Her magic doesn't feel like a guardian's," the man said, looking down on Charity's face.

"Yasmine, the picture," Devon called.

"It's in her pocket," Penny yelled, her voice thick with emotion.

Steve dug his hand in Charity's pocket and extracted the picture.

The man took the picture before showing it to his companions. "Where did you get this?"

Devon's patience gave out. "Do you know him or not? The vampire Vlad thinks this man is her father. If he is warrior fae—a guardian—she's one of yours, and she badly needs your help. She's dying."

"I will help her." An elf practically danced up to them, at once beautiful and aggravating, with its dramatic flair and musical voice.

"You've helped plenty," Devon growled, the force of his irritation driving the elf back a step.

The fae woman's eyes widened and a smile graced her face. "My, you are powerful."

"I'm an alpha, and you are wasting my time."

"I know exactly what to do with her," the lead elf said. His comrades waited behind him.

"You better back off, because I know exactly what to do with *you*." Penny walked up with tears and fire in her eyes. "You didn't help when we needed it. When it could've saved lives. So now you will back the ever-loving dingle dongs off." She turned to the fae. "This woman clearly has magical poisoning. Are you so stupid that you don't recognize one of your own? You should stop being such arrogant donkey dicks and help her out." She bent and scooped up Charity's sword before thrusting it at them. "This sword fits her magic perfectly. Does it also fit yours? If the picture didn't convince you, maybe this will."

The man didn't reach for the sword, but the woman behind him did—even as another of their group pushed forward to look down at Charity's face. "I've heard of magical poisoning. It hasn't happened in the village in…" She opened Charity's eyes with her finger and thumb, exposing the bright, unnatural blue. She sucked in a breath. "This is…" Her eyes darted up, meeting Devon's. "The magic has flipped. It has inverted, hasn't it? How does she still breathe?"

"My magic is keeping her on the precipice, but she needs help from your people," Devon said, not sure if he was ordering or begging.

The elf opened its mouth, and suddenly it jerked backward, swiping at its face. It screeched, now slapping, as though a swarm of flesh-eating flies had attacked it.

"I told you to back off," Penny said in a low, rough

voice.

"I don't understand." The man finally leaned in. "Has she not gone through the change?" He put a hand over her forehead.

"Do you not listen when your betters speak, Hallen?" the woman with the braid said, stepping forward to peer down on Charity. "Halvor warned us of this. Where is—"

"I'm here," someone said from behind the handful of fae.

The woman with the braid cleared to the side for an older woman to push in, jostling Hallen as she did so. She was out of breath, as though she'd been running behind them, unable to keep up.

"This is a healer," the woman with the braid told Devon. "She will know—"

The healer sucked in a sharp breath when she saw Charity's eyes. "She is in the change. Don't you feel it? She's at the crux of it. How old is she?" Her blue-violet eyes were strange, although they were a natural color, not like Charity's.

"Twenty," Devon answered.

"She's late. No one turns that late," Hallen said to the healer.

The healer let out an exasperated breath. "You're nothing but a boy. What do you know?"

"The Arcana turn at that age," someone whispered from the back of the group.

"Precisely." The healer motioned for Devon to follow her. "Hurry! Get a fire lit. This young woman is leaning into her grave."

"But this is impossible," Hallen said, hurrying to walk beside the healer. Clearly he was the leader of this scouting party. "We would have been told if the one we seek is connected with the Arcana."

"Arrogance and youth, a damned annoying combination," the healer muttered. She raised her voice, taking over. "Grayson, make up some draught. Ensure it's potent. And chase those nosey elves out of here. I don't need them looking over my shoulder, trying to steal the show for their finicky masters. And you can tell them I said that.

"Boy, give that girl to Hallen." The healer gestured at Devon. "Your magic has certainly helped her, but our magic will cure her. At this late stage, it will start with skin contact. Hallen, take her. Drop her and I'll drop you."

Devon hesitated, possessiveness freezing his limbs. He remembered what Karen had said, though, that he'd need to do what was best for Charity.

He released his hold, his heart breaking as he gave her up. Was this the point at which he should turn back? Was this the point at which he should say goodbye?

Could he?

"Devon, your pack needs your attention," Penny said quietly, her hand on his arm. "I've done all I can."

"Do not, under any circumstances, let the elves take

her," Devon said to the woman with the braid, who was lagging behind the others.

Her eyes slowly slid down his nude body. A smile pulled at her lips. "I have the same orders. We are reading from the same scroll, Alpha." If a tone could capitalize a word, she just had. "Now, see to your pack. We will take care of the girl until you join us at the fire. I am Kairi. If you have any trouble, see me."

"Fae, a word?" The elf Penny had attacked gave her a wide berth before hurrying to the woman's side.

Devon could barely suppress a sigh as he watched them walk away. He had given Charity over to her people, but he didn't have to leave just yet. They'd invited him to the fire, and it would be rude to ignore such an invitation. He wouldn't have to leave.

The rest of his pack sat in a circle, their heads down and their expressions drawn. Devon's feet turned to lead as he neared them, seeing the limp form of Dillon at the center of their gathering. His ribs had been crushed, that was evident, but Devon had seen shifters come back from worse. If Dillon shifted, then...

"How is he?" Devon threaded between his people and knelt by his beta. Macy cried softly, her arms wrapped around herself, her face buried in her knees.

"How is he?" Devon asked again, louder, panic giving his voice edge. Dillon was the first friend Devon had made as a shifter. The guy who had stood by his side as he rose through the ranks. Others had been jealous or eager to challenge Devon, but Dillon had always guarded his back.

"He died on impact," Emery said softly, his eyes downcast. "His heart has stopped. He's gone, bro. I'm sorry."

Devon stared down at his friend. At his confidant. His second. A great hole opened up in his chest.

"I did this," he whispered. He hadn't intended to say it out loud, but it was true—he'd pushed his pack to guard Charity at all costs. If he hadn't taken up this detail, Dillon would still be alive.

Devon felt a heavy hand on his shoulder. Steve knelt by his side.

"I heard Roger say that once," Steve said for Devon's ears alone. "And only once. You are a leader. You are responsible for your pack. But you can't protect them all the time. There are losses in every battle. You need to be the guy that leads his pack through the bad times. You need to internalize your guilt and pain and be strong for your people. Be their hope, or their vengeance. Every good alpha has been in your shoes multiple times. It comes with the job."

Devon stared down at his friend's crushed body, his limbs numb, his heart aching. He wanted to crawl into a hole and shut his eyes against this day.

"It's a helluva job," Steve murmured, looking down at Dillon. "And he was a helluva wolf."

Devon nodded, steeling himself, knowing that Steve was right. It was the job, and right now, he hated this job with a passion he couldn't explain.

"How are the rest of you?" Devon lifted his head and turned to the others. He needed to take care of the living before he could mourn the loss of the dead.

"A few of us hurt like hell, but we'll heal," said Andy, who sat in a pool of blood from a wound on his leg. Judging from that and the deep score down the side of his chest, he needed to pass out.

"Barbara is barely breathing," Dale said, and nodded to the blackened and bloody wolf who lay at his feet. "She's hanging on, though. She's had worse and bounced back. She'll be all right."

"She needs time," Cole said.

"She needed better leadership," Dale said, looking up at Devon. The glare didn't stick for more than a moment before the defiant shifter pulled his gaze away.

A fire crackled to life not far away, the fae working on that potion or whatever it was for Charity. A hush fell over the pack. Devon's power flared in his middle as he stared the larger, older, more experienced wolf down. He wanted with everything he had to answer the other shifter's challenge. To finally put to rest what Dale had started when they'd first met.

But now wasn't the time. His pack was grieving. *He* was grieving. Dale needed a pass, and everyone needed to see Devon grant it.

So he let the hard stare linger for a moment longer, letting everyone see that he registered the offense, and looked down at his friend one last time.

"Dillon always said that he wanted to go out like a

hero," Devon said, using everything he had to keep his voice steady. "That if he should die in battle, he wanted it to happen with honor. Well…" Heat prickled his eyes. Devon paused for a moment, collecting himself. "He did do it with honor. No one could've done better. He has been my best asset, and my best friend, and I will miss him."

Macy cried harder, hugging herself. Rod and Andy both stared at the ground, their faces ashen.

"Let's look after ourselves and the wounded, and let's see if we can use the fae's fire to send Dillon to his final resting place."

"We'll deliver his ashes to his family," Macy said between her sobs.

"Charity?" Rod asked, sorrow creasing the skin around his eyes.

"She's being looked after. One of them seems to know what is happening." Devon gritted his teeth. "Let's hope they can bring her around."

Devon didn't know what he'd do if he lost them both.

CHAPTER 23

"Second, they are bringing her in."

Romulus glanced up from his plans, which he'd been staring at all day without making progress. Halvor stood at the door of his work shed, straight and proper. Not bad news, then, thank the bounty.

Romulus stood quickly, walking from around his desk.

He'd received news yesterday evening that a girl of about twenty had been recovered, with inverted magic and eyes of an unnatural blue. According to the healer who'd treated her, she should've died months ago. She'd only survived thanks to a band of shifters and mages.

The report sounded far-fetched, but given the accounts he'd heard of her magic, the elves' interest in her, and the fact that she possessed a picture of Romulus himself, something that could've only been taken from the Brink... Well, waiting hadn't been easy.

"What news?" Romulus asked.

"She has been kept under a sleeping draught. Magic seeps from her in great waves, and she tenses whenever it surges. They believe she is trying to subdue it."

Romulus frowned. "That must be causing her great pain."

"Yes, and it pains those around her."

"Why keep her under? Why not guide her magic until she can be brought here and properly trained?"

A proud glimmer lit Halvor's eyes. "Those in the seeking party are not strong enough to guide her. Only with the power of the Alpha Shifter were they able to subdue her. He calls it balancing, but Kairi called it competing. He is overpowering her magic with his and the pack's magic to keep it from spiraling out of control."

"An Alpha Shifter?" Romulus frowned. "I remember stories of shifters. I would not think one of them could handle this charge."

"Some are stronger than others, as with anything. This young man, I have heard, is exceptional. I have also heard their magic complements ours, like the elders have always said. Those in the seeking party are all enamored by these shifters, especially the women."

Romulus waved the comment away. "The young women in this village are enamored by anything unique. How close is the party?"

"They will be here within the hour. Where shall I direct them?"

Romulus looked over his shed, filled with sunlight and flowers. It was the place he liked best in the world, the ideal spot to spend a tranquil afternoon. If there was one place he wanted to show his blood, it was this shed.

"Here," he said without another thought. "Take the tables and desk out and bring in a bed. Assemble the healers. Bring my mother—" He cut himself off. Maybe that wasn't the best idea. She was less than open-minded. Still, if this young woman *was* his blood, and she was as strong as these early reports indicated, they'd need another powerful anchor.

He finished with a nod. Halvor matched it and disappeared from the room.

Romulus's possible daughter was coming. He could scarcely contain his hope and fear.

AN HOUR AND a half and a lot of pacing later, Halvor turned up at Romulus's door again, his face strangely pale.

"What is it?" Romulus barked, impatience getting the better of him. He schooled his expression.

"We are nearly ready, Second. The runner has just returned. The party is nearly upon us. One thing…they are being followed by three elves."

Romulus frowned at his assistant. "They're being *followed* by three elves? Are they accompanying her in a protective capacity to ensure she is delivered?"

"We will know the particulars soon enough, but these elves stood by while the shifters fought a group of demons that had infiltrated the area. The shifters lost one of theirs and have another struggling to heal. The elves have repeatedly offered to take the girl since then, and are only kept at bay by a fiery mage." Halvor's jaw clenched, his disapproval practically screaming through the shed.

Hope flourished even as anger simmered. The elves were clearly reacting to the woman's power, which meant great things for her, but their eagerness to abduct her from her own people worried Romulus. In the past, they would've helped get her home at all costs. What had changed, and what did it mean for Romulus's people?

"Alert the First of this troubling news. Have the elves attended to when they arrive, and then turn them away."

"Yes, Second." Halvor excused himself.

Romulus looked down at the fluffy bed in the center of his remade work shed. Colorful light streamed in from the stained-glass windows, showering the white sheets. The fragrance of flowers was soothing. A fresh breeze wafted in.

He hoped this young woman found the space as rejuvenating as he did.

Not long afterward, he heard shouts. Footsteps tramped in his direction. He saw a group of people through the window, hastening his way.

His heart jumped up into his throat, and he scarcely knew if he should step outside to wait, or stay within the shed so as to appear calm and collected.

"She comes, Second," Halvor said, popping his head

in. His eyes were tight, his reaction to pain.

And then Romulus felt it, like hot, stinging needles along his skin and in the backs of his eyes. The healers surged into the room with their patient. Known to be the calmest of his people, they seemed unusually flustered.

"Bring in the Alpha Shifter," one of them shouted, supporting the girl's head.

"Spin her toward the bed! Spin her!" Alvine coached in a brash tone Romulus had never heard from her.

The group of four turned, and as they did so, Romulus got his first good glimpse of her. His breath dried up and his composure fled. He had to grab the edge of the bed to keep from going to his knees.

He didn't need to see her photograph. He didn't need to hear her story.

He saw it all in her face.

The set of her eyes and jaw matched that of his beloved, but every other feature spoke of Arcana blood. She had an uncanny resemblance to his mother, in particular, with the same dainty features and button nose, although her auburn hair, which crested to a widow's peak, had been inherited from his grandmother. He wondered if her eyes were a similar color, and if, when she was healed, the ethereal glow of her magic would bring every man in the village forward begging and pleading for her hand in marriage.

But he was getting ahead of himself. She was sick. Very sick. It was a miracle she wasn't dead.

"Where is the First?" he barked as a powerful, dark-haired man in a loose robe someone had clearly lent him walked in with a killer's grace. His deep-set eyes scanned the room, the woman, and finally landed on Romulus.

The confidence he saw there told him this was the Alpha Shifter, as did the rush of pleasing magic that filled the room.

No. Not pleasing…thrilling.

As though a heavy blanket was pulled back, suddenly Romulus couldn't wait to get to the battle yard. He couldn't wait to brandish a sword and fall headlong into the magic that gave his kind its namesake of guardian.

He struggled out of the feeling. His child needed him.

He allowed the strong shifter magic to flow around him, suddenly understanding how this Alpha Shifter had been able to turn the tide in the young woman's—his daughter's—magic.

"Hello," Romulus said, offering a light bow. "I thank you for escorting…"

"Charity," the man said in a rich, deep voice.

Color danced in Romulus's vision. His legs wobbled, barely holding him.

"There, you see?" Romulus found Halvor by the door, blocking a crowd of people that rudely lingered outside.

"I'm afraid I don't follow, Second," Halvor said.

Romulus tensed within the flood of emotion. "I told

my beloved—her mother—that if she honored me with the gift of a child, it would be undeserved charity for an impure soul. That I must beg, being as flawed as I am, and hope. She called me foolish at the time, but in the end..." He blinked away the sudden moisture in his eyes. "In the end, she gave me a child, and honored me with the name I would have chosen."

Romulus shooed Alvine from Charity's right side and gestured for the Alpha Shifter to stand to her left, as was proper for her protector.

The Alpha Shifter filed in without hesitation, not needing a verbal directive. How pleasing.

"We must seek more facts before we—"

Romulus made a small gesture, quieting the healer.

"The First," Halvor announced.

Antonia entered the room, regal and unhurried. Not for the first time, Romulus cursed the decorum that dictated their every action.

"Mother," he said, motioning for her to join them at Charity's head. The boiling desire to fight thankfully quieted in his mother's tranquil presence.

"Yes, hello. Thank you for the note about the elves." His mother's gaze lingered on the Alpha Shifter for a moment—a silent request for an introduction.

"I apologize; we are not yet properly acquainted," Romulus said to the Alpha Shifter.

The young man's jaw clenched and his body leaned *just so*—the Alpha Shifter was clearly as impatient as Romulus himself, but doing a terrible job of masking it.

"Devon," he said at last, and another gush of power drenched the room.

Romulus's mother sucked in a startled breath and forgot herself for a moment, looking down on Charity with wide eyes. Her decorum was slow in returning.

"Why wasn't I summoned sooner?" she demanded, turning to the healers. "This young woman is on her deathbed, with enough power to take you with her."

A sort of green magic rose from Devon like a mist, curling through the air before disappearing. It was gone so fast that Romulus almost thought he'd imagined it. Charity's magic was subdued quickly even as spikes of pain flayed Romulus where he stood.

His mother reacted blatantly again, turning her wide eyes on Devon this time. "My goodness. I had no idea your kind could handle this sort of onslaught." She didn't waste time looking for an answer. "Healers, quick, ready the draught to awaken her. Bring in more anchors. It will take the strongest in the village to turn her from this destructive path."

CHAPTER 24

Devon stood at Charity's side, his placement indicating something of value he couldn't quite pick up on, while subdued—though clearly excited—fae filled the room. These people communicated similarly to shifters, using their posturing and movements to relay most of their directives. It occurred to Devon that he'd probably fit in here better than Charity until she could get a handle on it.

That was, if they would let him. After the demon battle, and after they'd used the fae's supplies for a funeral fire, saying goodbye to their pack mate and friend, his pack had been assigned a spot slightly removed from the fae's fire. Not much removed—Penny hadn't thought anything of the separation—but Emery had noticed. He'd just smirked and shaken his head, happy to be aloof with a people who didn't value his company.

Devon didn't have that luxury.

These were Charity's people, without a doubt. The man in her mother's picture was standing opposite him, and he didn't look a day older than when the photo had been taken. This was Charity's new world. These fae already accepted her as one of them—he could see it in their concerned expressions. In the joy in her father's eyes. She'd have a new family, a new community. If Devon was ostracized from that community…

He pushed down his uncertainty and ignored the memory of Karen's words. That wasn't a concern right now. They had to get Charity out of danger.

He pumped out his power, mixing it with the incredibly potent fae magic around him, and pushed it through the link with Charity.

"We are ready, First," said a rosy-cheeked woman in a white robe. She cradled a plain wooden bowl in her hands.

"Close the door," said the woman who stood at Charity's head. Her grandmother, it had to be. She had auburn hair streaked gray at the temples, wise, knowledgeable eyes, and a few creases around her eyes and mouth. She looked like she was in her forties—like she could be Charity's mom. Clearly these people didn't age like humans. Or maybe it was the land that acted as a fountain of youth.

The assassin posing as the Second's assistant turned ever so slightly. He'd already been blocking the door, but he did so with a slightly more assertive stance. Clearly, he *was* the door.

"Second." The rosy-cheeked woman handed the bowl to Charity's father, who hadn't had a chance to introduce himself. He took it with steady hands, as though nothing whatsoever troubled him. These people were excellent at masking their feelings. In fact, it seemed to be expected.

"Now," said the rosy-cheeked healer as she took her place at Charity's feet. "Given the seeps and surges of her magic, it's nearing its peak. It is trying to flower into its true potential. This draught will help that." Her eyes flicked to Devon.

Ah, so this explanation was meant for him.

He minimally shifted to show that he was taking it in.

"She will awaken, and then we will get the first true example of her power," the healer went on.

"Second," the assistant at the door said, his posture regal and firm.

"Yes, Halvor," Charity's dad said, the quirk of his eyebrows indicating he was annoyed by the interruption.

"Hallen has grave warnings about letting Miss Charity's magic flower without the proper protections."

"Bring him," the First said, not looking back.

Hallen, his arrogance dimmed and his white-blond hair released from its hold at the back of his neck, appeared at Halvor's side. His face was hard and grave, an expression belied by the excitement in his eyes. He was clearly delighted to be getting an audience with royalty.

"Hallen led the seeking party and recovered this young woman who bears a striking resemblance to our family line," Charity's father said, his tone expressionless.

"That remains to be seen," the First said, not turning her attention to Hallen.

"What are your grave warnings?" Charity's dad asked Hallen.

Hallen explained what he'd seen Charity do in the battle with the demons. Specifically, he spoke of her explosive magic. He seemed impressed, although Devon knew she was capable of much, much more. She'd been worn out, working on the dregs of dregs.

"That wasn't all done by Charity," Devon corrected when Hallen was through, adopting the same tone. "One of the mages mimicked Charity's magic to attack the demons. The mage is unique in that way. But Charity can do everything he said, and additionally, she can create magical sunlight strong enough to burn an elder vampire's skin, she can form a ball of…electricity, I think it is, and propel it a few yards, and she can explode air from a spark, as Hallen saw, but with much more ferocity. She has very little control over her magic yet, but she's learning quickly."

The First and Second—actually, everyone in the room—stared at him with expressions barely masking their incredulity. Well, except for Hallen, who clearly wanted to kill Devon where he stood. Devon suspected they wouldn't become friends.

"And…how do you know all of this?" the First asked.

"I've witnessed it on multiple occasions, usually when we were fighting for our lives. She's only known she's magical for half a year or so—this is all new to her. Her magic is pretty incredible."

The First took Devon's measure, and even though Devon had tried to keep his tone neutral, he got the distinct impression she'd picked up on his affection for Charity. Given her suddenly frosty demeanor, two things were suddenly clear: she *did* intend to welcome Charity into their family fold, but she didn't want any attachment to undesirable outsiders getting in the way.

Something hot and uncomfortable lodged in Devon's middle. He pushed it away. Now wasn't the time.

"Yes, I see." The First looked down at Charity, and the room fell silent.

Andy's voice rose over the din. "What are they doing in there, surgery? Why the hell is this taking so long?"

The First looked around the room. "Alvine, do you surmise we have enough power gathered to gently guide her magic on the right path and counteract any…powerful manifestations of the magic she might have inherited?"

Alvine, the healer at Charity's feet, looked at the ceiling. "We have enough power, but if we don't move her outside, we won't have much of a shed left. If she has as much magic as the Alpha Shifter says she does, we'll need to direct any powerful discharge somewhere, and that will be straight up."

The First looked at the walls, and Devon got the impression she was calculating whether they'd hold up without a roof. "You've always wanted to expand. Alvine, proceed."

Charity's dad stared at the First for a long beat, and though his thoughts didn't bleed out onto his face, it was entirely too clear he was silently cursing. Instead of raising an objection, however, he bent to Charity, his gaze flicking up as he did so.

Devon moved in immediately, lifting Charity's head so her dad could deliver the sweet-smelling elixir to her mouth. It dribbled past her lips, and she coughed, spraying the liquid over them. The Second dribbled more, and this time half of it was swallowed and half coughed out around her chin.

"That should suffice," Alvine said.

Devon laid Charity back down, his eyes rooted to her face, his heart in his throat. Now was the point they'd been waiting for these long months. He'd gotten her to the finish line, and he had to trust her people could get her across.

"It is evident you care a great deal."

Devon almost didn't realize the words had been spoken to him. He looked up into the brown eyes of Charity's father.

"I recognize the look," the Second said. An old pain surfaced in his eyes. "Utter bliss. A devastating obsession such that you couldn't imagine living without it." A sad smile ghosted his lips. "She holds your whole heart in her hands, and you wouldn't want it back for all the world."

"Is it me, or did things just get really freaking personal?" Andy's voice drifted in. Clearly those outside could hear what was happening inside. A few of the spectators frowned at the interruption.

"I love her," Devon admitted, hoping his face didn't look as red as it felt. "I'd do anything for her."

"I hope you will remember that when the time comes," the First said, analyzing him.

"Like…*really* freaking personal," Andy said.

Charity heaved on the table before coughing and curling up. Her face screwed up in pain, and Devon prepared himself for the onslaught. Instead, a thick feeling of euphoria swirled around them like a cyclone, the fae stirring the air with their magic somehow, grabbing his magic and that of the shifters waiting outside, sweeping it all up and mixing it together.

"*Hmm*, that is nice," someone murmured. "Makes me eager for my bow."

"The thrill of battle," another whispered.

"Is that hers?" someone asked.

"No. The Alpha Shifter and his people."

And then the shower of agony did come, blasting out from Charity and magically flaying all of them. Devon gritted his teeth and held firm, receiving an equal dose of pain through the magical link—which he used to work his magic into hers. Everyone else staggered back with their arms up.

"Now is not the time for cowardice," Alvine shouted, the first to recover. She walked forward as though through a gale, clutching the edge of the bed. "Help her!"

Charity's magic gushed into the room as though from a burst dam, more than Devon had ever felt at one time. If this had happened a day ago, even an hour ago, he wouldn't have been able to help her.

The cyclone of magic spun faster, working harder to sweep Charity's magic into everyone else's, balancing it with sheer force. A tiny spark flashed light near the ceiling.

"Watch your head—"

The blast cut off Devon's words. The ceiling exploded upward, blown off by the force of Charity's magic. White light, purer than the sun, beamed down on them from several points, buzzing. Small surges of lightning hit the edges of the walls where they'd recently been attached to the roof.

Charity cried out, arching on the bed. Her hands came together above her chest, palms up, light glittering across them.

"Watch out!" Devon pushed himself back. Wide-eyed, everyone else followed his lead.

A fizzing oblong of electrical charge condensed into a sphere of light before rocketing skyward. Thirty feet or so up, it exploded, sending balls of fire shooting over the shed.

With that, the pressure died away. The surge calmed

and the awesome display of magic dimmed. In its wake, a pleasing euphoria tickled Devon's insides and flirted with his magic.

Charity's eyes fluttered open. Her head fell to the side toward him, as though she'd known he was there all along. Her smile was serene. "Wait for me. I need to rest now."

CHAPTER 25

STEVE WALKED BESIDE Devon, ever the brooding alpha. Against all odds, the younger man had accomplished his duty. Although the loss of his beta had shaken him, badly, he hadn't fallen apart. That was commendable. Steve planned to find something alcoholic in this incredibly beautiful faery wood and get the young alpha so drunk he couldn't stand up. They had the time.

When Charity was carried past him on her bed of white silk, she had a small smile on her face. A relieved smile. The big dogs apparently thought that was a good sign. The best sign, actually. All she had to do now was sleep it off, like a magical hangover. She was being brought to wherever long-lost royalty went, while they'd been invited to follow a dishy fae lady, Zana, to their temporary lodgings.

"She really blew their skirts off, huh?" Steve asked as they followed their sleek little guide, who kept throwing Devon shy glances. Steve was going to have to up his game if he stuck with Devon. He wasn't used to this level of competition. "Half of them looked like ghosts they were so pale. You and that pipsqueak warned them, but they still weren't expecting that much magic."

Bystanders stopped to gawk at the pack as they walked by, all dressed in flowy robes that made them look ridiculous. It was unbecoming, but at least it let his nuts air out. It could be worse.

"They weren't expecting half as much magic," Rod said, walking beside Dale, who wore an obstinate expression. "You didn't see the people at the back who took off running."

"That was probably to get water," Andy said, peering in an open door of a small house they passed. "Charity lit two trees and someone's house on fire."

"It was a work shed," said Zana, turning back and offering Andy a smile. "The Second has many. Though…he has less after today."

"We have very different ideas on what constitutes a shed," Andy muttered.

Steve glanced down a row of cozy-looking bungalows, the cobblestone path between them lined with flowers and hedges, green and well-tended. The elves favored magical gardening—everything perfect and similar—but the fae clearly nurtured their gardens by hand. A few weeds poked up between the cobbles, petals littered the ground, and sprigs stuck out every now and then. He liked Charity's people better for it.

They were at the outskirts of what the fae had called a village, but what would be called a town in the Brink. It almost reminded him of Savannah, Georgia. The large cobblestone paths appeared to be organized in a grid system, dotted here and there with bench-laden parks. Trees surrounded the community, weeping with moss, and dotted the landscape, natural and beautiful, like the people as a whole. The place gave off a…serene sort of feel, easy and comfortable. Relaxing. He wanted to find a patch of sun-sprinkled grass and have a nice, long nap.

"We have not seen magical gifts like that since…" Their guide shrugged. "I never have, though in times of battle, gifts were more plentiful, I'm told. Miss Charity, the Arcana in training, seems like a relic of that time."

"They didn't do much investigation to make sure she was one of theirs," Barbara said, limping badly, still covered in wounds and her face drawn. But damned if she wasn't rising to the occasion. Steve was glad for it. They didn't need to lose another one.

"The Arcana in training proved herself with her magic. That is not something that can be faked," Zana said.

"Will she get a title, like her father and grandmother?" Devon asked.

Zana swished her long hair, and this time when she looked at him, her eyes were heated with lust. He didn't appear to notice. "Yes, if she passes her tests."

"And those tests are?"

They turned right down a path that looked like all the others, except the houses were a little smaller, probably one-bedrooms with tiny kitchens and little to no living rooms.

"They ask the same of all of us—to prove we are accomplished fighters with a desirable skill set, and to embark on a quest." She smiled at him. "She is lucky—given her magic and her family, she will be highly regarded despite her halvsie status."

Devon frowned at her as they walked down the street, half of them trying to hide limps. They needed a rest badly.

"Halvsie status?" he asked.

"Half-human, half-guardian. Usually that would greatly reduce an individual's status. But she has an incredible amount of magic, and she is a result of the Second's quest. She'll make a good match and bring honor to her family."

"Ah." Steve shook his head and tried to peer into an open window to see what was going on in these houses. "Your system is set up like the elves'—kind of like the royalty in the Brink. Your level in society, your wealth, your…whatever—it all gives you status points. You guys marry within your station, right? High status doesn't marry someone you deem low status."

"Of course not." She frowned as she looked back at Steve. Her crystal-blue eyes widened and fire licked their depths, indicating she'd given up on Devon and was willing to move on. Steve ever so slightly turned his torso in her direction, indicating his desire to ride the bang-bang train. Her pink tongue wet her lower lip. "If someone of lower status works hard enough, and has the right skill set, they can elevate themselves. Someone born high can fall, if they are lacking. In the end, you marry someone with whom you match."

"That right? And what about outsiders? What's their status?"

Her lips curved and her hips swung as she walked. "Hopefully very...*very* fun."

Steve's dick tented his stupid robe, and he didn't mind if she noticed. If she wanted to try a shifter on for size, he was more than happy to oblige. It sucked for Devon, though. It was clear that a shifter didn't even have low status in the eyes of the fae—as outsiders, they had *no* status. They were a red light when it came to marriage, and from what Steve had glimpsed, the head lady was stuffy, at best. While Steve was in Candy Land, with promiscuous ladies who weren't looking for long term, Devon was in hell.

They crossed a wide dirt lane, and even though there were no fences or markings, it was clear they'd just left the village.

"You'll be quite comfortable here," Zana said, indicating a small grouping of cabins that didn't seem like they'd seen visitors in...a long time. The flower beds were empty, the grass patches were taken over by weeds, and some sort of natural brown wall had probably once started as a hedge.

"You are not so welcoming to visitors," Cole boomed, and Steve smirked. He hoped the whole village had heard it.

Embarrassment crossed Zana's face. "I do so apologize. We weren't expecting guests. I'll relay your displeasure immediately."

"It's fine," Devon said. Steve didn't need to have a heart-to-heart with the alpha to know he needed some alone time where he didn't have to keep all his crap bottled up.

They really did need that hooch. This place better have some.

"Thank you for your hospitality," Devon said, stopping at the edge of the little grouping of cabins.

The woman gushed, her cheeks reddening, and fluttered her eyelashes. Oh yeah, the young alpha had *game*. "Thank you, Alpha Shifter. We would like to make your stay as comfortable as we can. We know you are concerned for your charge."

Devon didn't so much as twitch, but he must've been shriveling inside. His *charge*. He was a guy expected to move on now that his charge was safe and secure.

"C'mon." Steve slapped his hand on Andy's shoulder because he didn't think Devon would've reacted well if he'd tried the move with him. "Let's get drunk, pass out, and sleep for two days. This will all look better a couple of mornings from now."

"I could use a drink," Macy said, her eyes bloodshot and her lower lip trembling. She had some shit to work through too.

"How about it, lovely?" Steve asked Zana. "Got anything that makes people a little squirrely?"

She blushed again. "Yes, of course. I'll have some sent over right away. Would you…like chaperones, or…?"

Oh yeah, Steve was going to love this place.

He winked at her. "Not this time. We need to decompress. Come see me in a couple of days."

"Sure. Of course." She took a step back, bowed, and jogged gracefully back the way they'd come.

"Snooty bastards," Cole said, glancing at the nearest cabin, which likely hadn't hosted anyone for twenty years. "Why would a people want to separate themselves from the world, do you think? What are they hiding?"

Macy huffed. "The question isn't what they're hiding. It's what are they hiding *from*? Did you see them in battle? No real warrior has such well-brushed hair. Sure, they were pretty good, but they're green as hell." She lifted her eyebrows at everyone. "Obviously they're not used to dealing killing blows. Practice in a field with a wooden sword doesn't make a warrior. Experience on the field of battle makes a warrior. And if they give me an opportunity, I'll prove it."

A tear leaked out of her eye. Her jaw clenched.

Oh yeah, she'd prove it. Steve hoped to hell she got an opportunity so the grief didn't eat her alive.

"With your permission, Mr. Alpha Shifter," Steve said, giving it the dramatic emphasis the fae seemed to, "let's get out of these stupid robes and hopefully get roaring drunk."

Devon stared back at the village, an island with a fragile bridge, and Steve knew he was wondering about the odds of visiting Charity. She'd been put in special, temporary housing while "suitable" accommodation could be arranged. They'd scoffed at Devon when he suggested that she stay with the pack.

"Yeah," he said, his eyes swinging to Macy. "Let's get drunk and remember all the good times with Dillon. All the achievements he'd been proud of. That he'd want people to remember."

"Or the times he'd be embarrassed that we remembered." Andy smirked, sadness in his eyes.

A tear dripped down Macy's cheek. "Tonight is for Dillon."

"Tomorrow…or whenever we wake up, we can pick a fight with the biggest, baddest fae in this place." Steve winked. "We have some aggression to fight out…and a reputation to uphold."

CHAPTER 26

CHARITY OPENED HER groggy eyes, blinking in the soft light of a bedroom. Her temporary bedroom, if she remembered correctly. She'd come out of the fog of sleep a few times over the last few days, confused and disoriented. She'd only been able to take in small amounts of info, and ask for Devon, before a surge of magic or fatigue pulled her under again.

This time, though, she felt a little clearer. The haze had lifted a little.

"Ah. I see you're awake." A man sat beside the bed—the man from the photograph, Romulus. His elbow leaned on the bedside table, his ankle rested on his other knee, and a book was lowered into his lap. He'd been close at hand the other times she'd woken up, either sitting in the room working or reading quietly, or not far away and quickly on scene. Every time he'd seen her, he'd showered her with smiles, sparkling eyes, and words of support.

He pulled his chair closer. "How do you feel?"

She frowned, needing a moment to think about it while surveying the rest of the room. In the corner, standing tall, was a lovely woman with a thick braid draped over her shoulder. Kairi, if Charity's hazy memory served. She or the attractive man—Hallen—were usually within the room, often in that corner, and always looking at her when Charity emerged from the rip tide of sleep.

Kairi nodded in greeting.

An earthy, delicious feeling flowed into Charity from her magical link with Devon before rolling back toward him. He might not be in the room, but he was in her body. It was more comforting than anything could be.

She turned her attention back to Romulus. It didn't look like he'd aged a day.

"My mother had a picture of you," she said, pushing through the fog clinging to her thoughts.

His smile was sad and excited at the same time. "Yes. How much do you remember of our previous chats?"

She frowned and wandered through her mental haze, looking for any memories of the last few days. She thought it was only a few days, anyway.

"How long have I been here?" she asked, her voice scratchy and her throat dry.

Kairi moved to the dresser across the room and poured sparkling water into what looked like beautiful blown glass. She seemed to know what Charity wanted before Charity had to actually ask for it.

"Five days now," Romulus said, entwining his fingers in his lap. "You're recovering very quickly, a testament to your high power level. You're reacting expertly to our magical guidance, as though you'd lived with us all your life."

Charity let Kairi help her to sit, her body much less sore and achy in comparison to the days before. She drank large gulps of water with shaking hands, draining the glass. She lowered back down, sighing.

"Where's Devon?" she asked.

"He is in the battle yard, testing his mettle against our people."

His words continued to flow, but she was still lingering on the last two.

Our people.

Warmth wrapped around her heart as snippets of hazy memory jogged forward. Of Romulus sitting beside her bed, uttering the words *daughter* and *darling*. His assertion that he was the man in the photograph.

That he was her father.

"You said I looked like your grandmother," she said, interrupting something he was saying. "Sorry, I—"

"You do, yes." He smiled, not at all bothered by her interruption. "Like your great-grandmother. She was a brilliant, formidable lady. Heralded as a fantastic leader. You seem to have inherited more than her appearance. You share her magic, too, but with an interesting adaptation. She couldn't rain down lightning, from what I've heard. I was but a teen when…" He paused for a moment, then apparently thought better of whatever he was about to say. "Our whole community is fascinated by you. Thrilled, and fascinated." Pride shone brightly in his eyes. "There can be no argument that you are one of us. You belong here."

The warmth around her heart squeezed before filling her limbs. She'd never really belonged anywhere, not even with Devon's pack. Yes, they'd welcomed her in, but she was an outsider. Different. She'd never fit into the nice schools, in her neighborhood—to hear that this man was accepting her, and that she had found similar people for the first time in her life…

Tears came to her eyes.

Romulus reached forward and put his warm hand over hers. "I am not sure if you remember our conversations the last few days, but given all I have learned, it seems I am your father. I did not know of your existence, or I would have been there every day of your life, watching you grow. Helping you along the way."

She swallowed down a lump in her throat. "Why did you leave?"

"I didn't know about you, and so didn't work as hard to resist the pull of the Flush. Of my people, and family. It flooded my very being. I hated to leave your mother, I truly did, but I could not withstand the beckoning of my home. Can you forgive me?"

Charity let her head fall to the side and her eyes take in the beauty outside her opened window, with the orange haze and gold filaments slowly drifting by. A bright pink flower bloomed within the frame.

She didn't really know how to feel. It hadn't been her that was left, this time. This situation wasn't like that of her mother, or her ex-boyfriend John. Romulus hadn't even known about her. And while it really sucked that he'd walked away from her mother, she couldn't very well begrudge a man for wanting to be with his family again. Especially as a magical person in a non-magical world. That must've been hard.

"Yes," she said softly, and she did, as much as she hated to admit it for her mother's sake.

He squeezed her hand.

She rolled her head back to look at him. "How are you keeping my magic at bay?"

"Ah. So soon you ask. That is great news for your recovery. What we do is guide it into a natural release. You see, as fae, we have a special relationship with the nature around us. When we are in harmony with it, our magic is in harmony. That harmony can be achieved in a lot of ways, but the best and most powerful way lies within our skill set. Some are healers. Some are builders. For me, it is the creation and cultivation of gardens. I construct the nature around me into a beautiful tableau and, in so doing, create harmony with my magic. I fuel my being, and give a pleasing release for any pent-up power."

"So...I should've been gardening this whole time?"

He laughed softly. "No, no. Skill sets are highly individual. We have yet to find yours. Have no fear, that will come. But that would not have been enough. We are also guardians. Many magical species have a subset of people designed for the protection of their kind. For fae, it is us—*custodes*. Or guardians, as I said. Combat balances us in both mind and body. It is what we are, and so does us the most magical good. It is very much a way of life."

"But..." She blinked through the oncoming headache. Something rang false in what he said. It tickled her memory of a hazy battle. Strangers beside her. Demons. Hesitation in flashing swords.

She shook her head. She couldn't clear away the dizzy confusion to call up the memory. Hell, maybe it was a dream. Maybe another hallucination. There was no way to say.

She switched gears. "I've been training in martial arts most of my life. Since I met Devon, and all this started happening, I've been battling vampires and demons. My magic has only gotten worse."

"You can fight?" His smile was triumphant. "Fantastic." He sobered in the face of her blank stare. "Not worse. More powerful. None of us could have waded through the manifestation of your power level on our own. In the human lands, I believe you have the saying 'It takes a village to raise a child.' That encapsulates the situation perfectly. When the largest portion of power manifests, it does so in fits and starts. It rages through the body. It boils, stews, then gushes, trying to find that harmony. Those with a similar natural magic, and with enough power, can use their own balance and harmony to guide the surges into a healthy release. Your Alpha Shifter seems to have found a way to dominate your magic, forcing it into his natural harmony. Unfortunately, that could not lead you to your own harmony, but it did keep you alive, and for that, he has my eternal gratitude."

She rubbed her temples. "So as soon as I learn the harmony, I should be fine?"

"Given the state in which we found you, the healers agree that you are on the precipice. So yes, when your magic calms, you will need to find the harmony, and then you will sigh in relief. I remember my own journey through magical adolescence...but those stories are for another day. You are tired. Come"—he stood and pulled the covers to her chin before tucking her in—"sleep. Rest. You are safe now. Take the time you need to mend. Your family will be waiting, when you are ready."

"Devon?"

Romulus smoothed the hair back from her forehead. "We need you a little further along before we allow his magic to incite yours." A look of confusion crossed his face. "It's strange. It's as though the shifter magic peels back a thick blanket, and out from under the blanket rises the feeling of glory in battle. The song of the sword. The thrill of the victory. The elders are being strangely tight-lipped about all this, even though many of them fought with shifters in our history." Romulus's nostrils flared. "Anyway. Devon is quite popular on the battle yard, as you can guess. The shifters are welcome there, at any time. But have no fear—just as soon as you are well, you can see your Alpha Shifter again."

Her eyelids felt like weights. She nodded, content for now with the swish of magic back and forth in her body.

"Sleep, my darling," Romulus said softly. "All will be well when you next wake."

CHAPTER 27

CHARITY OPENED HER eyes and stared at the beams in the ceiling, taking stock of her body. She didn't ache anymore. Not even a little. When she wiggled her fingers, then her toes, she didn't immediately feel tired. The stresses of the journey had finally worn off. She felt...whole. Finished.

The deliciously earthy feeling washed into her from Devon, and she took a deep, smiling breath. Like a stream, their magic coexisted, moving and drifting as it would.

She startled when she met the brown eyes of a woman who squatted on top of a desk against the wall. Kairi and Hallen were nowhere in sight.

The middle-aged woman crouched like a mad thing, watching Charity with one eye squinted and the other wide open. Her fingertips, sporting long nails, some badly chipped, dangled between her legs, barely touching the edge of the desk. She wore pink clogs, sockless, and flowing red pants.

"Hello," Charity said, rising to her elbows. They sank into the fluffy bedding. For the third time in the last two days, her head didn't immediately start swimming.

"Hello," the woman mimicked, and tilted her head to the side like a bird. The light from the open door shone through her fiery halo of hair. "You have met my nemesis."

"Hmm, mhmm." Charity nodded, because what else could she do? The lady looked like a villain from a comic book.

"She has steered you true, but you will think it false," the woman went on, and tapped her nails on the polished wood. "It will make for a standoff I have been anticipating for decades."

"Ah." Charity nodded again.

"I miss getting out. I don't get out much anymore."

"Oh. Is that right?"

"Yes. I wish to see the world with my own eyes. I wish to meet my nemesis."

"Right. Where's…ah…where is Kairi?"

"She stepped out to get you some spring water. I told her you'd be absolutely parched upon waking, and that you wouldn't wake for some time. She believed me…because she's crazy."

"Yes." Charity rose to sitting. Her head was still in the clear.

A pulse of her magic surged through her body then the room. Almost immediately, it bloomed and then drifted before dissolving slowly and flowing out the window to the world beyond. Only a soft pulse of her magic remained, humming within her.

The woman smiled. "You are delightfully pure, like the spring water you will soon suck down. Untouched by customs. Unconfused by expectations. Your purpose is crystal clear, and you will prosper because of it. Down with the woman." She raised her fist.

"In the last few days, when my magic surged, it took a second for everyone to help me...direct it. Although it kinda feels like dissipating rather than directing, in some ways."

"Yes. That is because they did not know it would happen."

"I see."

"Care to go for a stroll?"

Charity stilled. She'd been recovering and confined to the bed for a week and a half. A week of that had been necessary. The last couple days, however, she could tell she was being babied. It was a first in her life. She didn't much like it. But she was in a new place where she wanted to be accepted. She didn't dare refuse their care. Not even when the care was left to a crazy woman who either didn't know, or didn't care, what seats were for.

"Sure."

Charity slowly pushed the covers off her legs, eyeing the fire-haired woman warily. Moving ever so slowly, she turned and dragged her legs over the edge of the bed. She paused and smiled good-naturedly at the woman.

"Lovely weather, isn't it?"

"Oh yes," the woman replied. "The best I've ever seen. Even better than yesterday. Which was also the best I'd seen, only not anymore, since this is the best."

"Yes." Charity stretched her arms. "Where is everyone? Apart from Kairi, obviously."

"On the battle yard. Should I take you?"

Charity froze, then tried to act nonchalant. This woman was definitely crazy, and unlike everyone else, she didn't seem to have Charity's best interests in mind. Charity was ever thankful for it.

"Yup." She stood up, not the least bit dizzy. In fact, energy practically bounced around her body. She scarcely remembered how good it was to feel…well, normal. "Your nemesis. Tell me about her."

"You'll want to get dressed first." The woman jumped from the desk with grace despite her age, then walked across the room with a strangely jerky gait, almost like she was walking for the first time. It was the oddest thing…

After dressing in loose pants that felt like cotton, a tight black shirt, and strange bands that wrapped around her middle—Charity was taking a leap of faith regarding the fashion in this place by accepting the advice of a whack-job—she followed the woman out of the four-bedroom, two-bath "bungalow," as her guards called it. It was only temporary until they could find something "more suitable." These people were cracked. They clearly had no idea what she'd been brought up in.

The fresh air greeted her, laden with the smell and feel of nature, which seemed to bolster the currents of her magic. Another "bungalow" was opposite hers, and more down a small lane that would comfortably fit two bicycles. If they had any.

"My nemesis has a gift unlike any other, save myself," the woman said, affecting a sort of hobble as they turned right. She waved one of her arms over her head like an ape. "She is my polar opposite, and she will absolutely detest me. She will try to get rid of me at every turn, claiming Reagan has no use for me, since Reagan already has her."

Charity's blood ran cold. From what the others had said, Reagan spent hardly any time at all in the Realm, and she certainly hadn't been to the Flush. How did this woman know her?

Before Charity could ask, the woman was already rambling on.

"The joke will be on my nemesis when she realizes she needs me. She and I will be two halves of the whole. Two key pieces of a larger puzzle. Soon, we will learn to unpeaceably coexist. She doesn't yet know any of this. I can't wait to see her face when she finally *sees* it."

"That sounds... How did you say you knew Reagan?"

The woman held up a finger with a broken nail. Her knuckle had nail polish on it. "I do not need silly snowy balls and flashing symbols on picture cards, whatever they are. I merely need my concentration. And maybe a tea with mind alterants."

"Ah. Hmm." Charity was back to nodding as they turned toward a hedge with a small hole in the middle.

"Come on. We can slip past the jailers this way." The woman straightened up, walked normally for two steps, and then wove her way into the hedge, somehow managing not to snag herself.

"You're not leading me to slaughter or something, right?" Charity asked, jolting as a stick jabbed her. "You're not…taking me to the elves, or vampires, or anything?"

The woman cackled. "Yes, of course."

"Of course you aren't, or of course you are—"

"But not until your quest vision flip-flops a few times. No, that's not normal. Unheard of, actually. That's why it is so fun to be alive right now. I'd tell you not to tell anyone about that, but I'll be there when it does, and walk you through everything. Then your future will call, I'll finally meet my nemesis, and Reagan will no longer be able to hide."

"Umm…right." There had been too much to unpack in all of that, so Charity went with the largest issue at hand. "About Reagan. How do you know her?"

"My, my. You are very dense." The woman paused at the other side of the hedge. She hurried through the open space between two fences and the monstrous houses beyond, before half diving into another row of bushes.

"What the bloody hell am I doing?" Charity murmured to herself, peering out through the leaves to see if the coast was clear. Someone sauntered down the lane, singing to herself with a lovely voice. She'd soar to the top of one of those singing game shows in the Brink. Although what was the point of money and fame in the Brink when she could live *here*, in peace and beauty? She would have no need for money in the Flush. No need to make things better. Things were already perfect.

Charity ran across the opening and ducked into the bushes.

The madwoman smiled and turned to again lead the way. "I have *Seen* the woman called Reagan. I have *Seen* her father. Most importantly, I have *Seen* where they meet, and how." She ticked her finger back and forth. "But I won't give you details. I am the only one in all the worlds—up, down, side and side—who knows. That knowledge will eventually have a purpose…" She fisted her hand. "I can *feel* it."

Ah. So she really had no idea. Fabulous.

They emerged from the bushes in an entirely different part of town, with smaller houses and mediocre gardens. Charity looked back at the bushes. "Are those magical in some way?"

"You are in the Realm, love. *Every*thing is magical in some way. Just up here." She switched back to her strange hobble, this time with both arms waving above her like an orangutan.

"I'm going to get in trouble for going with you, aren't I?" Charity asked.

"You might get a lecture about your well-being from the new, proud, though inexperienced, papa. *I* am going to get in trouble." She looked down at Charity's legs as they made their way to a break in the cobblestone path up ahead. "How do you feel?"

Charity stretched, then grinned. "Despite being laid up in a bed for the last week and a half, I feel excellent. Better than good. I feel…"

The woman patted her arm. "Just wait. This ain't nothin' yet, honey. Now, here we are."

They stopped at the edge of a large green field teeming with activity. The dull sound of wood hitting wood thudded repeatedly. The graceful movement and tumble of bodies excited Charity in ways she didn't quite understand.

"Well, greetings, Miss Charity the Arcana."

Charity started. Steve lounged beneath a tree not ten feet from her. She'd been so completely focused on the fighting she hadn't noticed anyone else.

"And hello, you nut job," he finished.

The fiery-haired woman cackled as she walked to the tree with a perfectly normal gait. Which raised the question: why had she been walking like an ape?

"Steve, why are you naked?" Charity asked.

He shrugged. "All the girls wanted to see me fight in my animal form. Our magic and ferocity turns them on. Given that these mock battles are so much work, for so little reward, I figured I'd just show them a little ferocity in bed, instead. I don't need to change to do a little magical tickle, know what I mean?"

She just stared at him.

"I'm sure there'll be a round two soon." He touched his hand to his chest. "I'm a simple man, Miss Charity the Arcana—three women is my limit, especially these vigorous little fae. Those who were willing to share were left exhausted and satisfied. Those who wanted to wait for alone time are currently vying for Devon's attention, soaking in his magic. They'll be back around as soon as they realize he's not interested." He lay back, his head propped up on an elbow, and closed his eyes. "Thanks for bringing me. This is better than I could've dreamed. None of these feisty little vixens want me permanently. After a little pickle tickle, they are happy to wander away, no strings attached. Perfect."

"You're so gross," she said, really trying to be outraged, but laughing instead.

"Only when the situation demands it," Steve replied, unbothered.

"Did you do them right here, under this tree? Because if not, that still doesn't explain why you're naked."

He shrugged. "It's refreshing to saunter around in my birthday suit. I don't have to wear those…clothes."

Charity looked down at herself, not understanding what the big deal was. Then again, she had no fashion sense.

"And the men?" she asked.

He peeled an eye open. "They don't see us. That's not true; they see Barbara, Yasmine, and Macy just fine—especially Yasmine—wishing the girls were as willing as I am, but they don't see the men. We're nothing to them. Outsiders."

Charity frowned, hearing something in his tone that unsettled her. On the surface, it sounded like the fae were being a lot more hospitable than she would have expected—men were territorial, and the shifters were waltzing around naked, monopolizing the women. The shifters wouldn't have been so kind had the situation been reversed.

"So no fighting at all, huh?" Charity said. "Even in human form?"

"God no. What a hassle."

"And everyone else?"

"Well, Macy sent someone to the healer." He let both eyes drift open this time, studying her.

Fear bled through Charity. "Did she get in trouble? She was allowed to stay, right?"

He watched her like she was missing something.

"What?" she asked.

The madwoman patted Steve's chest even though his large shoulder was much closer. "Ignorance is bliss…until it is not."

"It worries me that I understand you," Steve murmured.

"Yes," the woman replied. "Your journey of finding love—"

Steve held up his hand. "Nope. We've talked about this. I don't want to hear anything about the future. I'd rather be surprised. And love is for fools, so quit knocking on that door." The woman cackled again, and Charity got the distinct impression that the crazy laughter was for show. Or it was drugs. "In answer to your question, Miss Charity the Arcana, Macy was applauded and her technique studied. They blamed the man she injured."

Across the way, Charity caught sight of a powerfully robust body that stuck out amongst the lithe, lean forms of those around him.

Devon!

He fought with a graceful savagery that made her blood pump. The sun glinted off his bare torso as he moved through fighting poses, blocking a thrust and delivering a blow that had his opponent staggering back. His loose pants, just like hers, clung to his sweaty, well-built thighs. His messy black hair swirled around his head, and she just knew his jaw sported that irresistible bad-boy stubble.

In fact, now that she noticed, a line of spectators waited off to the side, women all, dressed in revealing clothes and hanging on every sword thrust.

Possessiveness, hot and fierce, bubbled up through her. Her heart hammered, and not just because of the battle she desperately wanted to join. She craved his viciousness and determination, his confidence that nothing in the world would get through him to harm her. She craved the man who had laid down his life time and again for her, the alpha who could make her feel safe even when she couldn't protect herself.

"He's the only one still competing," Steve said before Charity could start off across the field. "His victories don't count, but he keeps going anyway."

Charity hesitated. "What do you mean, his victories don't count? Count toward what?"

Steve lazily waved his hand toward the field. "This is some sort of fighting competition for people who think they are fierce and literally have nothing better to do. It's tied to their status in the community, I think. Being that the Supreme Alpha Woman Magnet is not warrior fae, his victories do not count. He can advance, but so does the person who challenged him. And he does have to wait for them to challenge him. It's a bonus of some sort." He fluttered his eyebrows. "Or something, I don't know. But like I said, these fae like our magic. They like the feeling of fighting with it, so he has no end of challengers. The men want to best him, and the women want to fu—paint rocks with him."

"Paint rock—" Charity shook her head. She wanted to march across that field, challenge her love, fight him across the gloriously green field, and then drag him back to her bed and claim him. None of those chicks would be laying a hand on *her* goods. "Then why is he still doing this? It sounds stupid."

"You were resting and he wasn't allowed to wait by your side. He needs something to do with his hands. This is why love can really sour a good time. No offense."

"I'm done resting."

The madwoman's cackles followed Charity across the field.

CHAPTER 28

"Enough," Charity shouted, strutting past the women staring at Devon in rapture.

Devon flung his opponent back with ease. The male fae groaned as his head thudded down onto the field. Child's play. Devon had been placating the lesser fighter. Wasting time, as Steve had said.

Devon spun around, his slightly widened eyes the only sign he wasn't totally composed. His gaze held hers, but he didn't make a move toward her. Hell, he didn't even smile in hello.

She lowered her eyebrows into a scowl, not sure if she was angry or annoyed.

"Aren't you happy to see me?" she asked, bracing a hand to her hip.

His hard expression slipped for a moment, revealing a flash of intense longing. "Yes. More than you could possibly know. How do you feel? I didn't think they'd let you out of bed so soon."

"A nutter broke me out and brought me here." She smiled and took a deep breath as murmuring rose from the small crowd of spectators. "I feel amazing. Thanks to you. They said I should've died. You've really pulled ahead in our lifesaving competition. We're far from even now."

"They wouldn't let me wait with you. They said my magic would interfere."

"I felt you through the magical link. I just focused on that when I woke up." She took a deep breath. "He's my father. He says he's my father, in any case. And that I look like my great-grandmother. And that I have her magic. And that these are my people and I'll fit in here."

A soft smile pulled the corners of his lips. "See? The big dogs were right all along."

"I'm going to tell Roger you called him a dog." She laughed, so damn glad to see his face again. "I hear your wins don't count toward whatever fighting competition is afoot."

Anger sparked in his beautiful brown eyes. The green and gold specks danced dangerously. He shrugged to show his indifference, but he didn't even come close to selling it.

She grinned. "What do you get if you win the whole thing?"

"Can't. Only a fae can win the whole thing."

"But won't it be interesting if you beat the fae that wins the whole thing?"

He shook his head. "Not possible. Animal forms aren't acknowledged. I don't use weapons as well as people who've trained with them all their lives. Without my shifter form, there's only so far I can advance."

She laughed again. "Your involvement in the competition isn't acknowledged. What's the difference if you use your animal form or not? Just wait until you finally battle some fighters worth your time. I bet they'll be happy for the extra challenge of fighting teeth and fur. And if they aren't?" She shrugged. "Taunt them for being cowards. Easy."

A grin pulled at his lips. "I missed you."

"I know. Now let's see if you've learned anything." She launched at him, seeing his hesitation—his worry for her—and used it to slap him across the face. Speaking of taunting.

He staggered back, trying to put distance between them. She advanced, not letting him.

"Charity—"

"What do you think I am?" She blocked his weak attempt to shove her back, and this time she backhanded him. The slap rang out across the field. The onlookers gasped. She barely caught Steve out of the corner of her eye, striding their way with a big smile. "Breakable?"

"Charity, you're still recovering—"

She swept his legs out from under him and then kicked him in the side, easily dodging his attempt to grab her leg. Her speed surprised even her—now that her magic was functioning properly, she was faster than he was by a mile, on par with some of the vampires they'd fought. Her strength was every bit as impressive.

His magic pumped out of him, swirling around her

in an intoxicating blend. This was what she'd wanted, needed, and the thrill of the fight flooded her body. A lovely tune floated on the breeze, and her hand itched for the sword she'd left in her bungalow. She opened and closed her fingers.

He saw it. His eyes flicked to a spot behind her.

She turned, and suddenly he was there, grabbing her and tossing.

The bastard had finally decided to fight, and he'd started by fighting dirty.

Adrenaline coursed through her. She kept a laugh from bubbling out, and instead rolled over and groaned, acting like she was fatigued. Or hurt. Either would do.

Devon stopped the downward swing of his fist, buying it.

"Oh God, Charity"—he crouched down next to her, laying a warm hand on her arm—"I didn't mean to—"

She rolled and punched, catching him completely off guard. If he wanted to fight dirty, who was she to say boo?

Her fist slammed into his jaw. His head snapped back.

She spun on the grass and kicked, but by then he was onto her, trying to dodge. Her foot clipped his shoulder, the force enough to knock him off balance. It would do.

She hopped up and ran, reaching the wooden practice swords with him hot on her heels. She pivoted, caught his swinging fist, and pulled and then launched him over her shoulder and into the pile of practice weapons. She snatched up a blunted sword, palms tingling, and swung it at the center of his broad, muscular back. It wouldn't do much more than form a welt. She hit him again for good measure before dancing back.

He rose slowly, muscles popping along his powerful frame, his physique standing out like a deliciously sore thumb in the crowd of sleek, lean fae. His eyes were wild, ruthless, his alpha mentality having kicked into overdrive, and his whole person was bent on forcing his challenger to submit. On forcing his dominance.

Something deep and feminine inside her mewed to be taken, to be claimed as only an alpha could claim his female.

But the primal part of her insisted he prove his worth. That he earn his mantle as her protector here, for all to see.

She opened up and let magic gush out of her, confident her new countrymen and women could handle it. Part of her wondering why they weren't already up and by her side, sensing the call of battle on the air. Her magic filled her to bursting, and still she let it come, blasting out of her and covering the field in the feeling of budding flowers, growing plants, horses stomping on bloodied mud, and the agonized cries of a foe. She blended it in a heady mix, the beautiful and the ugly, the peace and the violence, and released it as a shock wave.

We are warriors. Come fight by my side.

Steve halted his advance, nearly to the gathering crowd of onlookers, and the humor dripped off his face. His eyes turned hungry.

The lion emerged.

His roar made half of those seated jump to their feet. The rest cowered from the might of his shifter form, not living up to the stories she'd heard of the warrior fae. Wondering if hiding away here in the Flush had dulled their abilities.

Steve, on the other hand, stared at Charity. Ready for a command. Ready to battle.

Devon saw it, and his eyes blazed. Charity was, in effect, pulling rank, and the alpha in him wasn't having it. This wasn't just about dominance and submission anymore—it was about the right to lead his pack.

She'd raised the stakes.

Game on.

Magic swirled around him. A green mist enveloped him, and then his wolf form emerged. He lifted his head and howled, long and beautiful, the wolf song.

Your alpha calls. Join me.

She felt the power of it well up from her toes. Felt the need to fall in beside him. Saw the previously cowering fae straighten up, then stand, like awakening from a dream.

Felt the smile spreading across her face.

"Now. *This* is a battle." She ran at him, stupid fake sword at the ready. Almost there, she shoved out her hand.

A spark flared right in front of him. He opened his mouth for some reason, and then he was flying, tumbling through the air.

She was on him in a flash, slashing down with the sword, aiming for his neck. "Honor system," she grunted out, trying to get in a slash that would have decapitated him.

He dodged away at the last moment, so much lither and more graceful in his wolf form. So much faster.

He snapped at her ankle, making her dance away, before surging up and slamming into her body. How a man could weigh more in another form than his human form, she didn't know, but the force of the tackle shoved her back.

She cut her sword through the air while she fell, not wanting to waste an opportunity. Her back hit the ground as her sword banged into his front leg. That strike would've lopped off his limb.

He rolled off her, and when he stood, he kept that leg held tightly to his body, honoring the strike. She shot him with another blast of magic, the spark alighting on his right side. Before it concussed the air, though, he spun and bit. The magic…unraveled, somehow. It died.

"What the…" She tried again, sending a spark toward his other side.

He turned and bit, chomping on the electrical ball of light. It zinged through his teeth before unraveling out around his body.

He'd figured out how to circumvent her magic. Was that a bonus of their connection?

Magic now boiled and built, bleeding acid into her body and leaking from her in waves. Bright white light buzzed through the sky, covering the whole field. Lightning rained down, narrowly missing a thick gray wolf—Rod—as he loped toward them through the grasses.

"Need a little help here," she yelled to the onlookers, all in rapt attention. None of them had stepped forward to help her, or offered to guide her in the use of her magic. They were transfixed on the fight.

Devon surged toward her.

Not stopping, she slashed at him, forcing him to change his attack path. A bolt of lightning zipped down next to him, singing his ear. He dodged in the other direction, his keen eyes tracking her as only a predator could.

Rod ran to join the fight, but Steve pushed forward, blocking the way. A yeti's roar made someone screech. Cole lumbered out into the field.

Charity struck forward with her sword, the feeling natural, the choice terrible. Devon dodged and lunged, his teeth clamping down on her sword arm, although not hard enough to break skin. She cursed and dropped the sword, blasting him with barely controlled magic. Only then did those around her come to her aid, swirling their magic around hers. Calming it. But not quelling it. Keeping it vibrant for battle.

Someone out here still knew what warrior blood ran through their veins.

Devon flew through the air, not having moved fast enough to extinguish the spark she'd sent at him. She picked up the sword with her left hand. It felt just as comfortable in her non-dominant hand. Just as dangerous.

With a manic grin, she charged, seeing the shifters spread out behind Devon, stopped in their advance by Steve. The fae, as well—a huge crowd now but kept to the sidelines so Devon and she could battle.

She slashed at Devon, a dummy attack, and sent a spark at his other side. He bit into it, and she lunged. Her blunt sword tip grazed his side.

He took the hit, that wound in real life hurting, but the pain didn't stop him. He'd fought through much worse. He kept on coming.

She pulled her sword back, getting into position for a strike, but he was already on her. He slammed into her chest, taking her down a second time. This time, though, his weight was centered. His teeth closed around her throat.

He was badly wounded and missing a hand, but he'd claimed the fight.

A proud smile lit her face. Heat licked her core. It had been a good fight. Next time, she'd take him, she'd make sure of it.

But now…she wanted him to take her.

"Take me to bed," she said in a husky voice.

CHAPTER 29

Devon wasted no time. He rose and picked her up, hugging her tightly to his chest. They'd fought for dominance what seemed like a million times, sometimes with words, sometimes with fists, but it had always been about finding balance with each other, establishing their places in each other's lives.

It had never felt like that.

That had been…

Words couldn't express it. Saying he felt like an alpha didn't do this sensation justice. He felt like a god. And he knew that, without her, he never would've risen to this level. He'd bested power even Vlad couldn't touch. Power that had the entire field of warrior fae gawking.

And now, as he looked into her eyes, and saw her pride in him…

He felt like a man.

Halvor and the Second stood slightly removed from everyone else in the field. Devon didn't know how much of the sparring they'd seen, but judging by their postures and the smug delight in the Second's eyes, they'd seen enough to know Charity had something special. Something even a full-blooded fae didn't have. Moreover, she knew how to use it in battle. Not just on this field with their fake swords and useless competitions—she could rise from near death, in a haze, and still fight demons to save her pack. She was magnificent, and now they knew.

One day soon, they'd tell him his time was up. That he was of no more use, and could return to his life. One day soon, he'd have to face reality.

Today was not that day.

He strode by them without a word.

"You are on the road to greatness," the Red Prophet shouted, crouching at the base of a large tree at the edge of the field. Her shock of red hair stood around her head like she'd stuck her finger in an electrical socket. "First stop, Bang Train!"

"She is a nut," Charity murmured as she ran her lips up Devon's neck. "And you need a shower."

"I'd love a shower."

Even with Charity cradled in his arms, the women they passed looked at him with inviting stares. They were very open in their sexuality, and almost aggressively open in their desire to bed a shifter. He found it harder to ignore the complete lack of regard from the men, who smiled and nodded at Charity, then looked away as though she were being carried by a donkey. Except on the battle yard or in meaningless sexual conquests, it seemed the fae were consciously trying to ignore the shifters and their obvious curiosity regarding shifter magic. It was almost like they'd been told the ways they could intermingle, but outside of that, shifter interaction was forbidden.

Something he wouldn't bother Charity with at the moment. His pack had decided that they needed to give her a fighting chance. Until she was secure here, they wouldn't bring up their bad living conditions, how they were treated, or Dillon. It was the last that was hardest for Devon to bear, but he agreed that if they revealed all, Charity would internalize the guilt, and quite possibly start blowing things up. Sometimes you really didn't know where her mood would swing, at least in her current magical situation. Until she was established here, they would lie low.

She ran a finger across his cheek. "I forgot how handsome you are."

"It only took you a week to forget what I look like?"

"No, don't be stupid. I've been inundated with very attractive people, but they are all so…manicured. So polished."

"And you prefer an unkempt knuckle-dragger?"

Her smile lit her up from the inside out. His heart dribbled down his ribs.

"Yes," she said. "I like the rough-and-tumble, smoking-hot shifter who has clubbed me and will now drag me back to his lair."

"Her lair."

"Fine, my lair." She captured his lips, opening her

mouth so he could fill it with his tongue. When he entered her house, the whereabouts he'd heard in passing from Kairi, Charity's assistant, he let her down gently in the foyer, her body sliding against his, before backing into the door to close it. He worked her pants, pulling them open before pushing them down over her hips.

Her fingers wrapped around his shaft, and he growled into her mouth. He used his foot to shove her pants the rest of the way to the ground. She shrugged out of her shirt and fumbled with the straps around her waist.

"Curse these things—" she started.

He tore one of the straps apart before unwrapping her. "Shower first?" he murmured against her lips.

She dragged him across the room, her lips needy and insistent. Her hands stroking just right.

The bathroom had a luxurious spa-like setup, the opposite of the camping-style facilities in the cabins the pack had been assigned. There was a stone stall for showering, and while there wasn't plumbing in the Realm, the fae had arranged a gravity system whereby water would be released from a flat spout. A large copper tub sat on four legs beside it, without a spout. Kairi was probably in charge of arranging warm water to be brought in for a bath. Through a half-door was a little commode, needing a bit more privacy, and a basin was set up opposite the shower, the water kept in a pitcher.

The wildly different accommodations were yet another reminder there was a distinct class system in this place—and while Charity was at one end, Devon was at the other.

Charity turned to pull a lever, pushing her tight, round butt against his erection. A surge of lust stole through him, and he slid his shaft between her legs, flush against her warm wetness, so ready for him.

"I missed you," she said softly, angling, trying to get him inside her. He didn't bite—he needed a wash before they went any further. "I know it was only a week, but—"

"I missed you too," he said, pushing her into the stone enclosure and pulling a fabric screen behind him. "More so because I worried about your recovery."

"Men. Always with the one-upping." She turned in his arms with a sweet smile.

Devon slid his hands down her wet hair as the warm water fell from the—bamboo?—spout three feet above them. It cascaded like a waterfall, shimmering against the blue-gray stone behind it and shining in the natural light from the many high windows.

"Where's the soap?" he asked, running his hands over the swell of her breasts and down her flat stomach.

She turned and bent to the canisters tucked into one of the corners of the stall. He ran his fingers down the middle of her sex. She sucked in a sharp breath and braced her hands against the stone, ready for him.

"Need to wash, love. I'm filthy."

"Then use your mouth. I'm clean."

He couldn't fall to his knees fast enough. He licked up her center, digging his tongue into her core before reaching to give her attention where she needed it most. He backed up, then spun her around before pushing her back against the stone and throwing one of her legs over his shoulder.

"Hmm," she said, leaning her head against the wall.

The warm water washed over his back as he sucked in her clit before swirling it around in his mouth. He reached for the canister, washing his hands before returning to her. He threaded a finger into her, then two, pumping in time with the swirling of his tongue.

She moaned and grabbed a fistful of his hair. "Oh God, Devon," she said in a breathy voice. "Harder."

He changed speeds, from slow and reverent to rough and fast. He flicked his tongue quickly before sucking her in again, pulsing with his mouth and plunging with his fingers.

"Oh God, *yes*." Her grip on his hair tightened. Her hips gyrated toward him. "Hmm, yes, Devon."

He moved faster, working her to a fever pitch. She tensed, her hip gyrations getting smaller. More intense. His fingers pumping her to the goal line.

She cried out. Her hips jerked, and she shuddered, climaxing. He licked, tasting her, as she shuddered again, releasing her fingers from his hair.

"Do I have a second to wash now?" he asked with a grin, standing up and slowly running his hands up her legs and over her hips. He bent to run his tongue across her taut nipple before sucking it in.

"Hmm, sure. But just one second."

He chuckled and grabbed the soap, working it over his body. But she pushed his hands away, taking over, sliding her palms over his chest, down his stomach, and over his shaft. He breathed out a sigh as pleasure coursed through him.

She ran her hands back up to his shoulders, then turned him, letting the water wash down his body before taking the same time on his back. When she'd finished, she handed the soap to him.

He applied it to her breasts and cupped them in both hands before letting his hands roam, refreshing his memory of all the secret places that made her moan in pleasure or flutter her eyes in bliss.

As the suds washed away, Charity sucked in his bottom lip and ran her leg up the outside of his thigh. She hooked it over his hip and leaned in, using her hand to guide his tip to her opening.

"I can't decide if I want you to pound your love into me," she murmured against his lips, "or if I want the tender side of the alpha you don't show anyone else."

His tip kissed her opening, and her hand fell away. Her leg tightened around him, and he pushed forward, entering her slowly, heightening the pleasure. He'd give her whatever she wanted, but until she decided, he wanted to revel in every inch of her. It had been an insanely close call—so close that he still had nightmares about losing her forever.

He pushed into her again and tightened his hold on her body.

"Hmm," she said, clinging to him.

"I want to do this in a bed," he whispered, turning off the water.

"I love you." She grabbed his shoulders and wrapped her other leg around him. His cock plunged a little farther into her, the fit perfect, the feeling exquisite.

"I will always love you. I will do whatever is in my power to protect you. Always."

She kissed him tenderly as he carried her out, grabbing a towel on the way. At the bed, he dried them both before pulling back the covers and lowering her onto the silky sheets.

She smiled at him, her eyes sparkling, her beauty amplified. "It tickles me that you take a second to get everything perfect before you fuck me."

He slid between her legs, rubbing his tip along her wetness. He braced himself at her opening and met her soft, deep, open eyes. The love he saw there humbled him, as did the silent invitation to share souls as they did magic.

"I'm not fucking you right now, Charity. I'm making love to you." He thrust his hips forward, groaning as she tightened around him, and sighed. "And I hate wet sheets."

She smiled as he started moving within her, deep, hungry thrusts that made the world drop away. Pleasure slammed into him, tightening his body as he delved deeper. Her hips swung up, meeting each downward movement. Their bodies slapped together. Her kisses were languid, full of feeling.

She moaned, her hips swinging up into his downward thrusts. He worked faster, the pleasure mounting. Losing control. Needing her with all of his person. Needing to claim her in a way that blocked out his thinking and called to his wolf.

Their combined power flowed and danced through the room. The pleasure pulsed higher, so intense that his cock felt like a live wire. He slammed against her, almost there. Right at the edge.

"Yes, Devon, *yes*!"

An orgasm slammed into him, so hard that black spots swam in his vision. So sweet that it dragged him under until there was no reality. No gravity. There was only the feel of her, her soft lips on his, her arms tight around his shoulders.

He groaned, his heart full, emptying into her. She cried out, shuddering, clinging to his shoulders.

He gulped for air as tingles ran his length, his cock still buried deeply inside of her. He pulled back, shuddered with a renewed tremor of pleasure, and slid it in slowly one more time. She shuddered again and moaned.

"You've upped your game. That was incredible."

He smiled, and his limbs melted around her. "It's been a long week of waiting. And imagining."

"As long as it wasn't a long week of practicing."

He chuckled softly. "I'm not that stupid."

He turned onto his side and gathered her up into his arms. She settled her head into the hollow between his shoulder and neck, and she sighed in contentment. He let his eyes drift closed.

Before sleep pulled him under, he heard, "After a little catnap, we'll have to see if we can top it."

CHAPTER 30

THE NEXT AFTERNOON, Charity sighed as she sank into her couch. She stared at a lovely painting with interesting colors and wished it were a TV. She wanted to shut her mind off. Her day had been hectic and exhausting. She'd met her new grandmother and been warmly hugged. She'd seen the Second—her *father*!—off and on, and each time, she'd been warmly hugged. She'd met members of the council, which helped run the community, and had been hugged within an inch of her life. Random strangers smiled and hugged her. In fact, the only person who hadn't offered her a hug was the Second's assistant, Halvor, who'd randomly punched her.

She much preferred the punch, and even more so the sparring that had followed it. It seemed Halvor would be training her instead of the normal trainers who worked with the village at large. Given the intensity of her fight with Devon, which her father and Halvor had witnessed, they thought she was worthy of training with the absolute best. That, or she was getting preferential treatment. She suspected a little bit of both.

She didn't argue. Halvor was incredible—lightning fast, perfect form, and fluent in moves she'd never seen before. He might never have seen actual battle, but he was no worse for it. The man was a living legend. Devon had better watch himself—soon she'd dominate him!

Her father suspected that her fighting ability and magic, not to mention the fact that she was the result of his quest in the Brink, would eventually make people blind to her halvsie status. That was apparently a very big deal with these people. They didn't say it outright—they were much too polite—but it constantly came up in conversation. She was so fast…for a halvsie. She had incredibly dainty and fae-like features…for one of half blood. Her magic was incredibly powerful…for someone with a human mother. They were mystified the human part of her hadn't dulled her fae magic.

She'd thought she'd gotten over the "for a…" hump by this point in her life, proving that she was more than her shitty upbringing, and yet here she was again. Only this time, it was her blood that was the problem.

She had to own that the people as a whole weren't quite what she'd expected. She'd thought she'd find a collection of fierce warriors that sat around campfires and gnawed chicken bones or something. Their living in closed-off domestic bliss wasn't exactly the image Roger had painted. Many of them never having seen a battle, when the Realm was such a mess, seemed more than odd. *Off*, somehow. Then again, could she blame them? She didn't relish going back through, and she barely remembered half the trip.

She took a deep breath and let her head fall back on the couch. Despite all the warm hugs she'd endured from strangers, and the difference in expectation, she really did like it here. She saw herself in these people. Their magic was like hers, and they also shared her same brand of crazy. Couples didn't just argue; they took their problems public and tried to kick the hell out of each other—the women as strong and capable as the men.

It felt like the pressures of her life had finally eased. She didn't have to struggle to survive here—she could just *be*.

A soft knock sounded at the door. It opened a crack and a smiling Kairi peered in. Deep purple marred her right eye, her punishment for allowing Charity out of her sight. Charity had been aghast, but Kairi had nodded in agreement, saying, "They went really easy on me."

She'd popped in last night to help guide Charity's magic. Right in the middle of an intense round two with Devon, Charity hadn't realized anyone had snuck in. It wasn't until after an earth-shattering climax that nearly made Charity black out that she noticed her assistant in the corner with her eyes squeezed shut, fingers in her ears, and a big smile on her face. It had been more than a little awkward.

"Hey," Charity said, waving. "What time is it?"

Kairi blinked and turned, looking at the sky. "Probably four, Arcana." She opened the door wider and walked in. Hallen, the other person who had been dogging Charity's heels, followed her in. At least *he* hadn't been on duty last night. "I just wanted to see if you needed anything," Kairi said.

Hallen stopped beside the couch, these people's way of politely asking to sit down.

"Yup, sure. Have a seat." Charity gestured at the other end of the couch.

Kairi giggled, something she did when Charity broke guardian customs in some way.

She giggled a lot.

"Yeah, I was wondering—"

Another knock sounded at the door. Andy stood in the doorway. Fatigue—or was it unease?—had created lines around his eyes.

Hallen, who'd been lowering himself onto the couch, straightened back up, partially blocking Charity's view.

"Yes?" Hallen asked, ever watchful of her. She was grateful for it, but the guy could be overbearing.

"I thought I'd just stroll by and check in on Charity," Andy said, keeping to the door.

"That is Miss Charity, or Arcana to those not in her family, and we are seeing to her, I thank you."

"Ew, Hallen, give it a rest, man." Charity waved her hand for Andy to come in. She'd put up with these people's formality and politeness all day. She needed a break. "Come in, Andy. Where is everyone else?"

Andy entered a little stiffly, though his smile was warm.

"Hey, Charity," he said, taking a chair to Charity's right. Hallen stiffened at the informality and moved to stand near the door. He wasn't a fan of things that weren't *just so*. "Haven't seen you in a while."

"Yeah, sorry about that. I was half-dead."

His smile spread and the tightness evaporated from around his eyes, as though a weight had been lifted. He relaxed into the chair.

"I was going to head over to you guys tonight and thank you for all you've done, but…" She flung up her hands and then dropped them again. "I'm exhausted. I've been doing the proper thing all day. Improperly, I might add. Do you think the pack would be pissed if I left it one more day? And are Penny and Emery staying with you guys? I haven't heard a peep about them."

"Penny and Emery are staying with us, yes. They tried to leave on the third day after we got here, but a bunch of elves were hanging around, I guess. Emery thought it safest to wait for the pack. The crazy Red Hatter thought so, too, so that ended that. Now Penny drags Emery around this place, muttering about complex magic and stealing stones out of people's gardens. And no, you don't need to head down there tonight. Half the pack has been…we'll say dating. They are *dating* in the evening, without going anywhere." He waggled his eyebrows. "If you know what I mean."

Charity rolled her eyes. "Really, Andy, you too?"

Andy rested a hand on his chest. "How dare you! I'm not like them, Charity. It's one woman for me, all the way. Sadly, it's taking many women for me to find that special one, but the search is on. One day..."

Charity chuckled. "Oh my God, stop. So you're settling in well here, then?"

The humor dripped away from Andy's face. He shrugged. "It's beautiful here, don't get me wrong. It's probably the nicest place I've ever been. But it's not my home, you know what I mean? These aren't my people."

Charity sighed and tucked a strand of hair behind her ear. She glanced at Hallen and then Kairi, standing by, listening to every word.

"Can you guys give us a minute?" she asked, wanting to let her guard down in a way she couldn't if they stayed.

Hallen stiffened, raised his chin, and sauntered out of the door. Kairi winked and followed, closing the door behind her.

"He always does that," Charity whispered. "When he stiffens like that, it means I'm doing something wrong, but damned if he'll come out and tell me what. It's so annoying. How am I supposed to learn?"

"Have Devon teach you. That guy has all the rules down pat." Andy paused for a moment. "Kairi is cool. She's not like the others."

"The ones you...date?" Charity asked with a grin.

Andy laughed. "Those girls aren't interested in talking so much as—"

"Never mind," Charity said, covering her ears.

"I mean, they *do* say a few words, like oh—"

"I said I didn't want to know!" Charity felt the tightness in her shoulders loosen a little. Andy had a way of chilling everything out. She needed that right now. "I know this place is supposed to feel like home, but…it's all so strange, you know?"

Compassion took over Andy's expression. He entwined his fingers—he was listening.

It was amazing how quickly she was learning to read silent cues. Though these people probably thought she wasn't learning quickly enough.

"I mean, if it was a pretty place at home—the Brink—that would be one thing. Like Montana, for example. If I suddenly had family in Montana, I'm sure I could acclimate pretty quickly. But…the sky is orange here. There's gold sparkly dust floating around. And…it's always pleasant. There are no clouds. No cold breezes to catch you unaware and make you curse the weather."

"That's what you're into? Cursing the weather?" A goofy grin slipped on Andy's face.

"I always thought California was just a little *too* nice, you know? Ninety percent of the time, the weather is lovely. Even in the winter, it's mild and pretty. Not like Chicago. Those sudden shifts in weather in California, however rare, made me think of home. They reminded me of how far I'd come. But here…it's like a fantasy land. I have no roots. I have no memory of where I've been and where I'm going. I'm a stranger, even though I fit in. Almost."

"Almost?"

"I have a human mom. It's something of a roadblock, apparently. I shouldn't be this good at fighting, this powerful, this…fae-like…"

"Ah. Yeah, they are pretty close-minded about anything different." He adjusted his positioning. She had no idea if there was a hidden meaning in there somewhere, and thankfully, he wouldn't expect her to. "But you know what, Charity? That's just because they're locked out here in paradise. There's nothing new here. No new ideas coming from different people. It'll probably be tough at first, but if anyone can shove them toward a different way of thinking, it's you."

She nodded, taking that to heart. "It's also weird calling a perfect stranger my dad. I never even called the guy I thought was my dad 'Dad.' And my grandmother is Grandmama? What am I, British?"

Andy burst out laughing. "I haven't met Grandmama dearest, but your dad seems really cool. He is personally overseeing the revamping of the gardens out by our…lodgings. He called them 'frightful.' He's got one helluva green thumb, that guy."

Charity laughed with him, feeling lighter than she had since she'd woken up in the Flush. Maybe she should go over to see the pack after all. Hell, maybe she should move in with them until she was a little more acclimated to this place. They could all figure out how to fit in together.

"You'll get used to all of this," Andy said, crossing an ankle over his knee. "Santa Cruz was probably weird at first, too, right?"

She shrugged, allowing herself to absorb the truth of that statement. When she'd first moved, she'd felt lost for a good month. That feeling had faded with time, but she'd never felt the situation was permanent. Never laid down any roots.

Maybe that was the reason she kept collecting little grievances like they were armor—this could be home. It was paradise. Charity belonged here in a way she'd never belonged in Santa Cruz, or maybe any part of the Brink. She had family here, people who wanted her around, people who wanted to teach her. Maybe this was what her mother had wanted for her. She had, after all, left that picture of her dad for her.

Thankfully, Devon belonged in the Realm as much as she did. His regional pack had a castle here, for goodness' sake. It wouldn't be so out of the question for him to stay here. For all of them to stay, even. The shifters were magical, these people were magical—if she could learn to fit in, she was certain Devon and the others could do the same. Devon could already read the subtle nuances of their unspoken language, and respond in kind. He was already nearly as good as this place's absolute best fighters, something Halvor had grudgingly acknowledged earlier when he'd put Devon on the short list of people Charity was permitted to spar with.

She smiled, and her magic flowered, filling the room with perfect harmony.

"Nice work, Arcana," Kairi called in through the window. "You handled that surge all on your own. You're starting to find your balance. Good work. You learn abnormally quickly, as the Second has noticed."

"You don't have much privacy, though," Andy murmured.

"It's just because of my magic," Charity replied, stupidly not having checked if the window was closed. *Oops.*

She took in a deep breath. She really did need to try a little harder. So what if all these strangers wanted to hug? They were caring, friendly people who were happy she was around—she should celebrate that.

"Anyway," she said as another knock sounded on the door. Familiar voices reverberated through the wood. "Come in!"

Her father pushed the door open with a pleased smile. "Look who I found," he said, stepping aside to make room for Devon. "The man who has the whole village talking."

Andy hopped up and offered a bow. "Second," he said.

"Fantastic, another of the pack. I saw you fighting today too." The Second—her *dad*—stopped beside the chair in the corner and waited, facing her.

"Yes, of course." She motioned to it.

Devon didn't wait to be asked, thankfully. He sat

down beside her on the couch. Andy reclaimed his seat.

"Hi," she said, threading her fingers between Devon's.

"Hey." He kissed her on the forehead.

"I must confess, it is exciting to see the Shifter Pack in action," her father said. These people had a way of emphasizing all things shifter. It was an unexpectedly nice gesture. "There is so much…" He fisted his hand and gritted his teeth. "And that lion! Or the… What is the white creature with the horrible face and long arms?"

"A yeti," Charity said with a smile.

"Yes, yes, of course." It was clear he had no clue what a yeti was. "Their roars are fantastically rejuvenating. Every time I hear them, I want to grab my sword and head to the battlefield. I have never met the shifter race before this, but I was able to pry information out of a reminiscent elder regarding the glory of battling with them. Our peoples were entwined for a large part of our history. I see why."

"Have you ever been in a battle?" Charity asked. "Like…with an enemy?"

The Second squinted a little, and she knew she'd said something wrong. "Thankfully, it is peacetime," he said. "There are no enemies to be had."

Charity tried to keep from frowning and tilting her head. Tried, and failed.

Peacetime? Some of them had recently battled demons. They were keeping a wary eye on the elves hanging around the edges of their land. It was anything but peaceful out there. He wasn't a stupid man. Even if these disturbances were new, they were there. For him to sweep them under the carpet made her wonder if they'd always swept issues under the carpet. And if so, why? What were they hiding from?

Not like she was brave enough to ask. She was still a halvsie. She couldn't raise a fuss yet. She couldn't ask questions that got squints and tight shoulders. Not yet.

"Then there are the wolves." The Second leaned back and rested his arms on the armrests, a sign he was settling in for a longish visit. It struck her that she'd been sending the wrong messages all day. "Their synchronicity is…"

He let his body language finish the sentence for him, leaving Charity in the dark.

"Translate?" she whispered to Devon.

"Spellbinding," he supplied.

"And it is something we can learn from." Her father shifted, and Charity was too tired to keep trying to read his cues. She leaned against Devon's arm. Her father saw it—he saw everything—and smiled benignly. "Forgive me. I forget that the human lands have a much more…vocal way of communicating. Why, I was scarcely understood when I was there. My dearest—" Affection took over his features, and an answering warmth filled Charity's middle. It had come as a relief to hear he'd genuinely loved her mother—that he still loved her. "Your mother, I mean. She had to speak for me half the time. I'll never forget. She always said, 'Use your words, darling.'"

Andy laughed, and his shoulders lost their tension again. He never had been good with authority figures, but clearly he was a little more relaxed around Charity's father. "That sounds like something Charity would say."

"Yes." Her dad gave her a fond look. "They have similar mannerisms. Sometimes I am transported to the past." Sadness took over his expression. "I wonder how different things might have been had I stayed just one more month. I regret leaving, now more than ever."

"It sounds like you couldn't have known," Charity said, shrugging it away. This talk of the past made her unbearably uncomfortable. She wanted a fresh start.

"Yes, of course," her father said, thankfully reading between the lines. Or he merely read her body language, which was probably broadcasting her feelings. "As I was saying, I am exceptionally impressed with the Wolf Shifters' synchronicity. They move together with a sort of…flowing grace. Halvor agrees, though he is reluctant to admit we could learn something from another magical species." The Second laughed as though that were a great joke. "They are as we strive to be, and I am not too arrogant to admit it. It has given us something to think about."

He nodded slightly to Devon, who rubbed his thumb along Charity's finger, his version of elated. Charity stopped herself from beaming in pride—she'd ruin Devon's confident nonchalance.

"Now. Charity. There is something I must speak with you about." The Second—*her dad*! When would she start thinking of him as her father?—paused for a moment, and Andy leaned forward to get up. Devon looked over at her.

Ah, apparently her father was asking to speak with her alone. She barely stopped herself from groaning. That meant more lessons in business, or etiquette, or some other thing she didn't feel like learning. When did the workday end around here?

"Andy, why don't you get us some tea?" the Second said. "Devon, would you mind popping outside and asking Halvor to arrange snacks for two more?"

Andy rose without a customary "yup!" Devon squeezed Charity's hand before stepping outside.

CHAPTER 31

"Despite the fact that it's against custom," the Second said once they were alone, "I am willing to allow your friends to stay, provided you won't be embarrassed…"

He was communicating without words again. She rubbed her temple. "You probably need them here just to translate half of your silences."

He laughed. "Use your words," he murmured. "Quite right, yes."

Andy stuck his head from around the corner too soon for him to have finished his task.

"What kind of tea are we thinking?" Andy asked in a small voice unlike him. "There are…like, eight hundred kinds."

"Oh, something floral, I should think," the Second said loftily. "A day like today calls for it."

"Is today somehow different from other days?" Charity asked.

"Of course. You'll see the changes, in time. It's a lovely early summer day. The most fragrant of flowers bloom at this time of year. I am in high demand."

"Right. I remember, because you're the village gardener."

"The gardening architect, we call it. I design and implement the natural places within the village, a skill set I am most proficient at, as I said. The actual planting and day-to-day management of the gardens are left to those with lesser, though still incredibly useful, skill sets." He paused as Devon returned and reclaimed his seat. "I was blessed to have a skill in such high demand. I mean…everyone needs gardens! What would we do without a place to sit and reflect?"

Charity nodded politely as Andy returned with a porcelain tea set, elegant blue flowers crawling up the sides of the cups. He set it on the coffee table, then stared at it helplessly.

"Maybe you would be more comfortable asking Kairi or Hallen to come in and pour?" the Second suggested.

"I'll ask Kairi," Andy said, heading for the door.

The Second—her dad—refocused on Charity. "And that is what I wished to speak with you of." He paused again.

"He's wondering if you're comfortable sharing confidences with me and Andy," Devon murmured.

"Oh. Yes, it's fine," she said as Andy re-entered, followed by a delighted Kairi.

"Now, to gain your title of Third Arcana of the Flush," the Second began, "you must prove your rightful place. As we discussed earlier today, it is widely agreed that your quest has already been established."

A tingle of fear worked up Charity's spine. She hadn't known what had shocked her more, that the hallucination she'd had in the dingy hotel suite was related to her "quest," and apparently a glimpse at her future, or that the crazy woman with red hair had seen the same thing and told everyone about it before they'd even met Charity. She'd had the details perfect, even down to the blurry people to the right and left.

The whole idea was ludicrous. Charity leading Roger into battle? Charity deciding the victor? She'd only ever looked out for herself, and now she was supposed to stand at the head of an army of shifters and fae? Not likely.

The only thing that stopped her from discounting the whole thing was Vlad. It seemed inevitable that she would face him again in battle. And apparently Lucifer was after her, too. What she'd thought was another hallucination—her fighting demons in a beautiful field—had apparently happened. Devon had given her the highlights, and although he'd been strangely tight-lipped about the whole confrontation, she'd gotten the gist. Lucifer was trying to drag her down to the underworld for a meeting. Yeah, right. Now that she was actually lucid, she wouldn't mind another crack at either of them.

Apparently, if her father and the Red Nutter could be believed, she'd get that chance. Though the First had seemed dismissive of the whole thing.

"The Red Prophet has defined your quest as life-altering. She is convinced it will affect us all, even if my mother questions the validity. If you complete it successfully…" His chest rose, and he beamed. That, she didn't need any help interpreting. It meant he expected great things. "But if you do not, your right to the title Third Arcana of the Flush will be revoked, and you will be held in shame."

"Right. So…no pressure," she mumbled.

"None at all." He smiled at her, not picking up on the sarcasm. "You have all of our people behind you. We will not let you fail."

Devon squeezed her hand, and she lowered her suddenly burning face. She had no idea why that sentiment should embarrass her when it felt so good to hear.

"A proficiency in fighting is also required of any Arcana," her father said. He raised his hands in triumph. "And you have already passed. That is exemplary for one so young. So far, your place is assured. There is just one more thing."

"This is the sticky part," Devon murmured, translating a silent message Charity hadn't even noticed.

"Every person of status in our humble little village has a skill set to benefit the people as a whole. It is a skill set that sets an individual apart. That defines them." Her father's smile was gentle. "I know your skill set will be highly applauded."

She frowned. "What skill set would that be?"

"That's what he's here to find out," Devon whispered, taking a cup of tea from Kairi—the steeping and adding of random embellishments made pouring tea a sort of event.

Charity took her own cup, worry eating through her. "Well…I've always only excelled at fighting."

"You're an excellent student," Devon said. "You made straight A's this last semester."

"Oh, that is something. A scholar." The Second sipped his tea, his eyebrows pinched. Charity didn't need translating to know that he was not overly ecstatic at the prospect.

She searched her brain for anything domestic or natural she did, since that seemed to be what these people were into. Flowers and painting and needlepoint—none of her schooling had ever prepared her for this stuff. Metal shop, wood shop, sewing—those courses had all been canceled due to lack of funding. At college, she was studying chemical engineering with a minor in computer science, something that would have set her up for lots of job opportunities with good paychecks in the Brink, but not something that could be applied in this setting. They probably didn't even know what computers were.

"You're an excellent cook," Andy offered. "Something I am reminded of both because I'm hungry, and this place could use you. They don't make plants taste nearly as good as you do, Charity. And the meat? A little ketchup, please. I need some flavor. Only, they don't have ketchup!" Andy stilled. He dropped his head. "No offense."

"They have people to cook. They don't need—"

"Cooking, did you say?" The Second scrutinized her. "Yes, your mother did outstanding things in the kitchen, I remember. Why didn't I think of it? Of course she would've passed on her mastery to her daughter, as my father passed his skill set on to me. Silly of me not to remember. Yes, that will do nicely. I was but a boy when our master culinary designer passed. We lost him early, sadly, and his excellence has not since been matched."

"I mean, I'm all right." Charity shrugged. "I'm sure I'm not..." But she couldn't finish that sentence. She was sure she *was* better than whoever had been cooking for her. Even without spices, the food should have had more flavor, but almost every dish had been overcooked to the point of being mushy.

"Yes, fantastic." The Second sipped his tea, and Kairi excused herself back outside. "Our annual cooking competition was disrupted when my assistant and his wife had an argument get out of control and broke many of the tables. Our master furniture worker is busy with new tables. He should be finished soon. I can always hurry him up. Let's have you enter the competition. That will be a nice way for you to win your place."

Charity's eyes widened, and she swallowed. What if she couldn't deliver? What if she embarrassed herself in front of everyone? What if she got so annoyed that they were worrying about tables and cooking and gardens, instead of what Vlad had said about what the elves were doing to people, that she accidentally kicked someone in the face? She still wasn't exactly stable; there was no telling what effect stress would have.

Devon squeezed her hand and bumped her shoulder with his. "You'll be fine. You'll win, hands-down."

Andy raised his hand. "I'll taste-test."

Charity took another sip of tea to hide her thought process, letting the flavors delicately flow over her tongue. As she pulled the elegant cup away from her mouth, she stared down at the light brown beverage.

An idea sparked.

Suddenly, she knew exactly how to make an impression. She hoped it was enough to solidify her place here.

She also hoped that those elves or demons didn't push into the Flush, grab her away from the battle ignorant village, and render all of this useless.

CHAPTER 32

"All I'm saying is, they have knives, made with metal, so why don't they have bedframes?" Andy paused and gave Rod a poignant look. "Right?"

He'd seen Charity's super-comfortable house two days ago, and she'd certainly had a bedframe. Of course, she lived in what was clearly the nice part of town. Since then, he'd barely seen her. The Arcana were keeping her incredibly busy, giving her etiquette tutoring, fighting training, and now monitoring her every move regarding this cooking thing. Without coming out and saying it, they had impressed upon Charity the severity of her failing, which Devon said was only part of what was playing hell on Charity's nerves. The other part she apparently shrugged off whenever he asked. It was anyone's guess what that could be. Something else was bothering her, though; Devon said that much was clear. Something about this setup, or her status, or these people wasn't jibing with her, but damned if she'd say what. It was annoying Devon something awful, and annoying the pack in turn, since it put Devon in a terrible mood.

"Visitors don't need to have digs as nice as Charity's, but a bedframe would be nice," Andy said.

This place was getting to him. The formality and underlying hostility drove him nuts. He'd even stopped seeing the fae girls. Apparently, screwing a shifter was some sort of sexual taboo. Even if he had a great night with one of them, the next day she acted like she'd never seen him before. It was screwed up.

Something was definitely up with these people. They were cool and normal when it was one on one, or on the battle yard, but within that village, no go. It was like someone had spray-painted *has a contagious disease* on all the shifters and none of the fae wanted to catch it.

"I don't think they like visitors," Macy said, standing next to Rod in the communal kitchen, watching him chop something resembling a carrot on steroids. Sorrow lined her features and bent her body. They'd all taken Dillon's passing hard, but Macy had been hit the hardest. She spent a lot of time by herself lately, walking around the village with Penny and Emery, or beating heads on the "battlefield."

Thankfully, after the fae boys heard of her connection to Dillon, they left her alone. Well, unless they wanted to incite her rage. And some of them did. Those usually ended up with the healer. The onlookers had smiles as the douche was carried away.

"That's an understatement," Rod said to Macy. "Has Devon said how long we're staying?"

"He's not leaving without Charity," Yasmine said

from beside the window. She was the only woman who'd partaken in the fae boys. Her interest had lasted exactly one day. She'd figured out early on why they wanted her, and it wasn't for her beauty. Turned out, she didn't like being a taboo conquest any more than Andy did.

She'd called Andy an idiot for taking so long to realize it.

"Are you saying he's going to stay?" Macy asked. Any hint of hostility she might've felt toward Yasmine had completely dried up. Yasmine had been Macy's shoulder to cry on most nights. Andy had tried to help—so had Rod—but something about a crying woman heaving against him made Andy get a hard-on, and that got awkward real quick, because this place's stupid pants and loose underwear showed everything off. Not everyone was as confident as Steve.

"Charity is going to ace that cooking thing, and then they'll welcome her in," Rod said. "These people can't cook for shit. As soon as she gets the green light, she'll want to stay. Bet you anything."

"Why wouldn't she?" Yasmine asked. "She's royalty. Real, honest-to-God royalty. Have you seen how the people treat her? They love her. They fawn all over her, halvsie or not. But Devon would never get the grandmother's approval. Hallen is Charity's intended match—"

The door swung open, admitting a tired Penny, followed by an aloof Emery. If it bothered Emery to be largely ignored by the fae, he'd never let on. Andy almost wondered if he preferred it.

"What do you mean, Hallen is Charity's intended match?" Macy asked, turning to face Yasmine. Rod stood between them.

"Oh yes, I heard that just today," Penny said, dropping a pile of rocks on the very little surface space this place had.

"Do you mind?" Andy asked, pointing. "This is my tiny cabin. Keep your rocks in your own tiny cabin."

"They're power stones. All of them!" Penny beamed at them. "They basically shouted to me from across that field with all the people fighting. I'll tell you something, Reagan would give her left arm to stroll through this place. She'd be tickled by their attempts to ignore her. She'd bring the battlefield to the center of their serenity circle, or whatever it is they do in the center green."

"We need to put that on our bucket list," Emery said. "Invite Reagan to the Flush to raise hell."

Penny laughed with glee. "Eventually she'll probably bust through the elves to get to us. She has to be going stir-crazy without trouble to find and then throw me into."

"Sorry…you were saying that you heard Hallen is intended for Charity?" Andy reminded her. Penny could get lost on the thought train and never return.

"Oh yeah. I was sitting in someone's front yard, analyzing a new plant I'd found, when I heard someone talking about it. No one closes their windows here.

You'd think they would want a little privacy. Anyway, they think he's a perfect fit because he's from a high-status family, has a great skill set, and has proven himself on the battlefield. They didn't say who he was fighting against, but I found it pretty surprising, since he hesitated with a kill shot when going after those demons the other week…"

She let that comment trail off, although Andy was pretty sure she'd voiced what all of them were thinking. Hallen was a coward, and worse, he was a stuck-up prick.

"What's his skill set?" Macy asked.

"Candle making," Emery said, picking up a candle from the shelf near his head. "The way he uses colors and smells is masterful, I guess."

"That's what he's heralded for? Candle making?" Andy said. "He can fight and make candles and suddenly he's better than Devon?"

"Devon can't make candles," Rod said. "He can just fight."

"I'm sure he could make candles if he wanted to," Andy replied. "He could rock this place with candles. Do you know why he doesn't? Because scented candles are only good for stinky bathrooms."

Macy and Penny burst out laughing. Emery pulled over a chair from the small round table and stationed it between Yasmine at the window and Andy's bed on the floor. He sat and looked out the window, keeping watch. What from, Andy had never bothered to ask.

Emery wasn't used to relaxing when he was in the Realm. Old habits…

"Where's Steve?" Emery asked.

"He was going to go pick a fight with someone who pissed him off earlier," Rod said, dumping the carrots on steroids into a pot over a magical blue flame.

"That's the other thing." Andy pointed at the flame. "Other types of fae make useful things. Like that flame. It's used for cooking and lighting—useful. But not these fae. Their job is fighting. That's their whole identity." He made quotes with his fingers. "Guardians." He dropped his hands. "But what are they guarding, way out here in no man's land? They're removed from the rest of their kind. You know, the useful fae. They are fighters…who only *practice* fighting. They sit here, ignoring the world, *not* doing what it is they're supposed to be doing, and yet *we're* the gross ones? We're the dirty, brutish race that is a stain on their society?"

"You should tell them that," Macy murmured.

"How could I? They pretend like I don't exist, unless one of them is dared to bang me, and then she's not interested in chatter, she just wants my dong." That comment got a smile from Emery, his first in a while. Too bad Andy hadn't been joking. He scrubbed his fingers through his hair. "I'm losing my mind here. How long do you think until we can go home?"

"When Devon realizes he'll have to make a choice and stay here with Charity, or leave without her," Yasmine said softly, staring out the window, "he's going to stay. I know it."

CHAPTER 33

"I HOPE YOU know how lucky you are that you were invited," Hallen said to Devon. The fae stood just outside an arch made of vines and flowers, leading into the greatly anticipated cooking competition, as Devon and his pack approached.

Charity had been stressing about this for the last week. She'd sampled all of the local cuisine, learning what the people here liked. She tried all the drinks, too, breaking her rule and even trying alcoholic beverages. And she pored over the ingredients Kairi brought her, familiarizing herself with the unfamiliar. She was at a major disadvantage, not knowing what flavors appealed to people, and everyone knew it. Her family had made it clear they didn't expect her to win, something Devon had to give them props for. They merely wanted to see if she had potential.

Charity wasn't one to do things by halves, though. She intended to win the whole thing. Devon had never been prouder of her.

He'd also never been so terrified for the future. With each passing day, Devon watched as Charity fell a little more in love with the Flush. She belonged here. She was welcomed, and loved, and people smiled as she approached. Laughed at her jokes. She was blending into their community perfectly—her sweet nature, tempered with the bite of steel, matched that of her peers.

She was drifting away from Devon's way of life.

Devon stopped beside Hallen. "Any time you want to challenge me, I'm right here." His voice was low and rough, anger brimming just below the surface.

Hallen scoffed and looked away. Devon had proven his prowess on their battlefield. He'd worked his way up the competition, allowed to compete in his wolf form. He'd only been beaten by two people: Halvor and his wife. Hallen didn't stand a chance, and they both knew it.

"Think Charity knows they're trying to set her up with that joker?" Andy murmured as they walked into a grassy area surrounded by little glowing orbs. Shrubbery surrounded the enclosure, and tiny glowing creatures, like lightning bugs, fluttered along the tops, creating dancing light. Excellently crafted, highly polished round tables dotted the grass, adorned by elaborate flower centerpieces and surrounded by silk-draped chairs. It looked like a setup for a wedding, or some other swanky affair.

Devon glanced down at his robe, horribly plain compared with the artful embroidery and shimmering fabric worn by the other attendees. The costuming people were clearly identifying Devon's pack as outsiders, as if that hadn't already been sufficiently drilled into them.

"No," Devon said, spotting a table at the very corner, somewhat removed from the others. That would be for his pack. At least the table was of the same quality as the rest. "She's completely blind to it. She thinks he's just like Kairi—an assistant. Someone to help her find her way and keep her magic level. She doesn't realize they have an ulterior motive."

His pack followed him through the fancy setup. This would be the first time Macy had seen Charity since they'd arrived. Macy hadn't visited her at the bungalow for fear she'd be reduced to a puddle of tears. Being that everyone else had visited, had made excuses for Macy, and Charity was half-dead at day's end, it had so far gone unnoticed.

They all knew that after this, that would no longer be the case. Charity had been distracted, but a girl like her didn't stay oblivious for long.

"Charity thinks these people will accept me as her mate." Devon huffed as he caught sight of the First Arcana, dressed in a robe embroidered with beads and gems. A sparkling tiara identified her status. "She seems to think they're keeping us at arm's length out of respect."

"If that's the case, she's got a long way to go before she acclimates to this place," Steve said. Halvor had told him in no uncertain terms that he must wear clothes to this event. Unlike the others, he took great delight in being the fae ladies' dirty little secret, the dirtier the better. "They are probably throwing shade at her, and she thinks they're complimenting her."

"Probably," Devon said. "And thank God. So far I've kept my cool every time that prick Hallen touches the small of her back, but only because I don't want to mess this up for her. I'd like to rip that fucker's arms off."

"Let her secure her place, then raise hell," Steve said. "I like this place as much as the next guy, but I wouldn't mind getting back to a nice steak and a bed I don't have to literally roll out of."

"See? Didn't I say I wasn't the only one annoyed with the bed situation?" Andy said in triumph.

The First noticed Devon, and her posture changed into one of expectation. She wanted to speak with him.

His heart sank and his palms started to sweat. He knew why.

"Go sit down," he told his pack. "I'll be there in a minute."

"Alpha Shifter, hello," the First said, her tiara catching and throwing the light. She stood in front of a raised platform holding a narrow table. The head table, no doubt, for the ruling party to look over their people. Charity would get a place at that table. She'd get a future that most magical people would kill for.

Devon bowed. "First, thank you for inviting us."

"Charity expressly requested it."

Ah. So they were making an exception for Charity.

"How magnanimous of you," he said with a straight face and no bodily sign of his sarcasm.

Her pursed lips said she read it anyway. "Yes. Quite." Her smile was false. "You must be relieved this day has finally come."

"And what day is that, First?" he asked as her assistant, a hard-eyed man with impeccable posture, glided in behind her. He stopped a little too close to her, their proximity speaking of an intimacy that wasn't strictly professional. No one had mentioned what had happened to her husband. It was as though they didn't speak of the dead, missing, or lost. Or maybe they just didn't air their dirty laundry to strangers, and Charity was still one.

"Why, the day your duty ends. After Charity's role in our society has been decided, you'll be free to seek your home. You must be missing it."

Devon's heart jolted in his chest. And there it was. Spoken aloud as though it wasn't the thing he'd been dreading since he'd heard Karen utter the words.

"The time will come when you need to make a choice. To save Charity's life—to give her a life—you must take the hard road, sacrifice your heart, and let her go."

"This is it, then," he said to no one in particular. "This is the big deciding moment in Charity's life."

The First's continued smile was thin. She did not enjoy speaking with those of "lower status." "This is it, yes. If things go badly here, Charity will, of course, always be welcome. She can stay as long as she likes—

we will make room for her. Unfortunately, with no desirable skills, she will have her title stripped and a gravely reduced status. Her living situation will change somewhat for the worse. This is to be expected, for one who is only half fae."

"Your people are harsh, First."

Her eyes marginally narrowed. He'd spoken out of turn.

He didn't give a shit.

"And if this goes well?" Devon asked, his heart beating too quickly and a sweat breaking out on his forehead. He felt eyes on him and noticed the Second standing somewhat removed, watching the interaction. Devon couldn't read his expression or body language.

"Then things will only improve for her. She will be celebrated as the Third Arcana and trained as part of our ruling force."

"And if the Second has a full-blooded heir?"

"Do not trouble yourself with our politics, Shifter," she said, her voice lowered, and shivers crawled up Devon's spine. "They are far above your ability to comprehend."

"You're awfully arrogant for someone with a warrior title and a penchant for hiding in the woods, away from danger."

Her eyes spat fire, but before she could respond, the Second was invading their group.

"Tempers are running high." The Second placed his hand on Devon's arm. "Mother, let me escort him back to his table. This is a big day for everyone. We're all feeling it."

After a long beat, the First said, "Of course. Please enjoy the competition, Alpha Shifter."

She didn't have to say the next words, although her tone said it for her: *Because it will be your last in the Flush.*

"Charity would be heartbroken if you weren't here to see her big moment." The Second slowly led Devon through the tables as people found their seats. They smiled and nodded at the Second, but no one acknowledged or even glanced at Devon. "It is hard to determine the best course of action in these situations. When I was in the Brink, the pull of the Flush became painful. I missed my people more than anything. I did not belong in the Brink. It was not the right place for me. And so, as much as it hurt, I left. I walked away from the love of my soul, from my beating heart, and have spent every day since regretting it, now more than ever."

The Second stopped next to Devon's seat, patted his back, and walked away as the first participant emerged from the arch. Even the fae's clapping was polite.

"What was that about?" Rod asked.

Devon watched the retreating back of the Second. "It sounded like he told me not to leave."

Macy and Yasmine frowned. Macy said, "He can't expect you to stay here. Not with the way you're treated."

"He's been pushing Hallen at Charity—we've all seen it," Andy added. "Why would he do that if he wanted you to hang around?"

"He probably wants you to give Charity a choice," Barbara said, leaning forward on her elbows to look across the table at Devon. "She'd go with you. Maybe she'd want to stay for a bit longer, but she'd leave this place with you."

"I agree," Dale said. "Roger wants her back in the Brink. You can make that happen. I vote you tell her it's time to go."

"You *vote*?" Devon said. "Since when is this pack a democracy?"

Dale and Barbara both visibly shrank in their seats, one helluva change considering their initial hesitance to submit to him as alpha. Devon hardly gave it two thoughts, his mind swirling on what the Second had said. On what Barbara had said.

He wanted to take Charity back with him so badly it hurt. He wanted her to officially move into his house and join his pack. He didn't want her to lose all of this—the warrior fae, the Flush—but did it need to be her new reality? Couldn't she come back for birthdays and Christmases, the way most people did with family?

The thought of leaving her behind made him want to throw up. Made him want to rip the table in two and go on a killing spree.

"You think she'd come back with me?" he asked softly, his hope so thick it was choking him.

"Yes," Yasmine said without hesitation. "This place is new, and she definitely likes it, but… She'd pick you. I bet you anything."

"She'd pick you in a heartbeat," Steve said, lounging back as a plate was set in front of him.

"She deserves a choice," Barbara said. "A woman would at least want the choice."

Devon stared off in the distance. Barbara had a strong point. Charity *would* want the choice. Sure, Karen had said he should leave, but *Seers* had a way of getting things wrong. What if this was one of those things? He didn't want to make the same mistake the Second had.

He didn't want to leave without the love of his soul.

"Here we go," Andy said excitedly.

Devon snapped out of his thoughts as a plate was cleared away from in front of him. Seven meals had come and gone and he hadn't tasted one of them. But now, as Charity emerged from the arch, his thoughts fled and he snapped to focus.

She didn't wear the loose, flowing garments donned by everyone else. Her robe was cinched in like a dress, though it covered the same amount of skin. The embroidered silk flowed over her body. Gems and stones glittered as she walked, catching the dying rays of the afternoon. A small headband ran across her forehead, sparkling like her grandmother's tiara.

She was the most beautiful thing he'd ever seen in his entire life, and the sight of her was enough to suck the breath from his body.

"Hello," Charity said, stopping near the long table overlooking the green. Her family and their assistants had left a single space for her. Charity's eyes roved through the crowd before stopping on Devon. Her relieved smile told him that she, at least, was pleased to see him. She needed his support. "I've done something a little different for you. We're going to start with a sampling of tea, which is now making its way to you. Pick whichever one you want."

"I love that dress," Macy murmured to Yasmine. "It's a good compromise between the Brink and the Flush. Nice work."

Devon frowned at them. "You helped her, Yasmine?" he asked. How had he missed that?

Yasmine shrugged. "She asked me about it a few days ago when I stopped by. I know my way around fashion."

"No contest," Andy said as an assistant neared the table with a tray full of china. Each small plate bore a teacup and a biscuit. They were so delicate that they looked absurd in the male shifters' hands.

"Served with your tea is my take on a biscuit. It will stay good in your homes for three to four days and should complement any of the teas. You can serve these to company, or have them around as a snack. They're also the perfect thing to serve as a stalling tactic if you have a guest who accidentally indicates she'll stay for longer than you had anticipated, and you didn't place a food order for her…"

Laughter filled the place, everyone knowing Charity was making a joke about herself.

Dale stuffed the rest of a biscuit in his mouth. "That tea is no match for coffee, but these biscuits are fantastic."

"Next we have a small salad dish…"

Devon watched the faces around him as Charity explained what came next: a sampling of a five-course meal, something she'd brought over from the Brink. Each dish was better than the last, so completely different to the things he was used to, and more delicious for it.

"She's got the plant life around here nailed," Penny said, for she and Emery, as fellow outsiders, had been squished in with the rest of Devon's pack. She munched through some sort of seed pancake. "If only she were a mage, we could really create some masterpieces together."

"You can just steal some of her magic for your spells," Emery said. "She's gotten the hang of it now, I hear."

"Well, yes, if Devon goes against my mother's *Sight* and stays with her, sure." Penny took a sip of a fruity, clear liquid in a blown glass goblet made especially for this dinner. The pack looked down at their hands. He'd told them of the session with Karen, and there were mixed views as to if he should believe it or not.

"Nice subtlety," Steve told her before winking.

Upon tasting the main dish, the First closed her eyes in utter delight, and a proud smile lit up her face.

All the feeling left Devon's body.

That was it. That smile was the nail in his coffin. Charity was *in*. This food, hands-down better than anyone else's—better than anything he'd ever tasted—would grant her admission into the family. She was officially the Third Arcana. Officially a member of the ruling party of a magical people held in the utmost respect in the Realm.

Officially on the road to lead a people and claim her mantle.

What the hell was he doing, contemplating tearing her away from this? How selfish could a guy be?

Karen had been wrong. The choice he faced wasn't against his heart. It was the easiest choice in the world—he would do anything to grant Charity a lifetime of happiness. Anything. If that meant walking away and leaving his heart behind, so be it. He'd live with his pain to see her smile.

But Karen had been right about something else: this went against everything he wanted. Because Charity was all he could ever want. He loved her with his whole person, now more than ever. To see her shine in her element was a rare treat that he would savor for the rest of his life. As she climbed the steps onto the platform where her family waited, she looked back at him, her smile bright, her eyes brighter. Even now, she thought of him.

He would do the same for her.

He ignored the pain and clapped along. Tonight, he'd say goodbye with his body.

Tomorrow would be the first day of the rest of their lives.

CHAPTER 34

"I DID IT!" Charity threw her arms around Devon, joy bubbling up through her and exploding all around her in the form of her magic. She'd mostly balanced it now, only needing help occasionally when a particularly powerful surge came through. "I won! I'm a complete outsider, I didn't know any of the fruits and veggies when I started, and still I won the whole thing." She couldn't smile big enough to express her excitement. Her father and grandmama, too, had been beside themselves pleased. "I earned a place here."

She unpeeled herself from Devon's front for a moment so she could lean back and look at his handsome face.

"Of course you did," he said, pride shining in his eyes. He traced her jaw with this thumb. "I knew you would."

"Was Dillon here? I don't remember seeing him," she said. Everyone else had already headed back to their lodgings, leaving Devon to wait for her.

"He and Macy..." Devon shrugged, an uncomfortable expression racing across his face. In a moment, it was gone. "You hungry?"

She frowned. Were Macy and Dillon having problems? Charity had let the competition consume her, not to mention the worry that it would be broken up at any moment by a flaming demon barreling through. Now that it was over, she needed to reconnect with her friends.

"No, I'm good," she said as he intertwined their fingers and led her out of the competition area. People smiled at her as she passed, congratulating her on her completely unexpected win. "I ate the food from the other competitors."

"Are you okay to just go home, or are you expected somewhere?" Devon asked.

She responded in the affirmative, and they turned the corner onto the cobblestone path that led to her temporary housing, but his choice of words stuck with her.

Home.

Karen's words came floating back to her: *"When you find your true home, you will know it."*

Night shrouded them as they ambled along the cobblestone path, the darkness brightened only by the dancing fairy lights above the hedges. Charity pushed in close to Devon, and he wrapped one of his big arms around her shoulders as she took in the beautiful scenery and well-maintained houses. Her dad's beautiful garden designs gave the place a peaceful serenity. The blooming flowers warmed her soul, something she'd never really thought flowers could do. The crawling vines, turning fences green, softened even the harsh boundaries.

But really, they were just gardens. Devon could have something like this at his house, surrounded as he was with nature. Now that they knew what was possible, the right gardener could probably enhance the natural beauty of his property.

No, the surroundings, beautiful as they were, weren't what made this place special. So what did?

My father. My grandmother. An entire village of people who want to get to know me. In the Brink, I only have a mother, and she ran out on me.

She slid her gaze to the ruggedly handsome man walking beside her with an easy, sure step and a powerful, robust body. A man who had been through hell and back to protect her. A man who she believed would do anything to make her happy.

She didn't just have a mother in the Brink, she had Devon. She had his pack. Hell, she even had Roger. Their loyalty was beyond anything she'd ever experienced. Beyond anything she might've read about in a book or seen on TV. It was real, and she'd be lost without them. She knew that now. They hadn't just saved her life—they'd saved *her*. They'd given her a bigger picture. She wasn't alone anymore—hadn't been since she'd stumbled out of that vampire-infested house without a clue.

When push came to shove, she'd be lost without

Devon. He held her heart. Home for her wasn't a *where*. It was a *who*. It was Devon and all the people associated with him.

How did that fit with what Karen had *Seen*? Was Charity supposed to convince Devon and his pack to stay in the Flush? Because the guardians were entrenched. They weren't leaving. Which was madness, because she wasn't sure they were really *living*. Their whole genetic makeup was rooted in protecting others, and yet here they stayed, practicing fighting with no risk, and doodling around with hobbies. She knew it helped their balance, but so would battling a foe or throwing dirt clods. After getting even a small hold on her magic, she wasn't sure her dad's explanation of the natural releases really jibed. It sounded made up, like it was a placeholder for their real magical balance: protecting others. Their job. The root of their freaking name.

They were denying their natural urges to kick ass so they could play with gardens and make tables for superfluous, though enjoyable, competitions. It was incredibly frustrating. They were wasting their talents!

And since she was officially a member with high status, now she could raise that concern. It was about time.

What had happened to her people?

"What?" Devon asked, probably hearing her scoff.

"Nothing. What are you guys up to tomorrow? What do you think about a picnic—"

"Fantastic, Third," a beaming woman said as she passed. She squeezed Charity's shoulder. "The best I can remember."

"Thank you," Charity said, smiling back. The woman walked on without seeming to notice Devon.

Charity frowned, glancing back at the woman. It wasn't like these people to be rude. At least not in an obvious way. Their rudeness was hidden in nuances that Charity usually missed or didn't understand.

"Do you know that woman?" she asked Devon.

"No, why?"

"You might've been a ghost to her. Is all the fornicating between your pack and the fae giving you guys a bad name?"

He shrugged, apparently unconcerned, but his muscles bunched for just a moment. Tension worked into his shoulders before he sighed and released it.

She'd opened her mouth to ask about it when he said, "You really outdid yourself, you know." He squeezed her and turned the corner to the lane that ran in front of her house. "Some of those flavors tasted weird, and still it was the best food you've ever made."

She snuggled into him. "Thanks. It's probably silly in the grand scheme of things, but I was stressing really hard about it. I just want to earn my place, you know? Demons might be infiltrating the Brink, and Lucifer himself might be waiting for me to leave this place, but for once, I just wanted to show I belonged somewhere."

"You do." He squeezed her again. "You do belong

here."

Kairi stood by the front door. She offered a thumbs-up, something she'd learned from Charity and did constantly now.

"Excellent work, Third." She pulled the door open, giving Devon a nod in hello.

Charity was relieved to see it. "Thanks," she said, as much for the inclusive greeting as the compliment. Devon guided her in front of him, his hand on her lower back.

"I like that," Kairi said to Devon, stalling him.

He caught Charity's hand to keep her close. "What's that?"

"You let her enter first. Or you hold the door open for her. All of you shifter males do that, it seems. All except the dimwitted middle-aged wolf with the scar."

Charity huffed out a laugh. She meant Dale.

"They call it being a gentleman in the Brink," he told her. "It's a sign of respect."

She nodded at him, turning back to the street. "I like it. It made me feel special when the lion did it for me earlier. I shouldn't have punched him."

"Why—" Devon shook his head and kept walking through the door. "Never mind. I don't want to know."

Charity shut the door behind them. "I meant to ask her why she is still hanging around when I have a firm grasp on my magic now."

"She's your assistant, isn't she? Set to guard you?" Devon gathered her into his arms and traced her jaw with his lips. "Though how she could protect you better than you could protect yourself, I don't know."

"We can't always protect ourselves, as you well know from the journey here. But I don't need her. I have you," she whispered, letting her eyes flutter closed. "And no one mentioned an assistant to me."

"They probably did through their bodily sign language."

She sighed as he kissed down her neck, his lips leaving a trail of fire across her skin. "I'm going to need a tutor in that, I think. It's exhausting trying to figure out what everyone is really trying to say."

He swung her up into his arms and carried her into the bedroom. "You'll get it eventually."

He laid her down on the bed and leaned over her, running his hand along the inside of her thigh, pushing up her dress as he did so.

"You have more faith in me than I do—*Hmm*, Devon." She arched back as he slipped his fingers into her panties. "Did you like the dress?"

"I loved the dress. You were a vision tonight, baby. I couldn't take my eyes off you."

She turned her back to him, and he unbuttoned the fabric. A moment later, the dress lay on the floor. She'd thought the dress a little weird herself, but given what he'd just said, she didn't plan to mention that.

"Make love to me, Devon," she whispered, pushing his robe over his head and tossing it to the floor.

"Your wish is my command."

She expected his lips on hers to be hungry. To celebrate her win and exalt in her joy. Instead, he was slow and reverent, touching her as delicately as if she were one of the china cups she'd served tea in.

He moved between her thighs and wrapped her in his arms, running his length along her wetness. Her breathing turned heavy, and she arched toward him, catching him just right. He plunged in to the hilt, gloriously filling her to bursting.

She groaned against his lips, savoring the feel of him. Soaking in the rightness of his body within hers. She was certain he was *the one*. He was the last man there would ever be for her.

"I love you," she said, and a tear slipped down her face.

"I will love you forever, Charity," he replied, his voice filled with emotion. "Never doubt me. The love I feel for you will never dim. I will always do what's best for you. I will always protect you."

She stilled, her arms around him, somewhat confused by the gravity in his tone. But a moment later, the moment swept her away.

He pulled back and pushed forward, so good at sensing what she needed. He thrust again, and she arched to receive him, desperate now, wanting all of him. Wanting his body to imprint on her as heavily as his heart had.

His arms held her close. She clung to him, swinging up her hips to meet his downward thrusts. Her labored breathing rang through the room. Her body wound up, impossibly tight.

"Yes, Devon," she said, ecstasy washing through her, pulling her under.

He crashed into her again and again, his control obviously slippery, hers nonexistent.

She wanted more of him, all of him. She swiveled her hips and moaned as he pounded into her. The pleasure was so sharp that it cut. So heartfelt that it nearly tore her in two.

Without warning, bliss slammed into her. She cried out from the onslaught of the orgasm. Wave after wave of glorious pleasure rolled through her, lifting her to a place where there were no words, just feeling.

Devon groaned, shuddering. He thrust one last time, and another barrage of sensations made the world go fuzzy. She clung to him and squeezed her eyes shut, her teeth clenched and her body tight, riding the tidal wave of pleasure.

Devon relaxed on top of her and buried his face in her neck. She kept her arms around him, loving this feeling of absolute certainty that had engulfed her being.

Finally, she knew what she wanted.

Finally, she had found her home.

Contented, she breathed a deep sigh, closed her eyes, and drifted into a deep sleep. Tomorrow, she'd finally pay a visit to the shifters' lodgings, and together they'd figure out what came next for all of them.

CHAPTER 35

Devon twirled the strand of reddish-brown hair between his fingers. Inky night could be seen from the window, the glow from the moon soft upon the ground. Charity's deep, even breathing spoke to her contentment.

After a small nap, they'd gone for round two, and immediately moved into round three. He'd wanted to savor every moment and get his fill.

He was an idiot. He'd never be able to get his fill of Charity. It was stupid to even try.

He breathed in the smell of her, floral, spicy, and feminine. It occurred to him that she embodied this place better than the people within it did. Most of the time she was kind, gentle, open-minded, and willing to compromise—but when she flipped and turned on her aggression, watch out. She was a perfect storm.

He loved her more than words could say. More than he'd thought possible. It was why this was so damn hard.

He kissed her on the forehead and his heart broke. Still, he forced himself to roll out of bed. Even if the *Seer* hadn't advised this path for him, he knew it was the right thing to do. She was destined for greatness—for royalty and leading her people back to their purpose. He couldn't let her strap herself to him and waste this opportunity. He was a mid-level alpha relegated to one part of the world. It was no place for a girl like her.

She belonged here in the Realm. In the Flush.

His eyes stung, tears threatening. He wanted to punch something. He half wished Hallen was waiting outside. One last shot at that asshole would at least give him an outlet.

Kairi offered him a sad smile when he let himself out.

"Don't you get a break?" Devon asked her, willing his feet to move. Willing himself to follow through with this…with leaving *her*.

"Not tonight," Kairi said softly, looking out over the quiet path. "You know, I could have stopped Charity from fighting you on the battlefield last week. I was there in time to intervene, and duty said I should've. Instead, I watched. Fascinated."

"That right?"

She nodded, scanning the path like she was ready for an attack. "I've watched how your pack has handled being treated lesser. Like something that should be banished but propriety dictates that it can't."

"From the sidelines, huh?"

"Yes." If she was embarrassed by that fact, she gave no sign. "I've watched how the Third handles all the attention. It makes her uncomfortable. She must have been a loner in the past, while your pack is used to being respected. It is a role reversal, this journey, is it not?"

He smirked. "You could say that."

"Yet she rose to the occasion, and so did you."

He frowned, fighting the desire to go back in and say goodbye to Charity one last time. "How did we rise to the occasion? We've been like ghosts."

"Yes. Against your nature, you accepted your position here. I've seen you battle, in real settings, not just practice. There is a ferocity in you that calls to me. It begs me to join you. When Charity fought, it took everything in my power to keep myself from running to her side. Yet, day to day, when you were so badly disrespected, you held your peace. You grieve for your lost, but you hold your heads high. It must've taken a great deal of self-restraint."

"We aren't animals; we merely turn into them." The words carried a little of the bite he'd held back.

"You are fierce warriors that can display self-restraint for someone you value highly. It was noticed. It has lent Miss Charity, the Third Arcana, more status, if that were possible. As has your prowess on the battlefield. You have helped her more than I think you realize."

"That was our duty."

She laughed softly. "Exactly. You have shown us what it means to follow one's duty for the greater good."

He shook his head, confused as to what she was getting at.

It was no longer his problem.

"We're leaving. Take care of her." He stepped away before stopping, pain ripping him apart. "She won't take this well. Please, comfort her. Tell her I didn't leave because of her, it was..." He didn't know if he was allowed to tell Kairi about what the *Seer* had told him. So he just said, "It was Fate."

Before he could take it back, Kairi said, "Fate. What a bullshit meddler, eh? Always screwing things up."

Some emotion he couldn't place rang in her tone. A spark lit her eyes. Again, he wasn't sure what she was getting at. It struck him that this confusion was something Charity experienced all the time around the fae. Around his pack, too.

"Help her," he said, starting away.

"That is my duty, and I will perform it as you would," she called after him.

The others waited for him outside the cabins, all but Steve in shifter form. The two mages waited off to the side, and the Red Prophet stood with them, dressed in a bright pink robe.

"We're out," he said, making a circle in the air with his pointer finger.

"They're not going." Steve tilted his head at the mages.

Devon didn't really care, so he nodded.

"But she is," Penny said, tilting her elbow to indicate

the Red Prophet.

Devon hesitated. "Why?"

"Without me, your blood will make the elves a lovely new print of wallpaper," she said with a grin. "I know the way and, more importantly, when to take which path. In return, you will feed me. I can handle the fire; you just need to make the kill."

"We'll be in animal form most of the time," Devon said, ducking into the cabins to make sure nothing important would be left behind. A small square of white stood out on the table. A folded letter of some kind.

Devon left it and backed out. Someone wanted to say goodbye to Charity, and since they couldn't do it in person, they'd written a note. Hopefully, whoever it was had said something about Dillon—shared his memory in some way.

Guilt ate through Devon's middle. He shouldn't be doing it like this. This felt sneaky and dirty. But maybe if he was a dick, it would be easier for her to let him go.

"This is the right way," the Red Prophet said when Devon rejoined them.

"That's going to get old," Steve murmured.

"I didn't tell anyone I was going, either. Boy, will that piss off Her Highness." The Red Prophet laughed, an insane cackle. "Her perfect little world is about to be cracked wide open. She knew this day would come. I was there when she had her quest. I wrote it all down. She's worked to fortify her walls, but puppies will eat through anything."

"How old are you?" Penny asked incredulously.

"Old as dirt, and about as clean. Most of us die in battle. Or did. Lately, no one dies at all. I haven't had a funeral cake in years! They're my favorite, too. The cooks think it is in bad taste to make one without someone dying. Our population is bursting at the seams. Many of us have left, trying to find a little excitement. No one told you that, did they? No one talks about those who leave. They are shunned, much like outsiders. You'd know something of the latter. But our people are out there, waiting for the guardians to leave the Flush. The tides are turning. The magic holding everyone hostage has been pierced with holes. Soon, it will be broken." She held her hand to her ear and cocked her head. "Can you hear it?"

"She's a nutter and my mother is going to hate her," Penny said, backing away.

The Red Prophet cackled.

"Whatever. Let's go. This isn't our problem anymore." Devon met eyes with Steve, wondering why he was slow to change.

"Can I talk to you for a minute?" Steve asked quietly, turning his back to the others.

Devon stepped away with him, feeling Charity's magic seep through their link, starting to change his mind. He wondered if he'd still feel her even when he wasn't in the Realm. He hoped so.

"You sure about this?" Steve asked quietly, like a beta would question his alpha. "Karen has been wrong before. I heard about a pizza incident, for example…"

Devon's guts churned for a different reason. He'd have to make adjustments when he got back. He'd taken big losses on this trip. Life-changing losses.

"Yes," he said. "This is the right decision. We don't belong here. They made that clear to us from the start. This is her shot at a good life, Steve. I'm not going to take that away from her. None of us are."

Respect shone in Steve's eyes. He nodded. "I just wanted to make sure you'd thought it through. She's going to be as mad as a hatter, and it'll be your fault if she blows shit up."

Devon's gut kept churning. "I wish she'd blow stuff up, but I have a feeling she'll react differently. You didn't see her in her mom's house. But she's a survivor. She'll pull through, and she'll rise to the best she can be."

"Her future starts in"—the Red Prophet looked at the gold-crusted moon—"some time."

Steve changed shape, and Devon followed.

Her future started now.

CHAPTER 36

CHARITY REACHED ACROSS the bed, only coming completely awake when she felt the coldness. She frowned and rolled onto her side, glimpsing the empty space that felt like it had been vacant for hours. Where would Devon have gone? She didn't know of anything going on in the village, and it only would've taken a moment for him to order breakfast.

She sat up and rubbed her eyes before stretching. Her body felt so gloriously sore. He'd given her all he had last night, and she'd lapped it up like a thirsty dog. She could go for another round this morning.

Kairi waited outside, and though she stood straight and tall, her eyes were lined with fatigue.

"Hey," Charity said as Hallen walked up. If he weren't too buttoned-up to grin, she got the sense he'd be beaming at her. "What's the good word?"

"What word?" Kairi asked.

"What?" Hallen said.

"Never mind. Hey, did you see Devon leave?"

"Yes." Kairi stared straight ahead. "He walked toward the shifter cabins earlier this morning."

"Cabins..." Charity murmured, staring off in that direction. "Did he say...anything?"

Kairi set her jaw, but didn't comment. Hallen practically glowed with satisfaction.

A dark premonition crawled up Charity's spine. Before she knew it, she was jogging down the cobblestone path.

Turning the corner, she caught Kairi and Hallen out of the corner of her eye, following her silently. They were nearly as slick as shifters.

"Third, hello!" a man called from his front door as Charity passed. "I look forward to your—"

She didn't politely stop to hear the rest of his words.

She *really* hoped she was overreacting. That the past was throwing shadows where there were none. She really hoped there was a good reason for Devon to have left her bed in the middle of the night. So why didn't Kairi feel comfortable talking about it?

"You have my best interests at heart, don't you, Kairi?" she called out as she jogged.

"Of course, Third."

"If a big mistake was in progress, you'd say something, wouldn't you?"

"Yes, Third. That is my job."

"A big mistake is in—" Hallen started.

Charity didn't bother glancing back. She wasn't asking him. She still didn't know why he kept hanging around. He didn't make himself useful like Kairi did, nor was he on the same fighting level as either of them.

She no longer needed his help with her magic.

Another dark thought wafted through her mind, stemming from her conversations with her grandmama. Little comments about suitable matches. About what status meant and how to achieve and maintain it. Approved smiles and knowing nods whenever Hallen accompanied Charity places...

Did her grandmama expect her to accept Hallen as a match? Not a chance. She had a love, and she would not settle for any other.

Period.

Devon had better be in the guest house. Or on the battlefield. He'd better not have run out on her in the middle of the night.

This had better be deeply ingrained paranoia.

"Which way?" she asked at the other end of the village, and guilt ran through her. She should know how to get to the pack blindfolded. She'd neglected them.

"Right," Kairi said. When they reached the next corner, she said without prompting, "Left."

The houses grew smaller and smaller, and Charity's guilt mounted until she reached what looked like a collection of shanties. They were neglected, tiny dwellings shoved out of the way. The gardens were being beautified, her father's signature touch obvious, so that was something, but other than that, they were barely fit for wild dogs.

Charity laughed sardonically as she registered the stillness of the ramshackle cabins. They felt abandoned.

Her heart pushed up into her throat. Tears clouded her vision.

"Wild dogs," she said softly, stalling outside of the closest shanty. The door stood open, but she already knew it would be deserted. "You put them in the backyard, like dogs. They were your guests, and you sequestered them here, in a shithole, while you celebrated the woman they risked everything to get to safety. And here you talk about politeness. About doing what's proper. About the *right way* of doing things."

Charity turned and threw out her hand.

"This is not the *right way* of doing things," she yelled, and the first tear rolled down her face. "When I was in a tough time, they put me in Devon's house. He bought groceries, protected me, welcomed me into his pack…and look how you've treated them in return. They brought you the Second's daughter, and you put them *here*!"

She marched inside as another tear fell. Then a third.

"Why would they want to stay when they were welcomed with this sort of red carpet?" she said to herself. There was barely any furniture. A teeny communal kitchen, a common area with a little table shoved in the corner. Doors led to other sleeping areas, in which dingy mattresses littered the ground. All empty. The robes the shifters had borrowed from this place lay in piles or folded and cast aside. Left behind. Like her.

That was when the strange hollowness inside her

finally worked into her awareness. The wrongness that she now realized had fired the paranoia. She could no longer feel the back-and-forth dance of her magic and Devon's. Had Penny reversed her spell?

Distance.

The thought curled out of her mind. An assurance greeted it.

The connection Penny had forged didn't work with distance.

"No." Her stomach rolled. "Please no, Devon. Please…" She was begging. Pleading.

But he wasn't there to hear her. None of them were.

A stark white square stood out on the dingy brown table. Paper.

She snatched it up, fumbling to open it.

It was from Macy, written in a clumsy hand.

Charity's eyes flew over the words, and guilt threatened to consume her. She sank to her knees. Sobs heaved from her middle.

"Dillon was killed," she choked out, her hands shaking so badly that she couldn't read the words. "Dillon—"

"Third." Kairi knelt by her side, her hand on Charity's shoulder. "Are you unwell?"

"Don't I look unwell?" Charity screamed, shaking the letter in Kairi's face. "Dillon died getting me here. He sacrificed his life for me. Why wouldn't they tell me? Why—"

But if Charity had made the short trek to their shanties, she would've seen Macy's grief. She would've known. And she would've seen the horrible conditions they were being forced to endure.

She could've fixed this. She could've organized a candlelight vigil for Dillon, and put them somewhere nicer.

"What a horrible bitch I've been," she said to no one, the tears coming quickly. "What horrible bitches my people are—putting guests in a place like this."

Was her not recognizing Dillon's death why her father, or why grandmama, ignored it also? They surely knew. Charity was in a daze when she came in—they were not. Why had they not honored the death of a man who fought bravely to keep their family alive? To bring the Third Arcana home?

"What is up with this place?" she seethed, guilt and anger turning her stomach. She rounded on Kairi and Hallen. "What are you hiding from? How could you possibly call yourself warriors? What do you do all day, but play with wooden swords and pretend at happiness? This is happiness?" She flung her arms wide. "Treating people like this resonates with you all? This is the identity of your people?"

Kairi's face turned red. Hallen raised his chin.

Two fast steps and she punched Hallen in the nose. He staggered back.

She laughed at nothing, and then threw up.

"Let's get you up," Kairi said.

"He's left me, hasn't he." It wasn't a question.

Charity's limbs felt like they weighed a hundred

pounds each. This was much worse than the situation with her magic. She'd had Devon to help with that. Now, Devon had left. He'd left her, just like her mother, then John—

"What is it about me?" she whispered, tears hitting the floor. Hallen staggered out, holding his face. "What is it about me that pushes everyone away?"

"My allegiance is to you, Third," Kairi said quietly. "To you alone. Your well-being is my duty, and thanks to the shifters, I know more about duty than I was ever taught by my peers. So I am not breaking my duty when I tell you that he didn't want to leave you. It was killing him. I could see it in every line in his face, every movement of his body. He did it to help you. To give you a fresh start. He thinks you'll be better off without him. They endured all this, without complaint, to help you. And your father saw it all. He internalized it. If you need an ally, turn to him. He will give you the world, Third. He has hidden his guilt, but it fills him still…and so does his longing to see the Brink again. It is there, waiting for you to call upon it." She paused and tapped Charity's head. "But if you plan to remake the mold of our people, your grandmama cannot get wind of it."

Charity tried to push back her grief, and her insecurity, and her abandonment issues, and focus on the problem at hand.

"What?"

She'd probably need another moment.

"Internalize your suffering, speak to your father,

and create a plan."

"A plan for what?" Charity said stupidly.

Kairi tapped Charity's head again. "We are warriors, Third, or we are meant to be. We do not curl up and die. We fight until our last breath. Decide your own fate, and *take it*."

Kairi straightened up, her piece apparently said, and left the room. Charity's heart ached for Dillon. For Macy, who had probably been raw with grief, wondering if Charity would come and speak with her. For Devon, who'd forced himself to walk away from their love.

Charity dizzied when she stood, and she realized she was still crying. Sobbing, actually. The pain cut down so deep that it felt like she was hemorrhaging inside.

"How could he do this?" She hugged herself around the middle, trying to grab on to Kairi's words, but the sentiment proved slippery. "He knew my struggle with being abandoned by my loved ones. He hugged me and told me he—"

She realized he hadn't assured her he would stay. No, he'd assured her he would do what was best for her.

That could mean a whole lot of things, subject to the speaker's opinion. *His* opinion.

That sneaky bastard. That *Seer* had put him up to this, Charity would bet anything. No wonder he'd never told her what that woman had said. He hadn't wanted Charity to blast him through the wall. He hadn't told her about Dillon, he hadn't told her what he planned on doing, and he certainly hadn't asked her what *she* wanted. He'd taken her life into his hands and treated her like a puppet.

Just like everyone else was trying to do.

Anger flash-boiled her blood.

Kairi was right—Charity wasn't the type to curl up and die. She knew who her home was. She knew what she wanted. And she no longer gave two shits about the *Seer* and her stupid ball.

It was time to take her life into her own hands. It was time to write her own destiny.

CHAPTER 37

Charity stalked out of the shanty, rage stretching her skin.

"'Don't tell Grandmama,' is that what you said?" She stared at Kairi. "Well, I have to be honest, it'll be pretty hard to hide this…"

She turned around and pulled forth a surge of power. Sparks lit up along the sides of the shanty right before the air concussed. Walls blew inward. The roof crashed down on top, exposing another catacomb of the horrible structures behind it.

Charity destroyed another one, but this time, she shot forth a ball of electricity and power. It slammed into a wall and then exploded in all directions, a blast of heated air rocking Charity back on her heels.

Wood burst into flame. Sparks flew in all directions.

One more surge of magic and the whole thing was down, flames licking old wood and catching like wildfire. The rest would be nothing but ash soon.

This time, she didn't have Reagan to calm the flames down. Hopefully they had buckets.

"Third, what—Why…" Hallen couldn't get the

words out. His eyes were saucers. "They were animals. They—"

She stalked toward him before pulling back her fist and delivering a punch. His head snapped back and his heels saw the sky.

"They are gentleman and ladies, and they are my friends. They deserved better than you gave them." Charity walked on. "Where is my father?"

"He'll be in his favorite shed, probably, or his house, Third," Kairi said, walking by her side.

People called out to them as they walked by, but she ignored them, intent on her mission. Her father was in his temporary shed, a nicer place than the shifters had called home.

No, not home. A resting place until she was settled.

He looked up, startled. "Charity, darling, what—"

"Devon is gone, did you know?"

His sag was slight, but the fact that she noticed it at all meant he was gravely disappointed. "No, but I wondered. I spoke to him yesterday, hoping to impress upon him the remorse he would feel…" He sighed and stood, coming around his table to clutch her upper arms. He leaned forward to look into her eyes. "He wanted the best for you. He decided that it would be best if you were here, with your people."

She felt her lower lip tremble under his supportive gaze. She shrugged his hands away, needing to hang on to her anger with everything she had. "Well, that's the thing about modern women. We don't like our men deciding what's best for us without our consent."

"I understand, honey, but these are the guardian lands, and—"

"Dad, I am glad I met you. I would like a relationship with you. But Devon is my home. He brightens up all my dark places. His pack, to me, makes sense. I belong with them. But there's more to it than that. We, as a people, belong with them. I know you can feel that. You've *said* you can feel that. They fight like we're meant to fight. I mean...we're *guardians*, right? Why are you called a guardian when you spend your days messing around with plants? Aren't there gardener fae? Or table-designing fae? We should be playing with swords to get our kicks, not thorny flowers. We've lost our way."

He stared down at her for a silent beat. Footsteps, barely heard, sounded right before Halvor gently knocked at the open door.

Her father's eyes darted back and forth between them. "What have you done?"

The knock sounded again. She shrugged.

"Yes, Halvor?" her father said.

"Second—" Halvor cut off whatever he'd been about to say when he caught sight of her. He composed himself, if a rock could be said to compose itself.

"Go ahead, Halvor. I doubt she feels bad for whatever she's done."

"The guest houses, Second. They are...destroyed."

Her father's eyebrow ticked up. "Destroyed? How—

ever did you do that?"

"I have magic. If you use it right, it blows things up," she said.

Her dad's smile beamed brighter. "I see."

"Do you?" Anger overcame her again. Her dad took a step back. "What sort of people treat their guests like garbage? How does that look on you as a people? Sorry—on *us* as a people?"

A small crease formed between his brows.

"Did people ignore them?" she asked, thinking about the woman who hadn't noticed Devon the night before. She was an asshole for not having picked up on this sooner. Her people were all assholes for thinking this behavior was right.

An embarrassed look crossed her father's face, gone so fast that Charity thought she'd imagined it.

"And all this halvsie stuff?" she continued. "You can't treat people like this, Dad. You *can't*. Right now the shifters—and a lot of people, I think—regard the guardians reverently, as warriors. They even call you warrior fae! If they knew you treated people like this, hiding in your natural nook far away from trouble while the elves torture people for info and the—"

He touched her shoulder and his eyes took on a keen edge. "What was that?"

"What was…what?"

"The elves…"

She frowned at him. How could he not know?

She explained what Emery had told them about the

elves' recent history of torturing and sometimes killing for information. Her father's brow lowered as she explained the elves had been randomly grabbing people to question.

"This is pretty common knowledge," she finished. "Ask Emery—though I guess he left. But he knows exactly what the elves are capable of. He put himself at great risk to lead our party through the wilds. If you can get hold of Vlad, I'm sure he'd love to fill your ears on the state of things. I mean…you *live* here—you should know all this."

Her dad's gaze zipped behind her, and something new moved within his eyes. A smoldering light, of sorts, heating to flame. Halvor had stood to the side of the space and listened intently.

Her dad's lips pinched together. It meant he was disappointed. "Thank you, Charity, for all you have said. Now, if you will leave me to speak with Halvor—"

"Yeah, sure. No problem. But, to be honest, I came here to give you a hug goodbye. I'm leaving—"

"No." She nearly snapped to attention, such was the force of his bark. "You will not leave."

Thankfully, she had a lot of experience rebuffing a powerful alpha.

"Sorry, Dad, but you can't stop me. Neither can your manservant-assassin. Unless you try to kill me, that is, but if you do that, you should remember that I can rain down lightning. I'll take your best fighters to the grave with me. We halvsies can be unpredictable fuckers."

Her father's eyebrow ticked upward again. That eyebrow could convey so many things. She hadn't a clue about half of them.

More footsteps. Halvor quickly ducked out to allow Charity's grandmama to fill the doorway.

"Oh, Charity," her grandmother said, out of breath and pale-faced. "Yes. I wondered… I've heard word that the guest houses are on fire. Blown to bits."

"Yes, Mother," Romulus said, a twinkle in his eyes. "We're planning some improvements."

"We're…" She looked back and forth between Charity and Romulus. "We didn't discuss—"

"I also need to speak with you about some logistical issues." He stepped closer and lowered his hand onto Charity's shoulder. "Charity and I need to leave within the next few days. We'll need supplies and to arrange adequate coverage for my governing duties. Charity was not able to finish her business with the Alpha Shifter before he moved on. I will, of course, need to chaperone her to the human lands."

"You're… You…"

"First," someone said, also out of breath. "The Red Prophet! She's gone!"

"No, dear. Check the trees," Charity's grandmother replied, annoyed. "Or that crawlspace in her house. She got stuck there last fall, remember?"

"She left a note, First. She's gone with the Alpha Shifter. She has decided to spend her days in the Brink, where the sky is blue and the ocean is purple."

Charity grimaced. The Red Prophet might be a little disappointed when she made it to the beach. Unless, of course, she got her hands on some acid.

"There." Romulus nodded triumphantly. "Now it cannot be denied. I will escort Charity to the Brink, both to ascertain the whereabouts of the Red Prophet and so that Charity can complete her business."

"We won't have Vlad's protection this time," Charity said, thinking out loud. "It'll be dangerous, and that's if the elves or demons don't find us."

"Elves or demons bothering our kind?" the First scoffed. "A *custodes* needing a vampire's protection? Ridiculous. We *are* the protection."

"Is this like when an old—I mean, out-of-touch person tries to figure out the internet?" Charity grinned. "They just don't understand things have changed and someone has to explain it?"

Her dad pressed his lips together, which meant he was holding back laughter.

Her grandmother's eyes flashed fire. "No," she said, taking a step back. A strange sort of heaviness pressed down upon the room. The desire to stay within this beautiful, natural place intensified. "I forbid it. The Flush is our home. Our people would do well to stay within it. There is nothing for us out there. We are not the royal guard, as the elves would like. We are not another species' doormat. We are the *custodes*, and we will decide our fate."

Music rang in those words. The will behind them tugged on Charity. The hollowness in her middle felt like a vast chasm.

Romulus sighed, his expressiveness not like him.

"You remember when you were away the last time, darling." The First stepped toward Romulus. "When you were in that tiny cottage in the human lands with that rosy-faced woman. You remember how much you missed it here."

Confusion stole over Romulus's expression. The air in the room thickened. The desire to head home, straighten up everything, and settle in for the long haul nearly stole Charity's breath. It was a feeling she'd never had before. Certainly not in Santa Cruz, and not even where she grew up, where Walt always sullied the definition of home. But here, now, she couldn't think of living any other place.

She was being manipulated somehow.

"Yes. She did have rosy cheeks, like she was blushing every time she smiled. It was endearing." His brow furrowed. "I'd nearly forgotten. How did you know that?"

"You talked about her a great deal after you returned." The First smiled, her condescension ringing loudly. She didn't much care for Charity's mom, that was clear. She was human, after all.

The air continued to push down on Charity. The desire to put down deep roots twisted in her middle, nearly as strong as the desire to protect her world, at all costs, from those who would rip it away. From outsiders.

Suddenly it made sense why that woman wouldn't look at Devon. Why the pack was pushed out to the edges of the community, out of the way. This feeling, which threatened to sweep her away, made that treatment more comfortable. Only one thing kept her head, and it wasn't her head at all. Devon had left with her heart. He had a place in her soul. No magic could touch that.

"This is false," Charity said, anger inspiring her stubbornness. She gritted her teeth. "This feeling is false." She stared accusingly at her grandmama. "Are you doing this? Can guardians create magic that messes with people feelings?"

"No, darling," Romulus said, confusion still weighing down his features. "That magic is mostly legend. None of my family has had it in many generations. No, what you are feeling is the call of these lands. It is powerful. You've been ensnared, as we all have. Mother is right. Maybe—"

Shaking her head, Charity took a step back. It wasn't these lands. This was magic, it had to be. And given that Charity could tell Romulus was telling the truth, it had to be from the First. But why was she feeling it now and hadn't before? Surely her grandmama would want to tempt her to push Devon away.

And then it hit her. Like a Mack truck.

"You kept me busy, and away from the shifters, as

much as possible," Charity said to her grandmama. "You hinted at your displeasure at them seeing me in the evenings. That wasn't because their magic would incite mine—it was because the shifter magic circumvents your magic somehow, doesn't it? On the battle yard, when Devon blasted his magic out, people awoke as though from a dream. I saw it. People begged to fight them. Begged to bed them. Was that because of sexual taboo or promiscuity, or because they wanted to feel normal? They wanted the fire that the shifter magic allows them to feel?"

"You insolent child—" her grandmama started.

"Devon and I had a magical link. His magic was constantly with me. Constantly protecting me from this...whatever this is. Only now that he's gone—that his magic is gone from me—do I feel it." Charity laughed and shook her head. "You're keeping people here, aren't you? You're basically trapping them here with your magic. What are you hiding from?"

"I never mentioned the cottage," Romulus said softly, almost like he was talking to himself, working something out. "Purposely. I didn't want you to know she was poor. How did you know..."

His voice trailed away. Pieces of the puzzle snapped into place. He studied the First.

"Those that have left...they've mostly been elders," he said. "Those that left had witnessed our history outside of this place, instead of just hearing about it. Those that have stayed are unnecessarily tight-lipped about the shifters. About why we stay here. About what happened to Grandmother and Grandfather in the royal palace." He shook his head slowly. "Tell me you aren't manipulating your people, Mother. Tell me Charity is way off base."

The First brought herself up regally. "It was decided. After your grandmother and grandfather were slaughtered in the royal palace, and I was newly in charge, my councilors agreed—we would gather our people together and live here, away from influence. Away from the unnecessary danger thrust upon us by those selfish, conniving elves. My magic was just blossoming at that time. My powers to sway my people were just manifesting. We all agreed that it was Fate. A divine nudge. I could protect us all. I could save us all. And so I did. Those that didn't agree left, yes, that is true. And some younger who slipped away without my knowledge. But this is for the greater good. Keeping my magic hidden was for the greater good—everyone agreed! And here we've lived in harmony. In balance."

"In boredom. Withering," Charity said. "Cut off from your one true purpose."

Romulus didn't seem to hear Charity. "But how did your magic reach me in the human lands?" His voice was wispy. He didn't want to accept the obvious.

"You are the Second. Your duty is here. You made a connection, your quest was fulfilled, and it was time you came home. End of story." The First pushed her hair off her face indignantly.

"And I suppose the advisors covered for you when you were gone," Romulus said. "I suppose they helped through all these long years to lie to our people, and hold them hostage, as you were clearly doing me."

"We are leaders, Romulus. We have a duty to our people."

"That duty is not lying, Mother. It is not drugging them with magic. It is not hiding from the ruling power in fear. In...*cowardice*. What you have done—what you are doing—is against our laws. Hiding magic is a punishable offense, especially magic such as this. How you kept it from us...from me..."

His mouth opened and closed like a fish's. He was, truly, at a loss. That much Charity could read.

"What did you expect me to do, Romulus?" the First said in a lowered tone. "I was nineteen and my parents had just died. Been killed, if you must know. Assassinated. My world was ripped out from under me. My magic was surging, battering me. Our people's numbers had been steadily falling, and after that bloodbath at the palace, going through us to get to the elf royalty, they were nearly cut in half. I saw friends die. I held them in my arms as they took their last breath. Something had to be done. Why else do you think the council crafted this plan and still, to this day, follow through? Our numbers now are higher than they've ever been in history. Our youth are growing up in peace and harmony, with long, happy lives in front of them. Because of me, they have futures. Because of me, we have a community. A growing, prospering community. This is what is best for our people."

Romulus blew out a sigh and shook his head. "Maybe it *was*, Mother. But times have changed. And clearly, it is time to assess that change for myself. *Without* your influence."

His nostrils flared and he turned to Charity, his movements precise, his anger probably about to blow his head off.

"Charity, darling, I am so very sorry. For all of this. Things…are not as they appear. As they should be. I beg of you, give me a couple days. I must speak to the advisors. I must formulate a plan. Then I *will* accompany you into the human lands. I would like to meet with the shifters. I would like to see what has become of the worlds in our absence. It is time."

"No, Romulus, I forbid—"

Romulus held up his hand, silencing his mother. "I understand that you acted in good faith, Mother, but now we must see if the people will forgive you. We must see if they still want to be led by you. That is our way, as you well know. The punishment will fit the crime, and the people will decide how severe that crime was. It is they who have been beguiled, after all."

Charity stood, struck mute. She had no idea, in coming here, that this would happen. That she would, single-handedly, uncover old wounds and deep secrets. That she might be responsible for the upheaval of the guardians, or even pulling her father out of the Flush.

"When you find your true home, you will know it. And with that home you must stay so that others of your kind will stay with you."

It was all so clear now. This had been her job all along. This had been her duty. She was tasked with goading the guardians—the warrior fae—out of the Flush so that they would join the magical world once again. Maybe her grandmama's fate was to grow back the numbers, and now, teamed with the shifters, perhaps they could sustain them. But regardless, Charity was the catalyst to push them toward their true purpose. And Devon had been Charity's tool in doing so. He'd shielded her when she was weak, and then pushed her to action when she was strong. They were working as a team, even now.

Devon was her true home, and she'd be damned if she'd lose it.

CHAPTER 38

"We've got incoming, Second," Halvor said, fitted expertly in the middle of their small group as they traveled the wide, manicured path through what Emery had described as a highway through the dead center of the Realm. The place everyone who was anyone walked.

Until now, he'd only set foot there once, before he was banned from the Realm.

Three lithe creatures walked toward them, practically dancing along the path. Their arms swished one way, their toes flipped a little when they raised their feet, and their hair flared out behind them without any wind. Elves. If a children's parade had followed behind them, complete with dragons and unicorns, it wouldn't have seemed out of place.

"They are *sojets*, nothing more," Romulus said softly.

"What are so-jets?" Charity hadn't quite gotten the sounds right.

"Elf foot soldiers," Halvor said. "Armed for battle, but fairly stupid. They follow directions to the letter, but aren't trusted with important information. Killing them is forgivable. Shows great prowess."

"Not anymore," Emery said, slipping past Hallen and Kairi, who walked to Charity's left, and into the middle of the group with Halvor. "Kill one of them, and their kind will kill your whole family."

"Nonsense," Romulus said pleasantly. His tense and ready body said his mood wouldn't hinder his vicious reaction should one of these things attack. "They wouldn't be able to kill my family. Mother may be getting up in years, but she can wield a knife better than Halvor. She'd have them split from neck to navel before they uttered a syllable."

A grin pulled at Emery's lips.

The rest of the guardians spread out, covering the path and ensuring their presence was known. Not that anyone could mistake them. Eleven of Romulus's guard had set out with them, including Halvor—assistants, basket weavers, and table makers turned fighting machines in their loose pants, snug shirts, and the leather bands around their middles. It was the same outfit the Red Prophet had first dressed Charity in. The rest had stayed behind. For now, the First was still in charge, but she was being held accountable for her actions. She would get time to explain herself. To open up the not-often-talked-about history that led to those decisions. She'd hope to win back trust.

While that was happening, Romulus would get a better idea of what was happening in the outside world.

He'd get an idea of the next steps, so when he went back, they could formulate a plan.

Kairi and Hallen had been sent along with Charity. Hallen was a little sullen, but he hadn't mentioned his black eye.

"Protocol?" Halvor asked Romulus softly.

Unlike the shifter formation, the leader here took front and center, advertising his status. The most vicious, advanced fighter of the pack hid in the middle, the place usually reserved for vulnerable people.

The guardians had no vulnerable people. Or so Halvor had said when Charity mentioned the shifter way.

Halvor was the secret weapon, as it were, and would explode out to attack anyone stupid enough to threaten the group. Charity had seen him in action twice so far, both times taking out the offending magical creatures by surprise and scattering them or killing them within minutes. The other advantage the maneuver afforded the most advanced fighter was positioning. He could explode out of any side if the situation demanded it.

"Charity," Romulus said, his fingers twitching. That meant *move closer, quickly.*

She took her place beside and a little behind her father. The creatures' dance-walk became less gaudy and more cautious. Their hair settled a little. They kept exactly the same speed.

"Yes, they've always had a flare for the dramatic," her father said, not slowing either. "They like people to notice them, including the grunts. Try to contain your movements. It is better when our adversary doesn't know what we are thinking."

She'd thought she *had* been containing her movements.

"Second," the lead elf said when they neared, her smile showing large teeth and her skin faintly sparkling in the noon sun. Given the others weren't also sparkling, Charity thought she must've used some sort of sparkly facial lotion or something. "It is exhilarating to see you emerge from the Flush. I am sure the king and queen will be delighted."

"Yes, of course they will," Romulus said, and it was as friendly as it was arrogant. "The First has been planning a visit for some time. We must pay our respects."

The elf's eyes zeroed in on Charity. "If you'll forgive the bluntness, Second, we have been instructed to take this…young lady in."

"Is that right?" Romulus looked down on Charity. "Newly dubbed the Third and already her presence is requested among elf royalty? My goodness. We knew she was a shining star, but this is encouraging indeed. Unfortunately, the royal invitation was not sent out ahead of you."

The elves shifted, clearly flustered. They weren't remotely as good at keeping their thoughts to themselves.

"Yes, Second. It is an honor. The invitation…is coming. I think." The elf took a small step forward and inched her arm out as if to reach for Charity.

"Well, once we receive the invitation, we will be sure to answer immediately with a suitable date. Now, if you'd be so good as to step aside, we have business in the Brink."

The lead elf swallowed. "Yes, Second. Only, we've been ordered to bring her in."

"I do so hate conversational redundancy," Romulus said, his small, annoyed movements somehow getting his point across more than his words. He was losing his patience, and a sword would end the monotony.

"We've got orders for that one, too." The elf on the right of the path, reminding Charity of a very pretty and dainty thug, pointed into the center of the group where Emery stood. "He's in breach. He'll need to be hanged."

The lead elf tensed, clearly knowing that was the wrong collection of words for the moment.

Romulus smiled. "Hanged, did you say?"

"Oh. Well…" The lead elf plucked at a large, ornate button. "Yes, Second. That's elf business, of course. The lad played a cruel trick on the royalty some years back. With his brother. They've been ordered to be hanged. I apologize, but it's the law."

Romulus laughed, surprising Charity. "What a hilarious joke," he said. "Hanged. Why, that sort of brutality only applies to treason or heinous crimes. Per the doctrine of the Realm, initiated some few centuries ago, a *custodes* of high status would've had to stand in judgment of the ruling. Though, I will admit, we've been somewhat absent. Tell me, what was this cruel trick that warrants such a horrifying public punishment?"

"He… Ah…" The lead elf rolled her shoulders, then her neck, looking for breathing room.

"He did an illusion," the dainty thug said. "I was there. The whole place was in an uproar—people yelling, the queen in a horrible temper, half the palace confused…"

"An illusion. Hmm." Romulus half turned. "Mr. Westbrook, please step forward, if you would."

Two fae parted to let Emery walk out with his shoulders slightly rolled, like a cage fighter ready to do battle. His jaw was set and his fingers moved. Penny stepped closer to the front of the group, her hands up near her chest and her fingers moving as well. They had a spell in the works, probably something nasty.

The fae resumed their position, enclosing Halvor in the middle once again.

"Now, Mr. Westbrook, please do elaborate on this trick you played with your brother," Romulus said.

"We did create an illusion," Emery said, his hard eyes focused on the lead elf. "We put a dead end were there wasn't one, switched the look of the hall, and confused…some of the palace."

"Yes, I see. And if one were to walk through this illusion, what would've happened?"

"Nothing. They'd make it through and immediately find their way again."

"No, that's the thing. It didn't look like you could get through it," the thug elf said, his thin and manicured eyebrows pinching together. "I was there. It was a dead end."

"We've established that it did, indeed, look like a dead end, yes," Romulus said, his eyes flashing with impatience. "That is the nature of an illusion, after all. How long did this…trick last?"

"An hour, tops," Emery said, his fingers moving more now. Penny scooted closer.

"I see the problem." Romulus nodded. "The guardians have been gone too long from the rest of the Realm, and it has allowed the elves to lose their sense of humor. How tragic. Well, at present, there is nothing we can do about it. We are needed elsewhere. But don't you worry, madam. Just as soon as we are able, we will meet with the elf royalty and work to re-establish our practices as the guardians of the Realm. Now, if you will kindly step aside…"

Romulus waited patiently. The lead elf picked at her button. The lesser elves around her, fair and tall, hair blowing elegantly in the breezeless day, tensed. The very pretty thug pulled out a long dagger.

A feeling like sandpaper slapped Charity in the face. Penny gasped and staggered backward.

Emery threw his hand out for Penny. "No, babe, don't—"

Halvor burst out from the center of the group. The elf on the left snatched a whip, of all things, from a holster on his back. The pretty thug brandished his dagger. None of the three reacted in time.

A slice of pink crackled through the air. It cut across the middle of the thug—the first to go for a weapon. He let out a high-pitched wail. Blood spurted in a plume.

The pink swept across the group of elves before tearing into the elf with the whip newly in hand. His face went slack. The whip fell from his hand. The top half of his body slid from the rest and toppled to the ground.

The two middle elves, including the leader, stared for one beat. Their eyes widened and a strange moan wheezed out of the leader. Both turned and ran.

Halvor was after them in a moment, followed by half of Romulus's guard. Small weapons gleamed in their hands.

"That was impressive—No, no, Charity." Romulus put his hand on Charity's arm to stop her from running forward to help the others. "Guardian leadership do not chase small-minded idiots. It is beneath us. Penny Bristol, I am in rapture. What truly fantastic spell work. Clean, pretty, and so very brutal." He half turned to look at her red face. She clearly hadn't meant to let that spell loose. "Was that what you've been doing while creeping through everyone's gardens?"

"Umm…no. That was a reaction to the elves' magic."

"Ah yes, I see." Romulus stared after his men and women. He clucked his tongue, and Charity must have been learning to read his gestures, for she knew what he meant—his people had not dispatched the two elves as quickly as they should've. They'd been cooped up for too long. "I am disturbed by what I've seen so far on this journey, and we've only just begun. We've been gone far too long. Power, unchecked, corrupts those who wield it. I fear a disease is plaguing the Realm, eating it alive from the core outward."

"The warrior fae—I mean, guardians, used to police this place?" Charity asked as Emery stared at Romulus like he was seeing him for the first time.

"Yes, though I confess, this knowledge came to me from scrolls and records. After the elves established law and order, our people needed very little protecting. Our duty as *custodes* had all but dried up. The elves, seeing this, offered us the role of guardians of the Realm. Our duties entail keeping the peace and protecting all the magical people. Our kind was also sought to protect the elf royalty and their palace. You heard, as I did, what happened with that. But rest assured, my dear girl, the time for hiding has come to an end. We need to remind the elves of who we are, and the duty we are meant to perform."

The fae returned, and though their faces were businesslike and they'd cleaned and stowed their weapons, their eyes shone with exuberance. They were finally doing what was in their blood to do.

Charity knew it was just the beginning.

CHAPTER 39

"Sir! They're coming! *Sir!*"

Roger looked up from his desk in the castle, adrenaline fueling his body. Beazie, red-faced and out of breath, pushed open the door. Her eyes were wild.

"They're just up the road. A whole group of them! She brought a whole entourage out of the Flush. She came for Devon, just like you said she would."

Roger kept his composure. He'd *hoped* she would. It was anything but certain.

When Devon had stopped by, not two full days ago, with the news that he'd left Charity behind, per his own judgment and Karen's instructions, Roger had wanted to wring the younger alpha's neck. Devon was hurting; any fool could see that. He felt the loss acutely, something Charity would've responded to. Except Devon hadn't explained himself to Charity. He'd left in the middle of the night, without a word.

If Roger hadn't had years to hone his self-control in hostile situations, if he hadn't trusted Karen's *Sight* implicitly, things might've escalated. As it was, he lamented Dillon's passing, listened to a brief account of their journey, and had to prevent a very strange red-haired woman from scaling the side of the castle walls just to see if she could reach the top.

Instead of Charity, Devon had brought back a fae lunatic.

"So the rumors were true," Roger said quietly, staring down at the papers on his desk without seeing them. "You're sure it's them?"

"Yes, alpha," Beazie said, cleaning her hands on her white apron. "They walk like...phantoms. Deadly phantoms. They are what I've heard they are, and Charity is at the head with a very handsome man."

"Thank you, Beazie. Let me know if they stop in—"

Alder appeared in the doorway, his face grim but eyes excited. He nodded, a subtle movement.

Charity had brought the fae.

"She's asked to meet you in the courtyard," Alder said without preamble. Beazie filed out of the way. "The Second Arcana is with her, along with a man that...I wouldn't turn my back on for all the world."

"Yes, thank you, Alder." Roger stood, feeling excited for the first time in a long time. Something big was underway. There had been more vampire activity than normal in recent weeks. More turnings. An elder was at work, and not one he knew—Roger had come to recognize Vlad's smug predilection for flouting the law right under the shifters' noses, Darius's ability to mask his illegal enterprises with the appearance of legitimacy. This was someone different, and he or she was a master—suave and quick, striking quickly and without warning. The new power player dabbled in sacrifices, too. Ritual sacrifices that screamed *demonic*, with circles and symbols and other things Roger didn't understand. He wondered if this vampire was perhaps the one who had hoodwinked Vlad and delayed Charity's journey to the Flush.

Roger needed some backup, and he really didn't want to rely on a bounty hunter, since Reagan was the only one who could probably do the job, and she was in league with a vampire herself.

He headed out of the castle with Alder on his heels. The crew stood to one side of the castle, with Charity standing in front with a man who shared her likeness but who didn't look old enough to be her father. The rest didn't fan out behind them so much as stand loosely clustered, with one person protected in the middle.

No. Not protected. That was for show. Somewhat hidden and incredibly lethal. This was the person Alder didn't want to turn his back on.

Emery and Penny stood off to the side, their expressions fatigued and postures anxious. They wanted to get home.

"Charity, great to see you again," Roger said, and he meant every word.

Her magic flowered around him, calling to his wolf. He could've sworn he heard battle drums in the breeze.

"Hi," she said, and sheepishly glanced at the man

next to her. "Roger, this is the Second Arcana of the *custodes*, out of the Flush. D-Dad, this is Roger, the alpha of the North American pack. He's the head alpha, over Devon, which is more like—"

"I can see the distinction perfectly," the Second cut in gracefully, a small tick of his head and a slight lean in his body indicating he recognized Roger as an equal.

Roger held in his surprise at the ease with which he understood the unspoken language. It seemed these fae communicated similarly to shifters. That would make working with them even easier than he'd imagined.

He just had to get them working together.

"You can?" Charity asked, confused.

"You may call me Romulus," the Second said.

"He can?" Charity said, now more confused.

"Welcome, Romulus. Would you care to come in for a drink?" Roger shifted his stance just slightly, speaking through his body as the fae was doing.

"How gracious, Alpha. Thank you for the invitation." Romulus made the title seem loftier, somehow.

"Please, call me Roger."

Romulus bowed. "I would love to take you up on that offer another time. For the moment, I think Charity is anxious to get back to her Alpha Shifter."

That must've been what they were calling Devon. Romulus had indicated he understood Devon was a step down from Roger's position. Surprisingly, however, he seemed to consider the step a small one. Devon must've impressed them. Steve had told him the younger wolf had come a long way. Roger needed to reassess the young alpha's pack standing, especially now that Charity had returned, her posture and air regal and confident. She was already donning her newfound status as Arcana royalty. The two would make a power couple. Roger had to make sure they were in prime position to use their potential.

"Of course," Roger said, returning the bow.

"Roger, I wondered..." Charity fidgeted with a strap that wrapped around her middle.

"They need a place to stay in the Brink," Emery said, his hands in his pockets. "I doubt you want Vlad taking care of it. He'll already be apprised of the situation."

"Yes, of course," Roger said. Emery had his finger on the pulse of the worlds, that was clear. "I already have some houses temporarily blocked off in Santa Cruz. They'll be comfortable until we can arrange a more permanent situation in the weeks to come."

"That is very kind." Romulus bowed again, deeper this time. Surprisingly, Charity bowed with him, if somewhat stiffer. She needed practice. "We are in your debt."

"Not at all. I thank you for looking after my pack while they were in the Flush."

"While we are on the subject of Vlad the vampire," Romulus said, "I would like to speak with him. He has...information that interests Charity and me, as well as an unhealthy attachment to my daughter. I'd like to set that to rights."

Roger allowed an aggressive smile to curve his lips. Judging by the fact that he'd killed elves without being hauled to the palace, he was capable of delivering on his threats. Assuming the rumors were true, of course.

"If I knew where Vlad was, Second, he would be eternally dead by now. But rest assured, in due time, he will find you."

"Ah. Yes, of course." Romulus's posture suggested his business was concluded. It was time they got going.

"If you use the nearest gate into the Brink, I can have transportation arranged for you," Roger said, taking a step back to clear the way.

"That is very generous, Alpha. Until next time."

"Roger, we're just going to…" Penny hooked a thumb at the fae. "We're going to hitch a ride, if that's cool."

He stepped forward to shake Emery's hand, then Penny's. "Thanks for getting them to the Flush."

Emery smirked. "You'll want to thank Vlad for that."

"Not likely."

Emery chuckled and took Penny's hand before following the others.

Roger watched them walk down the lane in their loose formation, nearly as synchronized in their movements as Roger's pack.

Nearly.

"What'd you make of that meeting?" Alder asked quietly.

"There is no way that group of warrior fae is retreating back to the Flush anytime soon. Especially not if Vlad shows up and gives them a reason to fight."

"Then I guess we'll have to hope Vlad shows up."

"Where Charity's concerned, it is not *if* with Vlad. It is *when*. Make sure they are comfortable. We'll support them until our peoples can come to an arrangement. Keep an eye on them, and let me know if Vlad or anyone else shows up."

"Should I let the young alpha know Charity has returned?"

Roger laughed, turning to the castle. "And spoil their battle? Not a chance. The hotter Charity's anger, the more fun Devon will have apologizing."

CHAPTER 40

As the Suburban pulled into the long drive, Charity could barely breathe through her anger and fear. Her dad and his people had been deposited in their modest houses, with gardens her father could barely stand to look at. Still, the accommodations were comfortable and welcoming, and it was incredible that the houses had been made ready for them at a moment's notice. Roger was putting the Flush's guest housing to shame, and Charity knew her dad felt it.

Charity had a bedroom in the house her father had been assigned, but she hoped she wouldn't need it. She *hoped* Devon had left for her own good—that he'd attempted to sacrifice his own happiness so she'd have a chance at a better life. She hoped, but part of her feared he'd left to free himself up. That his history as a ladies' man and player had finally come to bear, and he didn't want to be chained down.

She was about to find out. He'd get a thumping either way.

The truck pulled to a stop, and Steve glanced at her with a crooked smile. "Nervous, huh?"

"No, mad," she half lied.

He nodded and somehow affected a lounging position in the driver's seat. He'd been one of those chosen to pick everyone up from the portal. "What do you want me to do with your entourage?"

Charity glanced back at Hallen and Kairi, two people who would apparently be her shadows. Her father had politely, and very respectfully, threatened her with a beating should she try to evade them. She didn't want to be on the other end of that particular politeness. It hadn't worked out well for those elves.

"I guess just drop them off? I can call an Uber if…things don't go well."

"Oh, they won't go well. At first. Your dad's crew will need to make the alpha a bunch of new tables. But you won't need an Uber. You'll be staying the night."

She let out a shaky breath. God, she hoped so.

She pulled the handle on the door but hesitated a moment. Maybe a *little* nervous, yes. "You're still calling him alpha—does that mean you're still in his pack?"

Steve chuckled and leaned his big arm against the window. "I figure I better stick around for a while. If you and yours are joining up, I'll get more chances at a certain little fae that enjoys rejecting me."

"It is not a rejection," Kairi said with humor. "It is only that I would miss the sun whilst standing in the shadow of your enormous ego."

Steve leaned in closer to Charity with a sly smile. "One day she'll succumb, just you watch."

Kairi laughed delightedly. She enjoyed the game, clearly. As did Steve.

Charity rolled her eyes and stepped down from the SUV. *Mental note: don't ask.*

The late afternoon sun flared in the windows at the front of the house. The trees gently waved around the property. With some attention from her father, this place could be just as beautiful as the Flush. Maybe more so, with the crystal-clear blue sky and the pleasant sea salt on the breeze.

She'd missed it. She really hoped her dad could be happy here.

She really hoped Devon would let her stay.

"It is a beautiful house, Miss Charity," Kairi said softly, reading Charity's mind. She followed her to the house. "It reminds me of the Flush. Your wolf has chosen well."

"It's well situated within the nature," Hallen added, although it was clear the compliment annoyed him.

Charity reached the door and paused with her hand on the handle. Butterflies swarmed her belly. This was the moment of truth.

She pushed into the house, immediately greeted by the comforting smell of air fresheners and a scent that was uniquely Devon. Her gut pinched even as her heart surged. She hurried to the front room, desperate to see him again, to lay her eyes on the face she'd missed. It had only been a couple of days, but it was the longest they'd spent apart since they met. She'd hated it.

The house was soaked in a deep hush.

"What is that?" Hallen asked. "What is all this?" His wide eyes darted to the lamps, the laptop on the coffee table, and the fan on the ceiling.

"Get a hold of yourself," Kairi muttered out of the side of her mouth. "We're in the Brink. It's different. We'll figure it out later."

Hallen's mouth snapped shut, but his eyes still flew around the room.

Charity checked the kitchen, and again Hallen gawked. She checked the second living room Devon used as a meeting space, then the back bedrooms. All were clean and tidy, and his smell lingered, but he wasn't here.

Her heart aching, she found her way to the sliding glass door—the one that had been repaired after she'd tossed Devon through it.

"It will be okay, Third." Kairi placed her hand on Charity's shoulder. "He will provide you many strong children to carry on your muddied but powerful fae line."

"Goodness gracious," Charity murmured. "That's a bit much."

"He will be more powerful than the Head Alpha one day," Hallen said, mostly grunting. "He has more potential. He is a good ally for the fae."

"Something it must pain you to admit," Kairi said with laughter in her tone.

Charity ignored them, sweeping the backyard with her gaze.

"The Second will find this garden abominable," Kairi said. "Even I can see it is all out of—"

A huge black wolf pushed slowly through the foliage, its brown eyes rooted to Charity. Magic washed into her middle and then back out again, Devon's surge answered by her own. Apparently, after the link was broken, close proximity was needed to reconnect. She'd have to talk to Penny about that, but right now, she barely stopped from fluttering her eyes, his magic still so reassuring. It still felt so good. Lord, how she'd missed it.

He walked forward with his head held low and his hackles raised, a predator seeing someone unexpected in its territory. Someone he didn't want there.

Kairi and Hallen fell in beside her immediately, wary and alert, ready to draw their swords should the need arise.

A burst of green magic surrounded Devon before his human form rose from a crouch. She couldn't help but feast her eyes on his cut and powerful body.

"Why are you here?" he asked, his tone rough.

Uncertainty flared within her. Anger rose to mask it. "You didn't say goodbye, you prick."

He took a step toward her, his muscles popping, as though he were keeping himself from rushing her.

"Charity, the Flush is your future," he said. "You're an Arcana. You're fit to rule. You belong there."

She steeled herself and took a chance. If she was going to get rejected, it wouldn't be because she was vague about what she wanted.

"I belong with you," she said.

His chest deflated, as though he had just lost a battle. "Karen, the *Seer*, said I had to leave," he said, taking a few steps toward her before stopping himself. She could see it took him effort to do so. "I would've done it anyway. You deserve to be in that beautiful place with your people. You deserve a crown, Charity. I'd just hold you back."

Her heart broke and tears came to her eyes. Kairi had been right—he hadn't wanted to leave her, and it had cost him dearly to do so. She could see the pain vibrating through his body. Wow, had the tables turned from when they'd first met.

"Go inside," she said to Hallen and Kairi. "Go figure out the electronics."

"The what—" Hallen grunted, probably because Kairi had elbowed him.

They backed into the house, leaving Charity and Devon alone.

"Remember when we first met?" she asked, smiling through her trembling lips. "You thought *I* would hold *you* back. And yet you let me stay. You helped and protected me, even though I was a huge pain in your ass."

"It was my duty," he said, taking another step. "And I quickly saw it was worth it."

"It is still your duty. Is it not still worth it?"

He shook his head. "My duty was to leave. To walk away so that you could have a life."

Like a puzzle getting its last piece, it all clicked together. She laughed and looked a̶ overhead.

"Your duty was to drag me fae with me," she said, blinking th̶ we positive that Karen doesn't work for ̶ Roger wasn't resorting to Vlad's tactics?"

Devon shook his head, his eyes roaming her face. His hands balled into fists, clearly his attempt to keep himself where he stood.

"Do you know what the *Seer* told me, Devon? She said, 'When you find your true home, you will know. And with that home you must stay.' When you left, you took my home with you. You gave me no choice but to follow you."

"I don't…"

"Understand?" She stepped toward him, all her uncertainty melting away at the longing on his face. The blind hope he clearly didn't think he had a right to. "You are my home, Devon. You are the walls that protect me. The roof that keeps the elements from reaching me. The person who grounds me and assures me that I have a place in this world. The Flush was ugly and empty without you. The Brink would be, too. I was living a temporary life when I met you, chasing a future without putting down roots. You've changed that. I have found my purpose within your pack. I have finally found my people."

He took another halting step, as if he couldn't help himself. "But what about your father, Charity? What about your status and your position?"

came with me. I'm still the Third, and my fa- and his people are currently figuring out how to takeout in their borrowed homes downtown. hey've also picked a fight with the elves, I think. They killed a few of them on the way."

Devon's eyes widened and his mouth dropped open.

"I know, right?" she said. "My father didn't seem worried about it. I think Emery nearly shit himself with glee. He's always been really aloof, but not after that. Suddenly, he was on Team Fae. Given he and Penny are the most powerful mages in the world, and Roger is one of the most powerful shifters, it seems my father is already connecting us favorably in the Brink. It'll make it easier for them to stay for a while."

A smirk pulled at Devon's full lips. He took another step forward, nearly reaching her. "You're already thinking like a princess."

She shook her head. "I'm no fae princess. I'm a half-fae, half-human in love with a shifter. I'm an anomaly. I know you were trying to do what was best for me by leaving the Flush, but Devon, *you* are what's best for me. I don't care where I am, as long as I'm there with you. I love you," she whispered, tears streaming down her cheeks. "Please don't ever leave me again."

He rushed her, wrapping her into his arms and holding her tightly. "It nearly killed me to leave you." His breath was hot against the shell of her ear. The warmth of his body comforted her. His power and strength grounded her. "It tore me up. Please forgive me." He pulled back, and his beautiful brown eyes, the green and gold specks dancing, showered her with deep, heartfelt emotion. "I lost Dillon, and then I thought I'd lost you. Two of the most important people—"

His voice hitched, and he clenched his jaw to keep the emotion at bay. Her heart broke all over again. Sobs welled up for Dillon. For what Devon had gone through—what he was still going through.

"I'm sorry about Dillon," she said, putting her palms on either side of Devon's face. "I'm so sorry. I should have realized. Macy left me a note."

He nodded, his eyes glassy, clearly not trusting his voice to speak.

She didn't know what else to say. He wouldn't accept her guilt, she knew, and it wouldn't make anything better. So she simply wrapped her arms around him and held him tight, feeling him tremble against her. He'd been hurting but with no one to lean on. It was lonely being at the top.

Except now he had her. He was her protection when she needed it, and she was his comfort when he couldn't brave life on his own. Together they were each other's support through this crazy magical world. She said as much.

"I love you, Charity," he said, and captured her lips with his. "I love you so much."

She deepened their kiss, losing herself in the feel of him. In the thrill of his magic and his touch. In his wildness. "Take me to bed."

He swung her up into his arms and stalked across the yard to the back door. "I'll take you for forever."

EPILOGUE

THE SOFT EVENING light filtered through the clouds as Charity stepped from the large SUV. Macy and Andy followed her out, annoying Kairi and Hallen, who were supposed to be right behind her in all dangerous situations.

Charity held two notes in her trembling hands, her teeth gritted against her rising emotion. Both notes had been written by Vlad, the second having been delivered by a courier shortly after she'd settled in with Devon. Vlad had lived up to his word—possibly—by giving her the address of her mother as well as an invitation to travel there in his private jet.

She'd declined his invitation immediately. Any half-sane person would. But it had taken her much longer to decide what she wanted to do with the information he'd given her. She had a good thing going at the moment, and she just wasn't sure if she wanted to hear why her mother had left her and never looked back. Her father had insisted it was her choice.

Devon had asked her to move in permanently. She was no longer in a temporary housing setup; now she had a solid foundation with a man she adored. This was made infinitely more special when her father had exchanged Realm gold for Brink dollars and purchased a few houses for their people. He was already hard at work on the gardening, and Halvor was hard at work kicking Charity's ass in the guise of training.

The only thing that was still on the fence was how the warrior fae would coexist with the shifters. Roger had offered Charity her old job back, and Devon had mentioned that his people would be happy if she fought for the beta role, but after a word with her father, she'd declined both offers. First, Dillon's passing still tore her up inside. She'd had a good cry with Macy, and although no one blamed Charity, it would seem wrong to fill a hole *she'd* created.

Most importantly, though, she was an Arcana of the guardians—or *custodes*, if she wanted to be formal about it. She had duties to her people, and her people apparently had duties to the Realm. They could not join a pack, they *were* a pack, and the two peoples needed to communicate regarding the best way for them to join forces. Something the Red Prophet, who was staying with the guardians at the moment, kept muttering about. Well, that and her need to meet her nemesis.

After a couple of months, having missed the summer quarter and not long before classes started for fall again, Charity had finally given in to temptation with regards to her mother. Ultimately, it was simple—she just wanted to see her again.

She wasn't the only one.

Her father stepped out of the SUV parked beside hers as their backup, mostly shifters, emerged from cars, trucks, and SUVs, all massed together in the dusty parking lot in front of a large white building stretching out across browning grass. A sign arched over the front entrance.

Brackner's Home for the Terminally Ill.

The feeling left Charity's legs. She dropped like a stone, nearly hitting the ground, before Devon's strong arms wrapped around her and hoisted her back up. Her father looked down on her with concern.

"She's dying," Charity heard herself say through numb lips.

"Or she is a nurse," Devon said. "We won't know until we check."

"Yes, Charity, the Alpha Shifter is correct. We do not know the situation until we gain more information." Romulus put his hand on Charity's shoulder. "She might not be here at all. This could be an elaborate trap by my cunning elder vampire pen pal. He plans his strategies the same way I plan my gardens, I think. He aims for all the flowers to bloom at once. Night flowers, in his case, no less beautiful. I half hope he will meet us here. Why else would he recommend we come near sundown?"

Vlad was trying to woo Charity's father into his way of thinking—casting doubt on the elves and their dealings in the Realm. Letters were left in Romulus's yard, or in Halvor's pants, taunting them with what Vlad must've known the fae would deem their faulty security. He was silently telling the fae that they were rusty, and Vlad was...not.

Romulus refused Devon's offer to erect a ward. Charity had taken up nagging as a new pastime. It wasn't getting her anywhere. Apparently, the warrior fae had a problem with hardheadedness.

Roger waited at the edge of the parking lot in his tearaway sweatpants and loose white shirt. His people spread out around the vehicles, on full alert. The sun sank slowly toward the horizon.

"Shall we?" Romulus put his arm out for Charity.

They walked out from between the SUVs, Charity surveying the large white building in front of them. It stretched across the expansive property in the small Nevada town.

Emery and Penny drifted in behind Charity, having offered their help.

"This isn't a trap," said Reagan, who had not been invited but was apparently unwilling to be left behind. She stood a little removed from everyone, looking out over the grounds. "This is an offer of goodwill. He has nothing to gain by waging war on someone whose help he wants. He won't snatch Charity, either, and risk upsetting the Arcana." Her thick boots crunched on the dirt. "No, he sees what's coming, and he's working on his allies."

"What's coming?" Roger asked.

"Haven't you heard the red-haired nut?" Reagan grinned. It didn't reach her eyes. "War. The elves have been unchecked in their brutality for far too long. There's unrest. And if there is anyone to capitalize on unrest, it's Vlad. He's planting his garden, so to speak. When it blooms, it'll be a helluva show."

"A hallucination says I'll play a key part in that war," Charity murmured as they neared the building's large, scuffed, and scraped doors.

"We've talked about this, darling." Romulus patted Charity's arm. "It was not a hallucination; it is your birthright. One that will grant you much status. Now, let's turn our attention to the matter at hand. We have all the time in the world to discuss the coming war."

A shiver arrested Charity. She somehow doubted how much time they had, number one, and she didn't want to talk about it, number two. She didn't want any part of it.

She forced the situation from her mind.

Alder jogged forward to reach the door first as Roger fell in behind them, taking the back. His people moved in around Charity's party, covering the fae, who covered her. It should've been a cluster of chaos with so many people filing up at the entrance, but somehow, it worked seamlessly. If they'd needed any proof their two peoples could work together, this was a good example.

A tired and drawn woman looked up from a worn desk in the middle of a large, run-down space. Her gaze took in all the people suddenly entering the hush, and a spark of recognition lit her eyes.

"Yes, Miss Charity Arcana?" The employee glanced between the women of the group.

"Me. I'm Charity." The group opened up a little so Charity could reach the desk.

The woman nodded and ducked down, seeming to grab something from under the desktop.

"Goodness." An older woman entered from a hall on the right, her gray eyebrows winging up and a delighted smile on her face. "What's all this?"

"They're here to visit the Taylor plot." The woman straightened up with a beige envelope on which Charity's name was written in delicate, easily recognizable scroll.

"Plot?" Charity said, heat pricking the back of her eyes.

"Yup. Head back out the front door, hang a right around the building, and go through the fence." The woman used two thin fingers to point. "We've agreed to keep the grounds unlocked until nine."

"But plot… That's a grave, right?" Her legs didn't seem to want to move. Tears overflowed from her eyes.

"It's okay," Devon said, one arm around her waist. "It's going to be okay."

As they made their way to the cemetery, Charity caught sight of Macy. The shifter's eyes were haunted. She'd just been through this with Dillon, visiting a plot they'd selected so that people would have somewhere to mourn…

The rickety old gate stood open, rusty and tangled with weeds and dying plants. A sob ripped from Charity's throat when she saw the rows of neglected headstones beyond it. She clung to Devon as they walked through the gate, certainty pounding through her. Part of her had hoped her mother was living her best life somewhere. But Charity was too late; her mother wasn't living at all. Charity wouldn't get to speak to her again. She'd never get to hug her, or slap her. She'd never need to work up the courage to ask why she'd left.

Charity hadn't gotten to say goodbye.

"No," she said softly, tears drenching her cheeks. "It can't be. She would've at least reached out to tell me she was…sick. Maybe she's a groundskeeper, or…"

In another moment, though, they found the stone. The words weren't etched very deeply, but there could be no doubt.

Here lies Patty Taylor.

Tears obscured Charity's vision, washing away the dates. Washing away her remaining strength.

She sagged, but Devon held her tightly to his chest, and her father held her hand. His head was bowed. He was mourning, too.

"Here, let's…" Macy wove through everyone. She plucked the envelope off the ground, it having fallen from Charity's suddenly lifeless fingers. "Let's just read…"

Two pages came out, a faded white piece of paper

against the familiar beige of Vlad's stationery. Macy gently pulled them apart, her eyes moving quickly from side to side over the message on the beige sheet. In another moment, she handed the faded white paper forward, her eyes rooting to Charity's.

"Vlad rescued some of your mother's things from this place's basement." Macy's tone said her heart was breaking for Charity. "He will meet you back at the car with them if you call off the…shifters."

He'd probably called them "dogs," knowing Vlad.

"I can keep her safe," Reagan said, probably to Roger. "Vlad knows I can kill him, but that I won't if he plays nice."

"I can protect myself from Vlad." Charity hiccupped a sob. "I can burn him with sunlight and then blow him up."

"I'm starting to really like her," Reagan murmured to someone. "Think she'd want to do some bounty hunter gigs with us?"

Charity tuned them out, pushing away from Devon so she could take the paper. She recognized her mother's handwriting immediately, though it wasn't as delicate as she remembered. She wiped away tears with the back of her hand so she could read what it said.

Dear Charity,

Please forgive me. Though I don't know how you could. What monster leaves her darling girl without saying goodbye? I just didn't know any other way.

The doctor said the tumor was terminal and I would need looking after. I couldn't let that burden fall to you. Please understand. I would've killed your dreams. I left so that you could continue on. You're a survivor—this was the best way, I know it in my heart. It's the least I could do for the half-life I have forced upon you.

I do not have the money to send for you—charity pays for my lodging here—but even if I did, I don't think you'd make it in time. I am at the end of my tolerance for this sickness. I don't have the strength or the will for much more. So I write this note to beg forgiveness. To explain.

I have missed you every waking moment of this past year. I've thought about you every instant. I miss your laugh, and your smile. I miss our time together. I so wish I could've said goodbye to you. That I could've seen the woman you will grow to be.

I hope you are following your dreams. I hope your life is filled with laughter and love. I want you to know that I love you so, so much. You are the best thing that has ever happened in my life, and I am so very proud of what you have already become.

Charity shook her head. Her hands shook so hard that she could barely read the words. "She didn't sign it."

"She must've died before she could finish it," her father said, tears shining in his eyes. "She might've made a mistake in your eyes, Charity, but it is clear she left with you in mind. She did it to save you. Had I not left—"

"Don't," Devon cut in, instantly silencing Romulus. "This isn't time for guilt or the blame game. Her mother was trying to do right by Charity in the only way she knew how. Let Charity grieve."

Charity let Devon gather her up tightly, crying so hard that she could barely breathe. How could her mom do that? How could she leave, thinking Charity would be better off not knowing where she'd gone? How could she choose to die alone when she had family who would give anything to be with her?

But she'd said why, hadn't she?

You're a survivor...

Her mother had done what Devon had tried to do. She had sacrificed her own happiness so that Charity could chase her dreams. And Charity had done exactly what her mother had hoped. She had created the kind of life her mother would've wanted for her. Her mother would've been proud—and happy to sacrifice herself for Charity's happiness.

Why did that hurt so much more?

"I would've followed her, just like I followed you," Charity admitted, crying into Devon's shirt. "She knew that about me."

"She loved you very much," Devon murmured, rocking her. "She didn't abandon you. She didn't want to leave. She felt she had to."

"But she didn't." Charity fisted Devon's shirt in her hands. "She didn't have to."

Devon didn't argue, just rocked her slowly. She cried until she didn't have any tears left, then she hugged her dad and found a few more to squeeze out. Finally, after the sun was gone and the stars had made bright holes in the dark sky, Charity stilled and dried her face. She wasn't done being sad, but she was done making a show of it.

"Let's go see Vlad," she said, threading her fingers through Devon's.

Roger had cleared all his shifters away, giving her a large perimeter for her grief. For all their focus on propriety, the fae didn't understand personal space, and crowded around her as she led the way out of the grounds and to the vehicles beyond.

"We will mourn her together," Halvor said, walking directly behind Charity. Murmurs of assent sounded around them.

"And we'll get really fucking drunk while we do," Andy said.

"Charity doesn't drink, you dick," Rod said.

"Shut up," Macy added.

"He is there." Cole's words, uttered like a sudden crack of thunder, made Charity jump.

"Fall back," Roger said.

Devon nodded to Steve at his right and glanced at the rest of his pack. Dale had requested a transfer shortly after they'd returned to the Brink, but Steve, Cole, and Barbara had chosen to stay. They followed his silent command and drifted back with Roger.

Vlad waited where he said he'd be, holding a beat-up box and sporting an expression of compassion.

"I am sorry for your loss," he said as Charity neared.

Reagan and the mages split off to the side without a word. Vlad didn't spare them any notice. He only had eyes for Romulus and Charity, standing in front of the other warrior fae, battle ready.

Vlad held out the box. "I secured this for you. I thought you'd want to have it."

Romulus stepped forward to take it. He didn't flinch from the elder vampire or seem worried in any way.

Charity glanced into the box as her dad handed it back to her. A few items of clothing Charity didn't recognize, a beat-up sun hat, and some other effects her mom had left behind. The box wasn't even half-full.

Charity's heart hurt. She just wanted to go home.

"Thank you, Vlad," she said, and meant it. "Thank you for finding that note. It…means a lot."

"One last thing, to put your mind at ease. I did a little digging. I have reason to believe a *Seer* in her youth pushed her toward marrying Walt. This was after Romulus had left, of course. Now, whether this *Seer* was offering your mother a divine view of the future, or simply acting on her judgments regarding an unwed mother, I do not know. But in your mother's position, heartbroken—I beg your pardon, Second—and after seeing a man disappear into thin air, when he crossed over to the Realm, she probably took the *Seer's* guidance in good faith. Anyone would've done the same. Having taken a *Seer's* guidance yourself, I hope you don't fault her for that."

Memories of her mother visiting the fortune-tellers and palm and tarot readers drifted into Charity's head. They'd been entertainment when she was little, sure, but Vlad was correct. Her mother had watched her real father cross over into the Realm… Charity could see asking a person she perceived as magical for answers. She could also see a real *Seer* giving her the option to sacrifice her happiness for a more favorable outcome for her daughter. Devon had received such a telling. Her mother would've done it out of love, as Devon had.

More tears slipped down Charity's cheeks. The sadness she'd felt over the last few years changed, turning into something good. The people that loved her most gave everything to see her through. It was more than anyone had a right to ask for. Charity was truly blessed.

"Thank you," she said.

Vlad swept into a bow, debonair and perfect. "Please, let me know if you need anything. I am at your service." Vlad's gaze shifted to Romulus. "Second, so great to finally meet you in person. I shall have you over for dinner one of these days. I would love to get your opinion on some gardens I'd like to alter."

"Of course. We can make a night of it." Romulus offered his own bow, polite yet distant.

Vlad took a step back. "I won't keep you." He turned a little, now facing Reagan. "Miss Somerset."

"Vlad." She crossed her arms over her chest.

"I have not forgotten our exchange in the Lair. It has been on my mind of late."

"Oh, right," she responded. "When I spun you around like a top? That time?"

His smile was slight and sly. "One good turn deserves another. Shall I say hello to your father? He'll be around next week for a...meeting of the minds."

Her face closed down into a hard mask. She didn't respond.

"Next time, perhaps." He bowed to Charity again before zipping out of the area, so fast that it was startling. She never got used to it.

"He will be capable of quite the bloom, yes," Romulus said, eyeing Reagan as the shifters drifted back in. "Come, Charity—let's go walk among Devon's new and refreshing gardens and remember the good times. I want to hear more about your life growing up. It is time to lie within the shade of memories."

Feeling soggy and strung out, Charity let Devon and her dad marshal her toward the SUV. As she climbed in, her head spinning from Reagan and Vlad's exchange, she noticed the way Reagan and the mages were standing. Reagan in the front, at the position of power, with Emery and Penny behind, in a pyramid. A pyramid not unlike the hazy grouping Charity recalled from her hallucination. They'd stood halfway between the two forces, facing off with another collection of vampires she hadn't recognized.

She shook her head. All of that was a concern for another day. Or another decade, if they were lucky. Right now, she just wanted to clutch her mom's note to her chest and remember the good times, as her father had said. She had to admit that even though Vlad had made her life hell, she would forever be thankful for the closure he'd afforded her.

She entwined her fingers with Devon's and leaned against his arm, waiting for everyone else to load up.

"Thank you," she said.

"For what?" Devon asked.

She smiled, sad but her heart full. "For everything. For helping me lock down the life my mother always wanted for me. She sacrificed herself so that I might one day find you. Maybe she hoped I'd find magic one day, too. She would've thought it was a job well done, having me end up here. She wouldn't have been sorry. I can see that now. I can respect it."

Devon kissed her on the forehead. "She'd be proud of you."

She sighed and rested her head on his shoulder, having found her place, finally.